THE LONG CORRIDOR

Only one person was ever able to understand the tensions and frustrations of the Higgins' household. Jenny—with a compassion that only she was capable of—tried to soothe and help the unhappiness of Paul, the restlessness of her cousin Bett, and the confusion of young Lorna. Jenny was always welcome in their house because —when she was there—the hatred between husband and wife, between mother and daughter, grew a little less.

But Jenny—unattractive and lonely, had problems of her own—problems she never spoke of and that she tried to forget in a life of work and service to others . . .
Until the day came when the turmoil of Paul and Bett Higgins threatened to engulf Jenny's life as well . . .

Also by CATHERINE COOKSON
KATIE MULHOLLAND
KATE HANNIGAN
THE ROUND TOWER
FENWICK HOUSES
THE FIFTEEN STREETS
MAGGIE ROWAN
THE UNBAITED TRAP
COLOUR BLIND
THE MENAGERIE
THE BLIND MILLER
FANNY MCBRIDE
THE GLASS VIRGIN
ROONEY
THE NICE BLOKE
THE INVITATION
THE DWELLING PLACE
FEATHERS IN THE FIRE
OUR KATE
PURE AS THE LILY

The 'Mary Ann' Series

A GRAND MAN
THE LORD AND MARY ANN
THE DEVIL AND MARY ANN
LOVE AND MARY ANN
LIFE AND MARY ANN
MARRIAGE AND MARY ANN
MARY ANN'S ANGELS
MARY ANN AND BILL

The 'Mallen' Series

THE MALLEN STREAK
THE MALLEN GIRL
THE MALLEN LITTER*

and published by CORGI BOOKS
* to be published by Corgi Books

Catherine Cookson

The Long Corridor

CORGI BOOKS
A DIVISION OF TRANSWORLD PUBLISHERS LTD

THE LONG CORRIDOR

A CORGI BOOK 552 08493 X

Originally published in Great Britain
by Macdonald & Co. (Publishers) Ltd.

PRINTING HISTORY

Macdonald edition published 1965
Corgi edition published 1970
Corgi edition reprinted 1971
Corgi edition reprinted 1973
Corgi edition reprinted 1974
Corgi edition reprinted 1975
Corgi edition reprinted 1976

This book is set in Plantin 9/10 pt.

Corgi Books are published by
Transworld Publishers Ltd.,
Century House, 61–63 Uxbridge Road,
Ealing, London W5 5SA
Made and printed in Great Britain by
Richard Clay (The Chaucer Press) Ltd, Bungay, Suffolk

CONTENTS

Part One	THE FAMILY	9
Part Two	IVY	33
Part Three	JENNY	57
Part Four	BETT	86
Part Five	MAGGIE	186

THE LONG CORRIDOR

ONE

THE FAMILY

'Aw, Doctor, I'm as fit as a fiddle. Go on now and sign me off.'

'Not for another week at least, Annie; you're in no fit state to go cleaning and scrubbing.'

'There's no scrubbing these days, Doctor; you're behind the times. I only wield one of them polishers. Magic, they are.'

'Well, be that as it may. To wield one of them polishers you have to get out of bed before six, haven't you? And that chest of yours doesn't take to the early morning fogs.'

'Doctor.' Annie Mullen's jocular face became straight, and her glance equally so as she looked across the broad mahogany table towards the doctor for a second or so before she said flatly, 'I can't stand another week in the house, Doctor. She wants me out of it, an' I want to be out of it. It's been sheer hell this last three weeks. Nothin' said directly to me you know. Oh, no, she's too clever for that. She talks at you. You know the kind. All day she goes at it until my Harry comes home at night, and then butter wouldn't melt in her mouth. It makes me sick, Doctor, so do me this favour, will you, and sign me off. I'll take a lot of killin', really I will, but when me time comes I hope it's short and sharp.' Leaning further across the table now, and her voice dropping to a whisper, she added, 'You promised me once that when I was goin' I would have no pain. Do you still mean that?'

'I do, Annie.' His voice was as low as hers. 'Never you worry about that, you've got my word for it.'

After a single nod the old woman straightened up and, the smile returning to her face, she said, 'That's good enough for me.'

She watched him writing swiftly, and when he handed her the certificate she rose to her feet, and as she buttoned her coat she glanced sideways at him, as he also rose, and said, 'My old man used to say that your father, God rest him, looked tough, and talked tough, but there wasn't a better stitcher in the land, nor a kinder heart ... aw, an' you know what?' Mrs. Mullen now laid the flat of her hand on the doctor's chest. 'He's passed everything he had on to his son. Goodnight to you now.' She turned abruptly away and made for the door.

The doctor did not call after her, 'Aw, I've heard your blarney before, Annie'; he accepted her good opinion of him quietly, saying, 'Goodnight to you, Annie.' Then passing his hand over his chin he resumed his seat and pressed a button. And the door opened again and a man entered.

The doctor did not raise his eyes to the newcomer but consulted the card on his desk. Harold Gray, thirty-four years old. His eyes skimmed down the dates during which he had been treating the man over the last twelve months. Three weeks, five weeks, now four weeks. He looked up. 'Well, how are you?'

'Oh, you know, Doctor, not too bright.'

'Back better since you started taking those new tablets?'

'Well ... well a bit, Doctor, but ...'

'Ah, that's good, I thought they would do the trick.'

'But it's like this, Doctor ...'

'Well now, I suppose you're ready to go back to work.'

'But, Doctor ...'

'I gave you an extension last week that should have put you on your feet.' The doctor pulled a form towards him and began once again to write rapidly, and when he handed the certificate across the table to the man, Mr. Gray, wearing a resigned and solemn expression, got up from the chair and looking down at the doctor, said, 'It'll only go again.'

'You'll have to chance that. But try to remember that the last time it went you had an X-ray and it showed nothing wrong with your back. And the time before that, when it went you had an X-ray and nothing wrong could be found ...' He paused before ending, '... with your back. Goodnight.'

'Goodnight, Doctor.'

The salutation sounded like a threat, and Mr. Gray closed the door none too gently after him.

The doctor now gathered a number of cards from his desk, patted them together and sat looking at them. They represented people, all sorts of people: among them old Annie, with cancer eating her stomach and he was treating her for bronchitis, and she wanting to work until she dropped, which would be the best

10

way for her to end, and they both knew it. Then there was Gray. He wanted to spit. On the thought of this man he wanted to spit. He went out of the surgery, across a wide low waiting-room, pushed open a door marked 'Enquiries' and, throwing the cards on to a table at which sat a middle-aged woman, said, 'Anything else in?'

'No, nothing, not since Mrs. Ratcliffe's call.'

'I've a damned good mind to make her wait until the morning. . . . Neurotic individual.'

'We mustn't forget that the neurotic individuals pay on the dot, Doctor; and as you've said yourself, P.P.s are so few and far between these days we should pamper the ones we've got.'

A quizzical smile passed over the doctor's face, and, leaning his hands on the table, he bent towards his receptionist, saying, 'Your caustic memory will get you somewhere one of these days, Elsie; it's odd how you manage to remember all the wrong things I say.'

'I wouldn't call them wrong, Doctor.' Her smile was as quizzical as his own. 'Anyway, if I can remember all you say now after fifteen years I never will.'

'Fifteen years is it?' He straightened up and looked away from her back into the hall, with its big round table patterned with a criss-cross of magazines. 'Fifteen years you've been here? It makes you think, doesn't it?'

'Well, I wouldn't start and reminisce now if I were you. You haven't had anything to eat since one o'clock, so you'd better have something before you go to Mrs. Ratcliffe. Then there's Mrs. Ogilby. She's near her time; she might last till tomorrow, then again she might not.'

The doctor, still looking across the waiting-room, said submissively, 'As you say, Elsie, as you say.' Then over his shoulder he added on a sharper note, 'Leave that lot for tonight and get yourself home. If you ordered your own life as you do mine you wouldn't be so skinny.'

Elsie Ryan looked up at him and smiled her tight smile. 'Goodnight,' she said.

'Goodnight, Elsie.'

He walked across the waiting-room again in the direction now of a door marked 'Private'. Then almost as he was about to open it he turned slowly away, went past his surgery and out through another door into a courtyard. Here he stopped for a moment to look up into the star-studded sky. The moon was full and lit up

11

the frost-coated tiles of the outhouses surrounding the yard. He filled his lungs with the sharp cold air, then sauntered over the wide square blocks of granite that paved the yard towards the open gates, and stood looking out into the square. It was utterly deserted at the moment, which was unusual, for nearly always there were figures going in and out of the Technical College across the road. He turned his eyes towards the right, where the block forming the top of the square was taken up by the refrigeration plant. It was funny how things grew. Pearson had started with a little butcher's shop in the heart of Bogs End— the vicinity alone would tell you what quality meat he sold—and now he had the biggest cold storage plant for miles. It was said he was a millionaire, a millionaire who couldn't write his own name. Old Pearson had been a patient of his father's for years, and of his too, until Mrs. Pearson decided that they now needed a better setting for their wealth and had taken her coarse-mouthed, illiterate husband to the softer climes of the South. Still looking to the right his eyes passed over the Salvation Army barracks adjoining his own property. They, too, were quiet. No calling on God to come and jazz it up tonight. His lips moved into a tolerant smile. Did it matter how they called, as long as they had the desire to call, and the belief that they were being heard? Some folks looked on the Salvation Army with scorn and pity, but they weren't to be pitied. It was those who had thought themselves into the conviction that such simple souls were shouting to a deaf mute, it was these, he knew, who should be pitied. And he was one of them.

He looked to the left of him now, to the façade of his own house. Houses would be a better description, for Romfield House was really three houses knocked into one. Romfield House had begun when his grandfather, who had a taggerine business, made prosperous by the inhabitants of Bogs End, had bought the four-roomed, Georgian-fronted house in Romfield Square, which in those far-off days was on the fringe of Fellburn and not yet included in the vicinity of Bogs End. And it was in this house that his grandfather, the ambitious scrap dealer, had fostered his own son's desire to become a doctor. And when that son qualified he had bought him part of a practice in the best end of Fellburn. He had also, through time, bought the two houses adjoining his own—just as a business proposition this. But his doctor son had other ideas, and the outcome of these ideas was that the three houses were turned

12

into one. And later, he brought his practice to the house in which he had grown up.

In due course Doctor Higgins did for his son Paul what his own father had done for him: he encouraged him in the way he wanted to go, and eventually, during the last years of his life, he had the reward of working side by side with his son and imbuing in him a love not only for his work but also for practising it from this house. But such loves have a way of dissipating themselves. Scanning the quarried stone façade of his house the doctor told himself it was well overdue for a clean-up, but he would have to see the Reverend Conway about getting those iron railings mended, where they were attached to his end wall. These iron railings hemmed in the dilapidated drunken-headstone cemetery, and the equally dilapidated but sober St. Matthew's church.

This then was the Square. The Technical College along one side, the refrigeration plant along another; then the Salvation Army and the Church of England, with Dr. Paul Hugh Higgins's house in between them. These formed Romfield Square, a part of Fellburn that had now become attached to the slum of Bogs End. Not a desirable residence, many thought, for a doctor. But although he dwelt more happily in its past associations than he did in the present, he still felt himself at one with its surroundings, rough, even grim though they were, and with the inhabitants who were herded, even in new council flats, beyond the Square—the inhabitants who were part rough, part gentle; cunning, honest; bad, yet good. He felt one with them because he knew he had every recognized trait within himself.

He inhaled deeply again, turned his gaze from where the moon was creeping behind the group of chimneys on the Technical College and went back across the courtyard, through the door marked 'Surgery', which he locked behind him, across the waiting-room and entered the house proper through the door marked 'Private'. Here he stepped into another hall; a smaller hall this one, oak-panelled and warm looking. The red carpet covering the floor continued up the shallow oak stairway that rose from the far end, and after the stark lighting of the waiting-room the wall lighting of the hall lent a mellowness which was reflected from the two gilt mirrors flanking a side table and the various pieces of brass dotted here and there.

Having washed his hands in a cloakroom to the right of the staircase, he went into the room opposite which he called the

13

drawing-room but which his wife referred to as the lounge.

His wife was sitting in a deep couch before the fire. She did not turn her head on his apprach, nor did he look at her on his way towards the fire. Their lives had been separate for so long that each could pretend that the other wasn't there. But it was a pretence, and both of them were vitally aware of it, bitterly, irritatingly aware of it.

He leant his forearm against the edge of the high marble mantelpiece, the mantelpiece that she had wanted ripped out. He had stood firm against this as against most of the changes that would make the old house appear naked; you can't dress granite and oak up in pearl-grey paint and frills. He stood staring down into the fire for fully five minutes before, his irritation rising, he lifted his head and looked up at the large oilpainting of his father hanging above the mantel and said, 'Well, what about the meal?'

'It's waiting for you; it's on the hotplate.' Her voice sounded controlled, like that of someone trying not to lose her temper.

Still looking at the picture he asked, 'Has Lorna eaten?'

'Yes, she has. It's too late to keep her waiting for a meal until seven o'clock.'

He didn't ask, 'And you?' for knowing that he hated to have his meals alone she would purposely have taken hers earlier.

Paul turned from the fire and looked at his wife. He looked at her deliberately, as if trying to find something that had escaped him. It wasn't the first time he had done this, and it wasn't the first time he had told himself that he had always disliked little women. There was something, to say the very least, irritating about them. They were like little men, pushing, forcing the issue. Anything to make themselves felt, making up in aggressiveness their lack of inches. But of the two, give him little men before little women, with their grim determination and their ruthlessness. Yet these qualities were, he supposed, what usually made little women the best mothers and enabled them to rear successful families.

From the couch Beatrice Higgins raised her eyes, then dropped her glance quickly away from her husband's scrutiny. She couldn't think of anything in this world that she detested so much as his face, his square face. Everything about it looked square; his mouth, his nostrils, even his eyes, the grey eyes that at one time had held a certain fascination for her. His strong sandy hair, as yet devoid of grey, did nothing to enhance his

14

features. If she disliked anything more than his face it was his body, his big lumbering body. Big hands, big feet, chest like a bull. He was all bullish. A big, unthinking, uncouth bull. It was hard to believe that he was only forty-three, seven years older than herself. He could be twenty years older. Her thinking moved along a tangent—he could live another twenty years, perhaps thirty. Even the thought was unbearable and brought her upwards.

As she stooped to gather up her magazines from the couch she said, 'When you're finished put the dishes in the sink in some soapy water.'

'Put the dishes . . . What do you mean?'

Bett straightened up and, looking at him over her shoulder, said briefly, 'Helen's gone!'

'Helen's gone?'

'Yes. And for goodness sake don't keep repeating everything I say.'

There was a dull red glow creeping up beneath his skin. Her manner of speaking to him had the power to infuriate him. 'Well, be more explicit.' His voice was a low growl. 'Then I won't have to repeat what you say. Why has she gone?'

'Because I told her to. . . . Now go on and say, "You told her to?"' She moved her head further around and watched him grind his teeth. 'She used foul language to me, so I had no other option, she had to go. Her Bogs End education hadn't been neglected.'

'You were damned glad to get her. You never could keep a maid. And now when you can't get help for love or money you go and . . .'

'I go and dismiss her. Yes, and I'll do the same with your precious Maggie very shortly, so I'm warning you.' Now she was facing him, the pale skin of her face seeming to be pulled taut across her small bones, her blue eyes dark, giving evidence of rage.

'You just do that. You put your hackles on Maggie and that will be one time when you have gone too far.'

'If I catch her red-handed I'll dismiss her, and you can do what you damned well like. She's been robbing me for years, carting away stuff every night, packing it round her. Her bust is twice as big at night as it is in the morning.'

'Robbing you, did you say?' His voice was deceptively cool. 'Who pays for the stuff that Maggie takes, eh? I ask you that.

Now you listen to me.' He was growling again as he stabbed his index finger slowly towards her. 'When my mother was alive she always saw that Maggie's basket was filled at night, but when you took over everything was changed. But with Maggie, habits die hard. She's always had it and she always will. She knows that I know she has her whack, so I'm warning you, leave her alone.'

They stared at each other for some considerable time in weighty silence. Then Bett, moving her head slowly and her features twisting as if in pain, said, 'My God, Paul, one of these days I'll get you where I want you. I don't know how but I feel sure in here——' she placed her clenched fist on her breast, 'I feel sure that you'll be delivered into my hands some time or other, and then I'll make up for everything you've put me through. Remember that.' She gave a short, sharp bounce to her head, then turned from him.

As she made to leave the room there came the sound of the front-door bell ringing, and she went into the hall banging the door after her.

Paul turned and looked down into the fire. He was shaking slightly with the force of his feelings. He had no doubt that his wife meant every word she said, and did she but know it the weapon was ready to her hand. He turned his head sharply to the sound of her voice, high and pleasant sounding now, coming from the hall, exclaiming, 'Jenny. Why, where have you sprung from? Why didn't you give me a ring?'

When he heard the answering voice he made hastily across the room and, pulling the door open, he too became a different being.

'Hello, Jinny.' He always called his wife's cousin Jinny, never Jenny. 'Aw, it's good to see you. Why didn't you let us know? I'd have met you. Get yourself in.' He pushed the tall woman into the drawing-room.

'Give me your hat.' Bett spoke to her cousin as she extended her hand, and Jenny Chilmaid, laughing, pulled it from her head, saying as she said so, 'I'm going to burn it.'

'And not before time I'd say.' Bett looked down at the hat in her hand, and she rumpled it. Then almost skipping across the room, she cried, 'Come on, sit down. Sit down.'

Bett Higgins now appeared a pretty, vivacious creature, with sparkling blue eyes and a manner that seemed to set her whole body alight. She moved her hands when she talked, running them girlishly through her short, dark, glossy hair. The doctor's wife was acting at this moment as she always did when pleasantly excited. No one seeing her thus could imagine any other side to her—no one, that is, except the two people in the room, her husband and her cousin.

Jenny Chilmaid was the opposite in every way to Bett. To begin with she was five foot ten, and thin with it. Her clothes hung on her as they would from a wire coathanger. Her face, like her body, was long, but unlike it, it was in proportion in that it had a good bone formation. Her straight-lipped, wide mouth, a fine pair of deep brown eyes, and a head of tow-coloured hair, drawn straight back from her forehead into a bun in the nape of her neck, would undoubtedly have given her some claim to attractiveness, if it hadn't been for her main feature, her nose. This took the pattern of her body, being much too long and too shapeless to escape comment. When people looked at Jenny Chilmaid they looked at her nose. Bett was looking at it now as she said, 'Tell me, what's happened? Are you on holiday? Where've you come from today? From Havant?'

'Yes.'

'Well, why didn't you let us know?'

'Oh, well. It's a long story.' Jenny smiled from one to the other before pursing her mouth and adding, 'And I could do with...'

'A cup of tea.' Both Bett and Paul ended the sentence for her, and it appeared as if there was no dissent between them. As they all laughed, Paul said, 'And a cup of tea you'll have, Jinny. And in two shakes of a lamb's tail. That's if you keep all your news till I get back. I won't be a minute.'

He, too, was changed. As if a boy had come alive in his large frame, he hurried out of the room, and as he did so Bett sat down on the couch beside Jenny. Then emitting a sigh that relaxed her, she said, 'It's good to see you again.'

'And you.'

'Have you finished that job?'

'Yes,' said Jenny briefly.

'Good, then you can stay for a while.'

Bett sounded sincere, and she was, for Jenny was always helpful. She would be a godsend with Helen gone. And what was more, life was always easier when she was around the place. She had a way of anticipating your thoughts, at least about

17

chores and the grind of running a house. Added to this she acted as a buffer between her and Paul. 'Come on,' she said now, 'tell me about everything.'

'Oh, I don't want to go over it twice, Bett. Wait until Paul, comes back, eh?'

Bett raised one shoulder; then she looked from under lowered lids at her cousin. She fancied she sensed a change in her, but she couldn't quite lay a finger on what it was. She still had that quiet withdrawn look, not a reserve—there was nothing in her to reserve. She had worked out her cousin's character years ago: there was neither high passion nor low cunning in Jenny. She was a neutral; fitted for the things she did best; nursing people and doing tiresome odd jobs unobtrusively. Now and again she had thought it was a pity she hadn't married. But then she wouldn't, would she, looking as she did. Still it was an ill wind, and she was glad to see her at this moment. And the big fellow was always more civil when she was about. He always wanted to rate good with Jenny ... the kind, considerate doctor.

'How are things with you?' Jenny rested her cheek on the back of the couch and watched Bett reach out and take a cigarette from the box on the table to the side of her, and pat it on the back of her hand before saying, 'That's a silly question to ask.'

'Well, it's eight months since I saw you; a lot could happen in eight months.'

'What! Between me and him? Could you imagine anything good happening between us?'

'Aw, Bett, it could if you tried.'

Bett struck the lighter, then applied it slowly to her cigarette, and she drew on it once before she slanted her eyes towards Jenny, saying, 'I stopped trying years ago. I've told you before I'm not the humble type to go crawling. I tried it once and I was kicked in the teeth.'

Turning her head towards the fire, Jenny said very slowly, 'I've thought a lot about you both over these past few months, and you know, Bett, I'm sure if you had talked to Paul in the first place everything would have straightened——'

'Shut up, Jenny.' Bett bounced to her feet. 'Look, you haven't been in the house a minute, it isn't like you to bring this up. What's the matter with you? Anyway, you know better than anyone that the pattern was cut years ago and nothing can alter

18

it. He goes his way, I go mine.'

'And Lorna?'

'Lorna is fifteen, Jenny.' Bett's voice was quiet now. 'In two to three years' time she could be married, and that will be the end of that.'

They held each other's gaze. Then Bett, her glance dropping away, reseated herself on the couch and there followed an awkward silence until Jenny said, 'How is she? I'm dying to see her.'

'Oh. In appearance pretty much the same as when you last saw her. I can see no change in her, outwardly at least, but she's reaching the difficult stage. Yet that's to be expected, I suppose. Her mind's on sex at the moment.' She thrust one slim leg out as if kicking something away. 'How anyone can want their schooldays back is beyond me. Talk about a breeding ground of false values. When I listen to her prattling on I could explode. But'—she gave a mirthless laugh—'her dream-world was a bit shattered last week. One of the girls in the fifth form—not in the sixth, mind you—got herself pregnant. It's Fay Baldock. You know the Baldocks ... the chemists. He's got a chain of shops now. Well you can imagine how Poppa Baldock reacted when the father-to-be was discovered to be a seventeen-year-old grammar school boy whose family live up in the Venus block, near the pit. Really, the Baldocks have my sympathy, for there's nothing to choose between the lot that live in the Venus block and the Bogs End crowd.... Bogs End!' She screwed up her face. 'Oh, how I hate all the muck and squalor.'

'But there's no muck and squalor there now, Bett; most of the old streets have been pulled down.' Jenny was smiling gently at her cousin.

'That makes no difference, the people are the same. Some of them have twenty pounds a week and more coming in, but it hasn't changed them one jot. They look the same, they act the same. They have their cars now and go abroad for their holidays, but they just have to open their mouths. Do you know'— she leant forward and motioned her head in the direction of the kitchen—'she, Maggie, she brags about her son earning thirty pounds a week and yarps on about him taking his family to Spain last year, and all the while she's helping herself to anything she can lay her hands on in my kitchen.... Oh, it boils me up. And he won't do a thing about it. And you know that daughter of hers, Lottie, who used to spit when she talked, you remember?' She raised her brows. 'Well, she's married a fellow who's manager of the big electrical works, a new place. Can you believe it? ... Her. And then there's ...'

Jenny was looking at her cousin as if she was paying attention to her every word, but she was actually not with her at all, for she was thinking how odd it was that Bett should have such ideas about herself, and the width of the gulf between her own upbringing and that of Maggie's daughter, for instance. Also she began again to think of the freak storm, that spurt of nature which had been the deciding factor in their being brought up together.

It had happened on a day in nineteen-thirty-eight when she was twelve. The two families had decided to go to Wales for a seaside-caravan holiday, and for five glorious days the sun shone down on them and they lazed on the sands, or went swimming; sometimes the brothers, taking a small boat, went out fishing. It was on the afternoon of the day before they were to return home that the freak storm occurred. The sky became overcast making it like night, then the wind came with terrifying swiftness and what had been gentle waves were lashed into gigantic mountains of water. Jenny could recall how her mother, crouched on the floor of the caravan, had held her tightly in her arms as she prayed. And beside them had crouched Bett and her mother. She remembered Bett, who was only nine then, saying, 'Daddy'll get wet, won't he?'

The next morning they had found the remains of the boat on the rocks along the coast, and three days later the brothers' bodies came in with the early morning tide, and strangely they had lain only four feet away from each other, and about two hundred yards from where they had set off in the boat.

After the numbness of the shock wore off and loneliness hit them, the two widows decided it would be better if they joined forces and pooled their small resources. So they rented a four-roomed downstairs-house, as it were termed, near the children's school, and Jenny's mother resumed the office work she had been doing before she married, while Bett's mother returned to the stocking counter in Weaver's Drapery store in the High Street, at which she had started years previously when she was fifteen.

The arrangement worked amicably enough for two years, until Jenny's mother, still lonely in heart and with not much will to live, gave in to a severe bout of influenza. And so Jenny, at the age of fourteen, was left with Aunty May.

Under the circumstances Aunty May had been kind to her, although she did take all the three hundred pounds that her mother had saved from her father's life insurance. But then, of course, Jenny knew, even without Aunty May giving her to understand, that she had to be fed and clothed until she could work. Jenny had learned one lesson very early in life. It was: if you made yourself useful, people put up with you. She had made herself useful to Aunty May, and also to Bett, and they had both accepted her usefulness without question. Should anyone at times, as they did, praise her for her industry her Aunty May, and her cousin Bett, would always say, 'Oh, Jenny's made like that.'

But Jenny knew that she hadn't been make like that. There had been lots of things she had resented doing, especially for Bett, for she knew that her cousin looked upon her as a kind of servant, at best someone who should make herself useful out of gratitude for a home. Deeply she had resented this, but she had the power to hide it. She also had the power to hide the pain that her reflection in the mirror caused her. And in her teens she had dared to protest against the reflection, for there was Bett, dark, vivacious, pretty, referred to as a live wire and a spark, attracting attention wherever she went; holding people with her bright chatter, apparently happy about everything in life that affected her, except her name. The name Chilmaid had become a source of irritation, even shame, to Bett from the time when she was fifteen and a boy, punning the name, had said, 'Bet you're a chill maid.' She had come home in tears that day, and from then onwards her name had taken on a kind of phobia. She wanted rid of it, and the only way to be rid of it was to get married. It was on this same day, when Jenny had tried to comfort her, that she had rounded on her, crying, 'It's all right for you, you look like a chill maid and always will.'

There are some things, silly things, that burn deep into the mind, and even when they heal with the years you can still feel the scars. Jenny hadn't realized how deeply she had resented, even the scars, until she had talked to Ben. Ben had been like a dredger cleaning her mind.

As her thoughts drifted over the years she was suddenly aware of Bett's voice.

'Jenny, listen. What's the matter? ... You're nearly asleep. Are you tired? I don't believe you've heard a word I've said.'

21

'Yes, I have. You were saying that James Knowles had come to work in the new laboratory attached to the Burley Group and had called in last week.' Jenny smiled.

'Yes. Yes, it was that, but you looked miles away.'

'Is he still with his wife?'

'No, he divorced her.'

'You mean she divorced him.'

'Well, whichever way it was, they're divorced. You never did like him, did you?'

'No, I didn't. I could never stand a man who wanted to tell you a dirty joke before he'd been in your company two minutes.'

'Oh, don't be silly, Jenny.' Again Bett rose to her feet. 'James just does that to you because he knows it shocks you. I'm sure he doesn't do it to anyone else.'

'Shocks me!' Jenny's eyebrows moved into points, lengthening her face still further. 'Four years on hospital wards, and a good part of the last ten spent nursing men ... I'll take some shocking. No, James Knowles talked to me as he talks to all women. He's dirty. There are men like that.'

'Jenny.' Bett was smiling tolerantly at Jenny now. 'You're so naïve; sometimes I think you're younger than Lorna.'

When Jenny made no comment on this Bett turned from her and threw her half-burned cigarette into the heart of the fire. And at this point Paul entered the room carrying a tray.

'There you are.' He put the tray on a table on the opposite side of the hearth from his wife, and sitting down beside it he poured out a cup of tea, and handing it to Jenny with exaggerated ceremony, he said, 'There you are, ma-dam. Cream off the top of a new bottle and two lumps, and if you take my advice you'll improve it with a little dash of whisky.'

'This is one time I'm not taking your advice.' Jenny took the cup from him. 'Thanks, Paul.' Her eyes smiled at him. Then looking him up and down, she said, 'I do believe you're losing weight.'

'I am.' He nodded at her brightly. 'I've lost half a stone this last month, down to fourteen two.' He pulled his trousers away from his waist. 'I'm terrified they'll drop off in the street, or, worse still, at the clinic. Not that the mothers would mind, but ooh! Sister Reilly. Imagine! How did that woman ever become a Sister, even a nurse? She should be in a closed order.'

Jenny had at one time worked with Sister Reilly, and what Paul had said struck her so funny that she laughed with him loudly, until, seeing Bett's straight face, she let her laughter fade away. That was another thing she had learned. In a divided house you laughed with the woman if you wanted peace.

Yet need she bother now? Was caution necessary any more? Did it matter any longer if she annoyed Bett or not? Yes, yes it did. For it was true what Aunt May had said, she was made in a particular way. She had always wanted peace, and she had bought peace, and the price had meant the submerging of her own individuality, so deeply that bringing it to the surface again would, she imagined, be almost an impossibility.

'Well now, I'm waiting. Come on, let's have your news.' Paul pulled his coat sleeve up and looked at his watch. 'I've got half-an-hour. That includes my eating time; say ten minutes for that. Can you get through your lurid life story during the past months in twenty minutes?'

'I think so.' Jenny straightened herself, pressed her back against the corner of the couch, then wetted her lips preparatory to speaking again. But no words came, and after looking from one to the other and shaking her head she lowered it, and putting her cup down on the little wine table at her side she took a handkerchief from the pocket of her suit and blew her nose.

'What is it?' Paul asked quietly. 'Are you in trouble, Jinny?' He was sitting on the edge of his chair now, leaning towards her. Bett, too, had also moved towards her from the other end of the couch.

'Is Mr. Hoffman worse?' Paul narrowed his eyes as he asked the question.

'He's dead.' Jenny again blew her nose. It had a loud sound as befitted a large nose.

'Oh, I'm sorry. But then'—he nodded—'in a way I suppose it was best. He's been bedridden lately, hasn't he?'

Jenny inclined her head slowly. And now Bett put in, 'I've never seen you upset like this before. Somehow I thought you had got used to people dying.'

'You never get used to people dying.' Paul was not so much answering his wife as making a statement.

And Bett, going on as if she had not been interrupted, said, 'You're not worried about getting another post surely? Why, you're as rare as gold dust these days. If it's a job you're after there's one waiting right here any time you like, you know that.' Bett's smile was accompanied by an expansive movement of her hand which indicated the whole house.

23

Jenny looked up at her now. 'I won't be wanting another job, Bett. You see ... well, Benjamin Hoffman was not just my patient, he ... he was my husband. We were married six months ago.'

'Jinny!' Paul fell slowly against the back of the chair, and he pulled his chin in and pressed his head to the side as if to bring Jenny's face into focus.

'Is it so surprising that I should marry?' She was addressing him pointedly, and the question brought his big head thrusting forward. 'No, no, my God, no. Only why didn't you tell us? It isn't like you to hold out on anything. You never said a word in your letters.'

Jenny picked up her cup and gulped quickly at the tea, and after she had swallowed she said, 'I ... I meant to, every week I meant to, but somehow I just couldn't write it down. And then the time passed so quickly, and he became so ill.'

Paul stopped himself from asking the question, 'Were you happy?' It was unlikely that she was happy, other than in her job, being married to a partly paralysed bedridden man. And yet, who knew but that she was happy. It surprised him that in an odd kind of way he felt saddened by the idea that Jenny could be happy married to a total invalid, an old, total invalid, for in spite of her looks he knew that she was very much alive inside. If she had been happy it meant that she was reconciled at thirty-nine to middle-age and was becoming grateful for anything. It hurt him to think she had reached that stage; she deserved something better. She'd had no life.

'When did it happen?' he asked now.

'About a month ago.'

'A month ago?' Bett put in quickly, her voice high. 'You mean he died a month ago? Well, where have you been all this time?'

'Oh.' Jenny smiled weakly. 'There was a lot to see to. I sold the house and the furniture. I just kept a few good pieces. I did ... I mean I'm going to do all that he wanted me to.'

'Had he money?' It was a soft enquiry from Bett.

'Yes, but——' Her face took on a stiffness. 'But I didn't marry him for that. I didn't know what he had ... what he was worth before I married him. In fact I thought he was afraid I would leave him because his money was running out or something, and it was one way to keep me.... At least that was how I thought for a little while, and then I found out that he ...

24

well...' She shook her head and lowered her gaze again. She could not say, 'He loved me'; it would sound too ludicrous to these two people who knew all about her, who were all the family she'd had until Benjamin had made her his wife.

'Well! He had money then? Go on.' Bett had screwed herself to the edge of the couch until she was almost sitting in front of Jenny. 'I mean real money?'

Jenny gave a little smile. 'I suppose you would call it real money; my share was forty-seven thousand.'

Bett did not repeat the sum, it was as if she had been stunned by the force of the amount. Forty-seven thousand pounds! A man had left that amount to this long, thin, odd-looking creature. Oh, granted she was kind, and good, and thoughtful, but what what else could anyone be who looked like her at thirty-nine. You had to be something different to make up for a face like Jenny had. Yet a man had married her and left her forty-seven thousand. It wasn't fair ... IT WASN'T FAIR. Bett remembered that when her own mother had died and left her five hundred pounds she hadn't offered Jenny a penny; and she could have done because it happened just after she had married Paul when she had the idea she was sitting pretty for the rest of her life. If only she had given her something.... Oh, what was the use. She lifted her eyes up to her husband; he was standing over Jenny holding her hand, saying, 'If anyone deserves a slice of luck you do, Jinny. But tell me, what did he want you to do? You said he wanted you to do certain things. Aw, don't cry.'

Jenny was crying unrestrainedly but quietly now, the tears running unchecked down her unmade-up sallow cheeks. 'He ... he wanted me to enjoy myself.'

'Good for him. I wish I had met him; he sounds like a man after my own heart. Had he any relatives?'

'A son. He came over from America for the funeral. He ... he seemed pleased that I had married his father, ever ... ever so pleased.' Jenny's head moved as if she still couldn't believe this fact. 'I ... I thought he might question the will but no, he even seemed pleased about that an' all. He had the same amount but he doesn't need anything. He's got a big bacon-curing business of his own. He's a widower himself and no children.' She smiled as she cried, and her tear-drenched face looked odder still. 'He said that if ever he became ill he would send for me, solely on the recommendation of his father's letters. He ... he made me

25

laugh. In a way he was very like his father because we laughed a lot, Ben and I, and he said, I mean the son said, it would be a funny thing if I were to marry him an' all.' Her voice cracked, her face falling into painful lines, the tears spurted from her eyes, and from her throat were forced hard, broken sobs.

Paul, sitting on the edge of the couch, put his arm about her and drew her head against his chest, and looking towards his wife he said softly, 'Pour a drop of brandy out.'

Without demur Bett did as she was bidden. Going to the cabinet in the far corner of the room she poured a good measure into a glass and brought it back to the couch. 'Here, dear, drink this up,' she said.

Jenny gulped at the brandy, then drying her face with a large handkerchief Paul held out to her she said, 'I'm sorry; I didn't mean to go on like this.'

'You go on as much as you like, it'll do you good.'

'Your room's still ready for you,' said Bett now. 'I'll switch on the blanket and you have an early night; you'll feel better in the morning. Then you must stay and have a long rest.' She smiled sweetly down on her cousin, and Jenny, looking up at her, nodded and said, 'Thanks, Bett, but ...' She hesitated. They were kind; they were both kind. Jenny's mind evaded the knowledge that Bett's kindness, in particular, was a self-seeking kindness. Also she didn't dwell on Bett's invitation for her to rest; there was no rest for anyone in this house. The emotions were too taut, but at this moment she would sooner have stayed than say what she had to say. 'I've ... I've got to go up to town tomorrow, Bett. Thanks all the same.'

'Well, what's in that? You can come back in the evening.'

'Oh, I don't mean Newcastle, Bett; I mean London.'

'London!'

'Yes.'

'What are you going to do in London?'

'I've a bit of business to see to.' Jenny turned her eyes from Bett and glanced at Paul where he was still sitting on the edge of the couch, and he said, 'Is it the money? Isn't it settled yet?'

'Oh, yes, that's all right. It's ... it's just something I'm going to do.' She dropped her eyes from his and muttered under her breath, 'Don't ask me what it is, it would appear so silly. I'll be back in three weeks and then you'll know all about it.'

'Is it such a mystery? Can't you give us an inkling?' There

26

was an impatient note in Bett's voice, and before Jenny had time to answer, Paul, looking at his wife, said, 'It's Jinny's business. She says she'll tell us later, so we'll just have to wait, won't we?' He rose from his seat, his eyes still on his wife, and as he watched her face tighten he warned himself to go steady, not to start her off and Jinny not in the house five minutes; so changing his tone and forcing himself to smile, he said with weak jocularity, 'She's holding out on us. It's my guess she's going up there to open a night club.' He turned his smile on Jenny, and she, closing her eyes, said, 'Oh, Paul! A night club ... Me!' Then again, 'Oh, Paul!' She sniffed on a laugh and blew her nose once more.

As Paul, about to carry the joke still further, bent towards her, the drawing-room door opened and a young girl came in, crying, 'Mammy, have you seen...?' Her voice stopped with her feet, and then, her expression stretching her mouth wide, she cried, 'Aunt Jenny! Why, Aunt Jenny!' In a bound she was on the couch, her arms about Jenny, repeating all the while, 'Oh, Aunt Jenny.'

Jenny, holding her close, buried her face in the young girl's soft, jet-black hair. Then after a moment, pressing her away, she scanned the face that looked like a warm wax cameo. She had never seen anyone with skin like this girl's, nor a face like hers, a face that seemed built without the support of bones. The eyes were almond-shaped and grey, the upper lids full and smooth, lending to the whole an oriental look. The lips were not bow-shaped nor yet full as in young girls. They appeared somewhat shapeless, yet the mouth looked soft and fascinating. Jenny had always loved to watch Lorna talk, simply to see her lips move.

'They told me you hadn't grown,' she said, casting an accusing glance from Paul to Bett. 'Why, you've put on inches.'

'I have? You think so, Aunt Jenny? Coo! Good-o.' Lorna's vocabulary was girlish and her voice slightly husky. She galloped on: 'When did you come? Why didn't you come upstairs to my room? How long are you staying? ... Ooh!' Again she had Jenny enfolded in her fierce young embrace, and moving her cheek against her aunt's, she said, 'Aw, it's lovely, it's lovely to have you back.'

'Well, stop rumpling her like that,' Bett put in sharply; 'and get your feet off the couch.' She slapped at her daughter's legs. 'And you can stop kidding yourself that you're going to have someone waiting on you hand and foot during the next few weeks because your Aunt Jenny is leaving in the morning.'

'Aw, no!'

'Aw, yes.' Jenny was laughing now as she nodded back at Lorna's horrified expression. 'But I'll be back in three weeks or so.'

'Three weeks! Then you're not going on another job?'

'No, not this time, not for a while.'

'What do you think?' Paul had dropped on his hunkers by the side of the couch and taken hold of Jenny's hand. 'Your Aunt Jenny's married now.'

'Married? You? . . . Oh! I didn't mean it like that, Aunt Jenny. It's wonderful you being married. Fancy you married.' She opened her mouth wide, but emitted no sound. It was a gesture from her childhood. It usually followed amazement or surprise, and undoubtedly she was surprised now. Then she said, 'Does it mean that you'll not be able to come here like you usually do?'

'No, it doesn't. In fact it means that we're going to see more of her.' Paul thrust his other hand out towards Lorna. 'She'll likely be living with us, won't you, Jinny?' He wagged her hand as if to bring assurance from her, and she answered him rapidly, saying, 'Oh, now, Paul, Paul. We'll have to see.'

'Oh, yes, yes, Aunt Jenny. Oh, that would be simply marvellous. Oh, we'd have some fun. . . . But . . . but what about your husband?'

'Well,' Jenny said, evenly now, 'he died.'

'So soon? Oh, Aunt Jenny!' She looked sad, and Jenny said, 'It's all right. We'll talk about it some other time. . . . Now it's your turn. Tell me what you've been doing?'

'What's she been doing? I can tell you that,' put in Paul. 'Chasing the boys. At least, a boy. And not such a boy either, he's as tall as me. Brian Bolton. You know, the Mayor's son. Ah! ha! You didn't think I saw you. "Can I carry your school bag, Miss Higgins?" '

His teasing was checked by Lorna giving him a push, which caused him to overbalance on to the hearth rug, and as she went to pounce on him Bett cried, 'Stop it! Stop that horseplay!'

Her voice had the power to sober them all, and Lorna, hitching herself back on to the couch, took hold of Jenny's hand while Paul, straightening his coat as he rose to his feet, said, his voice flat now, 'I'm going to have a bite, and then I've one or two calls to make. I'll likely see you before you go to bed, Jinny,

28

but if you want to get off early I'll see you in the morning. What time do you propose leaving?'

'I was going to get the twelve o'clock from Newcastle.'

'I'll run you there.'

'Thanks, Paul.'

He went out of the room, across the hall to the far end, and entered the kitchen; and there, taking a covered plate from the bottom oven of the Aga cooker, he placed it on the Formica-topped table by the kitchen window, where was set a knife, fork, and cruet, and slowly and thoughtfully he began to eat. And as he did so the pleasure of seeing Jenny again faded and he became filled with irritation.

He hated eating in the kitchen. He didn't mind occasionally, such as last thing at night when he would scrape up something for himself, but even then he often put it on a tray and took it into the drawing-room, for the radiator in the dining-room was always turned down after lunch. 'A waste of fuel,' she said. The new order was: meals after six o'clock would be taken in the kitchen ... of course, provided Maggie had gone. He raised his eyes from the plate and looked around the kitchen. It had a clinical look, almost like the operating theatre. The big old easy chair with the sunken bottom was no longer in the corner, nor was the old pouffe that his mother had brought into the kitchen so that Maggie could put her legs up for half-an-hour after she had done the dinner washing-up. In place of the chair and the pouffe stood a washing-machine and spin-drier, and on the other side of the stove near the window stood a five-foot-high, naked-looking fridge. The old dresser had gone and in its place was a cabinet of frosted glass with drawers that stuck unless you used both hands to close them. And under the big working table in the centre of the room stood four plastic-topped stools.

The change, in the kitchen alone, since his mother had died was drastic. It was a wonder Maggie stuck it. Yet he thought he knew why she stuck it, and the knowledge warmed him.

He gathered up the dirty dishes and was on his way to the sink when Lorna put her head round the kitchen door. 'I thought you might have gone.' She came into the room at a run, adding, 'I've got a good Mrs. McAnulty, Daddy.'

As he turned the tap on the greasy dishes he glanced at her and smiled, saying, 'I haven't time for a Mrs McAnulty now. I've got an important call; I should be there.' He continued to look at her. He thought she had finished with the Mrs.

McAnulty game, as she hadn't broached it for some time. It was a game that had started years ago when she had demanded he play patients with her. He had been quite willing to let it die a natural death as she was fast growing up, at least she should be, but she was still a very young fifteen for these days. And he was glad of it. Oh yes, yes.

'Aw, it won't take a minute. It's a good one.'

'When I come back,' he said.

'I'll be in bed.'

'All right.' He nodded, then lifting a detergent carton from the draining board he squeezed some liquid into the water, after which he reached for a towel on the rail by the sink and wiped his hands. 'Well now.' He turned to her and adopted an exaggeratingly long countenance, and in a sober tone said, 'Good evening, Mrs. McAnulty.'

'Evenin', Doctor.' Lorna too had taken on a pose; she was now imitating the actions of what she imagined was an agitated patient.

'What can I do for you, Mrs. McAnulty?'

'Am bad, Doctor.'

'I can see that, Mrs. McAnulty. Tell me about it?'

'I've got hydro-ceph-alus.' She had difficulty in pronouncing the word, and as she finished Paul put his head back and let out a bellow of a laugh. 'Hydrocephalus. That's a beauty. Where did you come across that one?'

'Ah! ha! Ah! ha!' She was laughing up at him, wagging her finger in his face. 'There's more where that comes from. Just you wait; you've met your match at last, Doc-tor Higgins.'

'I should say I have. Well, Mrs. McAnulty'—he resumed his stern pose—'what are your symptoms?'

'Well, Doctor, me head's grown so big'—She demonstrated with her hands held level with her shoulders.

'You can say that again.' As Paul made this aside in a low voice, she cried, 'Aw, behave and listen. Listen.' Then slanting her eyes to the ceiling she concentrated her attention there as she went on, 'The disease made its appearance when I was six months old, and the water collected inside my head, and the bones not yet being set allowed it to form a kind of bag and it grew bigger and bigger until my head was as big as my body....'

'Poor soul.'

'Aw. Listen, will you? They thought at first it was only rickets, but it wasn't, I had dropsy of the brain, known to the uninitiated as water on the brain ... Doctor.'

Paul thrust out a hand and gripped her chin, and, laughing again, he said, 'Very good. Very good. Where did you find it?'

'Oh, I've bought a gem of a book. It's called *The Family Physician*. I got it on Rankin's Bookstall for three shillings. It's got one thousand one hundred and seventy-six pages.'

'No kiddin'?'

'It's a gem. Mr. Rankin said it might be worth a lot of money if I keep it a little longer. It's got a picture of St. Thomas's Hospital in the front and a wonderful coloured paper skeleton. Well, it's not really a skeleton, it's the whole body in flaps right into the be-owels. Coo! Doc-tor, it's beautiful.'

'It sounds it. I'll have to have a look into this gem. But, Mrs. McAnulty'—he was walking from the kitchen now with his arm around her shoulder—'I wouldn't go searching for medical books at present, not unless you have a consultation with Dr. Higgins first. Understand?'

'But it's a gem, Daddy. Really, it's a scream. It gives you all the diseases and all the cures, and there's six frousty pictures of old men in the front between bones and things. One is Sir William Jenner, Bart., K.C.B., M.D., F.R.S., and some. Oh he looks a holy terror. Some look sort of human but he looks as if he could eat you, like that Professor Wheelan you used to tell me about, remember?'

As he got into his coat in the hall he said to her seriously, 'The information is bound to be very dated, and quite a number of methods obsolete. We'd better look at it together some time, eh?'

'O.K.' She wagged her head at him. 'But it's all practice. In one part it says a nurse should not be so young as to be giddy nor so old as to be useless. And you know, Daddy, it says a woman should stay in bed for three weeks after she's had a baby, and rest on a couch each day until the end of the month. It's a scream, isn't it? Mrs. Price was out at the end of a week.'

'Ah, but then, don't forget Mrs. Price is a doctor's wife.'

He laughed down on her. 'I'd better see this great find of yours. And I wouldn't look upon it as practice yet.'

'Oh, all right, but it's priceless, Daddy. Aunty Jenny'll laugh her head off. I was on my way to get it to show her. And oh, isn't it lovely to have her back? And fancy her being married.' Her voice dropped to a whisper now. 'Fancy Aunt Jenny being married, Daddy. She's lovely, but ...'

In the act of picking up his bag from the side-table he paused and, turning and facing her squarely, said, 'Your Aunt Jinny is lovely, there's no buts; never judge by looks. Start early in this, Lorna, and practise it. Every time you see someone like your Aunt Jinny, say to yourself, she's only like that outside, and the outside doesn't matter.'

'Yes, Daddy. I didn't mean anything, I ... I love my Aunt Jenny.' Her voice was sober.

'Good enough then.'

As he turned away she walked with him to the front door, and there she said, brightly now, 'Oh, I forgot to tell you, Daddy. Miss Charlton said I should sail through the exam. I came out second in maths in the mock. I could have come top if I'd paid more attention, I know I could, but I will in the real thing. I told her that I'd finally made up my mind to be a doctor and she's all for it. She's lovely is Miss Charlton.'

'That's fine. Keep it up.' He pulled his hat on, pressing the brim down over his brow. 'Now get inside or you'll catch cold; it's cutting out here.'

'Goodnight, Daddy. I suppose I'll be in bed when you get back.' She reached up, and he bent down and kissed her. Then she went into the house and he into the car, and as he started it up, and drove with less than his usual caution out of the Square, he repeated to himself, 'A doctor. She wants to be a doctor.' It was laughable really. Yet no, there was nothing laughable about it. It just gave you food for thought, a lot of thought.

TWO

IVY

It was ten minutes past eight when Mrs. Ratcliffe's companion let Paul out of the front door. 'Thank you for coming, Doctor, she'll be better now,' she said.

He made no answer to the last, but jerking his head, replied, 'Goodnight, Miss Thompson.'

In the car he sat for a moment debating whether he should go straight to Ivy's or call in at the club. The thought of the club brought his teeth together. He didn't feel like the club to-night.... Councillor Ramsay with his constant, 'Now this is 'ow I see it. Fair's fair like.' And the regulars. Parkins from his solicitor's platform looking down on Ramsay, despising him but needing him, for Ramsay's business siphoned money into his pocket. Then old Beresford with his weedy body and outdated medicine. Paul's mouth twisted as he remembered Lorna's find, *The Family Physician*, by the sound of it late nineteenth-century. He wouldn't be a bit surprised if old Beresford used a similar one as a reference book. But it was the thought of Beresford that told him he must visit the club first, that it would be policy to go there as often as possible in the near future if he hoped to get on the short list for the assistant physician's post at the hospital when Travers retired, which would be some time in the New Year. He hated the idea that he was nervous of Beresford, that some part of him feared his power. Beresford was near retiring, but until he died, Paul knew, the old man wouldn't get over the fact that twice he had failed to be selected for such a post. The first time, in Newcastle, he had been made to feel like a small fish in a big pool. The second failure was even worse, when they voted in favour of a younger man. He had never again applied but he had put his disappointment to use. He had turned it into a whip to flay his own kind. It was a well-known fact that there would be more than one happy doctor in Fellburn when old Beresford disappeared from the scene.

Paul had never liked Beresford, nor had his father before him, and he would have despised himself if he had felt the slightest inclination to butter him up now. Yet he warned himself not to antagonize him in any way, for the old man had power in his hands, the power of a church-going moralist, the power of being a close friend of Bowles, the surgeon, who was on the Regional Board.

As he entered the lobby he met the Mayor on the point of leaving. Bolton was a man Paul liked, for he carried his mayoral chain with the usual quality of humility, which was likely one of the reasons he had been re-elected three times; this triple event had never happened before in Fellburn. Paul looked on Bolton as a scrupulously honest man, he did not think of him as 'a worthy man'—that was Parkins's phrase, and in an odd way, he surmised, it summed up for Parkins Bolton's worldly standing, which took the form of a double fronted stationer's shop.

'Hello, there, Doctor.' The Mayor had never called him Paul, nor had he himself called the Mayor Harry, and this in itself he felt engendered a deepened mutual respect. He did not take to the bandying of Christian names; Christian names were for friends, not for the acquaintance of an evening, as was often the case. Yet he would not have minded being called Paul by a man like Bolton.

'Hello, Mr. Mayor.' It all sounded very formal, but they both smiled warmly at each other. 'Finished your day's grind?'

'No, not quite, I'm just going to collect Mrs. Bolton. We have to look in at a dance ... in aid of the old people's fund; but it'll only be a look-in, I've a full programme tomorrow.... And you, Doctor, are you finished?'

'Just one or two calls. At least I hope so.'

'So do I for your sake. Well goodnight, Doctor. My regards to Mrs. Higgins.'

'Thank you. Goodnight, Mr. Mayor. Goodnight.'

He passed from the hall into the bar, then took his drink into the main club room.

Parkins was sitting to the right of the fire, in the chair of honour you might say. It was one of a pair of enormous brown leather chairs with outsize wings, a chair that forced you to walk to the front of it to see its occupant properly, and when Paul saw Parkins's thin body almost lost in it, he paused before saying, 'Oh, hello there.'

'Hello, Paul. . . . Busy?'

'So, so. At least during the day. No epidemics at present. But there's been quite a lot of night shift these past few weeks.'

'I don't know how you do it; that would drive me mad getting up in the middle of the night.'

'You get used to it.' Paul looked around. 'Very quiet tonight.'

'Yes. There's a special committee sitting late, fighting that Labour bloke, Skiffings. He's for running up more blocks of flats in Bogs End. How in the name of God these fellows get on the council in the first place beats me.'

'By the same token that they want to put up the flats: they say they'll give the voters what they want, and in Skiffings's case he does just that. Anyway, I suppose we need opposition to keep us on our toes.' Paul said 'us' but he didn't mean us, for he had almost voted Labour last time, and with the election coming off soon it would be a pretty near thing this time. In fact, he knew that, with the present set-up, Labour would be almost sure to have his vote. Yet there would have been no issue about his voting if Butler had become Tory leader instead of Home. A man gives his life to a cause and as payment gets a kick in the backside. He didn't like that. He himself always believed in paying well for services rendered.

'Here a minute.' From the depth of his chair Parkins motioned Paul to him with a lift of his thin chin, and when Paul stood over him he said in a low voice, 'Just a word in your ear. . . . You know old B's assistant, Rankin?'

'I've never met him; I heard he had one.'

'Well, he's just down from Bart's. Bright boy; taken the lot, I understand, including your pet tangent. . . . What is it?'

'Neurology.'

'Ah yes, neurology. Well, by old B's account he's swept the board with that and all the modern isms and ologies they're packing into them up there now. What I'm trying to say, Paul, is that old B's betting on him and is already singing his praises to the board, and Travers not yet with his notice in. But you know how thick he is with Bowles. I thought I'd tip you.'

There came into Paul's chest a restricted feeling that gave warning of his quick rising anger, and it was with an effort he said coolly, 'But the fellow hasn't been in the town five minutes, nor has he a practice.'

'I've got news for you.' Parkins deliberately reached out and took a sip from his glass of whisky, and returned it to the table before saying, 'Brace yourself.'

Paul waited.

'B's going to let him have his.'

'What!'

'S'fact.' Parkins jerked his meticulously brushed head and raised his eyebrows and showed a face full of concern, behind which Paul read the enjoyment his solicitor was experiencing in delivering this blow, this velvet-padded blow. Straightening up he looked hard down at him as he said, 'I think you're a blind jump ahead, Roy. You see Beresford can't hand over the practice to anyone he likes, that's decided by the local executive council. The days of selling practices are over. Since he was in practice before nineteen forty-eight he'll be compensated, but as for handing on his practice to whom he likes . . . Well, as I said, you're a . . .'

'Oh, I'm not a jump ahead, Paul, blind or otherwise. Oh, no. I know quite well, oh I know in ordinary circumstances you can't sell your practice now. But this is the point: you do know that there's only you and old B standing alone in this town, all the rest are working in twos and threes. Well, it's my idea, and I think I'm right, that old B's tactics are going to be in the form of a bluff. He's not quite due for retirement yet, but it's my guess he's suddenly going to give up, ill-health. That's why he has Rankin. There's not enough doctors in the town, as you know, growing as it is, and the three new factories going up, so what will happen? He'll propose Rankin and that, as I see it, will be that. So you'll need all your wits to get over that old codger. You'll have to keep on your toes, Paul. I'm just telling you. Thought I'd put you in the picture. And this isn't all surmise or hearsay about Rankin, no; I may as well tell you I'm speaking from good authority.'

There was a fury straining to burst from him. Parkins talking to him with that damned superior air as if he was giving advice to a sixth-former going out into the world. He forced himself to smile at him and say nonchalantly, 'Oh, I'm not worried, I think I'll manage. Beresford likes licking cubs; I consider I'm past that stage now.'

As he walked away Parkins put his head round the wing of the chair and asked, 'You off already?'

'No, I'm just going to have another, but I must be on my way soon, I've some calls to make. . . . And then there's the night shift looming up.' He laughed, and had the satisfaction of seeing a puzzled expression on Parkins's face as it was slowly with-drawn behind the wing once more.

Five minutes later he was in the car again. His anger now spilling over, he swore under his breath as he drove out of the club yard. 'Damn and blast them, both Parkins and Beresford.' He wouldn't stand for it, he wouldn't. He had worked for years towards this appointment, and he was damned if Beresford was going to get the better of him now by pushing a pup under his nose. Yet what could he do?

The question was still with him when he drove round the perimeter of the market place, along by the park, past the foot of Brampton Hill, then up the long steep road that led to the cemetery, and beyond the slag heaps. He was now in the country, his headlights picking out the low stone walls, the hedges, the lone cottages. About two miles south of the town he turned the car into a narrow lane and brought his speed down to ten miles per hour, and when, after about half a mile of driving, the wheels went into the comparative softness of frost-covered turf, he drew the car to a stop. Before getting out he switched off the lights, then went towards the bungalow.

There was a light on over the porch and another in a window to the left of it, and as he entered the gate the front door opened and a young woman stepped into the light and greeted him.

She looked about thirty, of medium height and plump build. Her hair was brown and wavy and fell down each side of her round face on to her shoulders. Her face was pleasant, rather than pretty, and her smile wide and warm. Her voice too was warm, although thick with the northern inflection when she said, 'I thought you weren't going to make it.'

'I didn't get out until rather late; I was held up.'

As he went to put his arm around her she stepped back from him into the porch, and as he followed he looked down at her, his face crinkling with enquiry. But as soon as she closed the door she lay back against it and held her arms wide, and he went into them and pressed her to him, kissing her with a hard dry kiss. When it was finished and she rested her head back against his arm, he looked at her closely. 'Why did you do that ... I mean move away just then?'

'Oh.' She wagged her head. 'It just struck me the other night that anyone behind the far hedge could see us.'

'Out here?'

'You never know. Arthur Wheatley, you know him who

37

farms at yon side of the road ... well, he comes over here shooting.'

'But he's no right; they're your fields.'

'Well, they're let to him for grazing.'

'But he shouldn't come into the paddock, that's not let.'

'Aw.' She took his hand and drew him further into the room. 'You can't stop these fellows wandering round. Farmers are like Peeping Toms; you find them in all odd places, and they always seem to have a right to be there.' She turned swiftly to him again and once more they kissed. Then as he moved his hands down her back he drew his lips from hers and said quietly. 'You've got nothing on underneath, you'll catch your death. It's freezing out.'

'I've just had a bath and you know I never catch cold. I'm as strong as a horse.' Her round blue eyes twinkled up at him. 'But if you like, I'll go and put some clothes on, Doctor.' She pursed her lips on the word doctor, and he jerked her to him and muttered, 'Oh, Ivy, Ivy.' When he buried his face deep in her hair she said softly, 'In a minute, in a minute, but look....' She pressed herself from him and pulled him to the couch that was drawn up before the red-stone fireplace, and pulling off his overcoat she said, 'Have you had anything to eat?'

'I had a bite around seven.'

'I've got some casserole steak in the oven. I just did it on spec. Do you fancy a bite?'

He looked up at her, then said meaningly, 'There's not much time.'

'There's time for everything.' She rubbed her finger gently across his lips, and he caught at her hand and put his lips to her broad, hard palm and muttered into it, 'Aw, Ivy, you're a lifesaver.'

'Here, give me your shoes.' She bent down and undid his shoes, then swung his legs up on to the couch. Her hands were strong, her arms thick and as he fell back and she bent over him to undo his tie the lapels of her dressing gown fell apart and exposed her firm full breasts, and before she tightened her girdle he laid his fingers gently on her warm flesh. At his action they both smiled and, their hands gripping, they held fast to each other for a moment.

When she left him to go into the kitchen he lay still, letting out one deep breath after another until he had the feeling he was sinking through the bottom of the couch. This was peace,

peace. What would he do without Ivy? Go mad. Stark staring mad.

'Were you very busy last night?' Her voice came to him from the kitchen.

'Yes, up till ten, and then I had a call at half-past three this morning.'

'No! You must be feeling dead.'

'I was, but not now.... Oh, what do you think, Ivy? Jinny turned up today.'

'Oh, that's nice.' Ivy's voice was high. 'Oh, I'm glad; she's an oiler of wheels is Jenny.'

'You'll never guess what. She's married.' He twisted his head round the side of the couch as he heard her come to the kitchen door, and he looked at her from an almost upside-down position as she exclaimed, 'Jenny married!'

'Yes. It surprised me, but I was glad.'

'So am I. I always thought that when you got past her face she had everything. Mind ... I'm not meaning that nasty like, about her face, you know I'm not, cos after a time you didn't notice her nose or how she looked, you just liked her. I don't think anybody could help likin' her.'

'That's what I think.' He lifted his head back on to the couch and Ivy returned to the kitchen. After a moment he called to her, 'And she's rich. Well, comparatively so. Anyway, I wish I had what she has, stacked behind me, with no calls on it. It would be good-bye National Health, thank you very much, sir.'

'Did you say she's rich?' Ivy was at the door again.

'Yes, forty-seven thousand. I suppose you'd call that rich.'

'He's given it to her?'

'No, he died and left it to her.'

'Well! Well!' She came walking slowly towards the couch, and when she looked down on him she said, 'It's romantic, isn't it? And fancy all that happening to Jenny. MISS Jenny.'

Paul raised his eyebrows and nodded. Then he spoke of the woman whose image had been evoked by the word 'Miss'. 'She's not pleased at Jinny's news. Oh, she pretended to be, but she's as green as grass. And she had another disappointment. She thought she was in for some free labour, but Jinny's off to London in the morning on some business and she won't tell her what it is. She didn't tell me either. But apparently her husband wanted her to do something and she's going up to town to do it and we'll know about it when she comes back. It's all very mysterious .. and nice for Jinny.'

'Good luck to her.' Ivy screwed up her face as she smiled at him; then added, 'Come on, sit up and have this, it's ready. I'm bringing it in.'

She brought the tray into the room and placed it on a low table before the couch, and she sat close beside him as he ate, and every now and again he would turn his big head towards her and nuzzle her or butt her forehead with his own. At one point he stopped eating, and with his voice devoid of all rancour he stated calmly, 'Old Beresford's all out to do me down over that hospital appointment, so I've just heard.'

'No! Oh, no! But what can he do?'

'Oh, he can do a lot. And Parkins is with him.... You know.' He stopped eating and wagged his fork at her. 'I often wondered why I didn't like Parkins, and the reason came to me tonight as he was talking: it's because he doesn't like me. Simple, isn't it?' He smiled. 'Yet I liked his father; he was a nice old fellow, witty; should have been a barrister. His turn of phrase was lost on the locals. But his son is a different kettle of fish; there's a mean streak in him.' He was looking towards the fire now, the fork still poised in his hand, and he seemed to be talking to himself rather than to her. 'It's funny how often, when like meets up with like, whether they are good, bad, or indifferent; there's always a greater chance of harmony between them than if they team up with their opposites. People yammer on about the success of opposites, but they are only going by externals. It's the traits and characteristics that tell in the long run. That's why Parkins and Beresford hit it, and they'll queer my pitch if they can.'

'But what can they do?'

'Oh.' He brought his attention back to her. 'Oh, old Beresford has an assistant, a bright boy I understand. He's got him lined up for the post. Beresford's a vindictive old swine. He never liked my father, they were poles apart in every way.... Liking again, you see.' He nodded at her. 'And he likes me less, but he's never been able to do much about it until this opportunity came up. He must be congratulating him. I can see him in church on a Sunday thanking God for giving him another chance to act as His deputy.'

He laughed, expecting her to join him, but her face straight, she said, 'But you've got the qualifications. Look how hard you've worked. I don't know much about how these things are

40

settled, but surely they can see you're the right man for the job. Everybody wants to be on your books.'

He laid down his knife and fork and, cupping her chin in his hands, said, 'If they were all like you, Ivy, they would. But the ones who want to be on my books never get on committees. You know, it's one chance in a hundred when the right man for any job gets it, Ivy, and in this town it's you scratch my back and I'll scratch yours. But even then you've got to be ... my kind of fellow, you understand, before I'll scratch you.' He squeezed her chin, then picked up his knife and fork again and went on talking as he ate. 'This, they would have you believe, is the age of the classless society. Ha! ha! ha! God, people are more class-conscious than they were in my father's day, and more conscious of being class-conscious, if you follow me. I pity any fellow in this town who wants to get on in one of the professions unless he's a member of the right church ... or the reigning body of councillors—thank God they can't stay put for ever—or a member of the Conservative Club ... of which I am a member.' He bowed his head ironically to her. 'I know it's no use griping, the same kind of thing goes on in every town, but oh, they're so pie in this place, so holier than thou.... Aw, old men who have forgotten they were ever young make me want to throw up.'

When he stopped speaking she made no response, and after a moment he pushed the table to one side. Then turning to her, he put his arms about her and looking into her face asked, 'What is it? What's the matter, you're quiet all of a sudden?'

'Nothing.' She was smiling broadly. 'What could be the matter?'

'You're not going to start worrying about what I've just told you.'

'Of course not, why should I?'

'Oh, I know you.' He took his hands from her and turned his body round and sat on the edge of the couch, his elbows on his knees, his hands clasped between them. 'I shouldn't tell you things, it only starts you worrying. I tell myself I won't....'

'Oh, darlin', give over, you can tell me anything. If not me, who else?' She was in front of him now, pulling him to his feet. 'Come on.' Her voice was tender and her smile warm as she led him to the bedroom, and there, her actions appearing natural and unembarrassed, she took off her dressing-gown and got into the big double bed. Within a minute he was beside her, holding

41

her full, firm body to him. After a moment of relishing the feel of her he looked down into her open face and said, 'I mean it, Ivy. Every time I say I'd go round the bend without you, it's true.'

'And Doctor, dear.' She was laughing at him. 'I always say to that, there's another road round the bend, don't I?'

'You won't get tired of me, Ivy?'

'Tired of you?' She strained her face away from his. 'Aw, don't be silly. Me get tired of you!'

'But I feel I'm taking your life, your young life; you could marry. Any day in the week you could marry.... What's his name?'

'I know that.' She wagged her head mischievously. 'That makes me think I'm giving you something worth while.'

'Oh, I-eevy.'

'Aw; I love to hear you say, I-eevy, like that. You know you've got a beautiful voice. That's what I fell in love with first, your voice.'

'You trying to...? Aw, we're wasting time.' He pulled her to him fiercely.... And fiercely she responded to him....

When, later, he lay with his head between her breasts, they were past talking, and as she had done so many times before she heard his breathing become deeper, and when he gave a gentle snort she knew he had gone to sleep, and as she had done before, she would let him sleep, for perhaps ten minutes.

She lay gazing over the top of his big rumpled head towards the orange glow of the table lamp. Her body was relaxed and at peace, but not so her mind. She had heard him say many times that the body was what the mind made it. But so often, as she had lain as she was doing now, her being satisfied, her mind would start at its niggling worrying, and it was never worry for herself but worry about and for him. And in this connection her worries were many and varied. She had no doubt that her body could hold him for many a long day, but she often wondered if the day came when a man wanted something more than a body, say a woman with a mind, one who could talk about things.... But then, he had got a woman with a mind. My God and how. And look what they had done to each other. Although she loved this man as she had never imagined loving anybody in her life, she did not exonerate him from all blame for the situation that existed in Romfield House. He had never told her the beginning of it, the real cause of it, but there were times when, before she had come to mean something to him, she had blamed him for the separate rooms, for the body hunger in Bett Higgins's eyes. She had noticed the body hunger the first day she had started working there. It was odd how that had come about, her starting to work there. She had only been married three years when George had taken ill. It had started with pneumonia, brought on by working in all weathers, getting wet and the clothes drying on him, all in an endeavour to make a market garden out of four acres of poor land. And he was just beginning to see daylight when he went down with that cold; and that was the beginning of the end. He was dead within a year. All the time he was ill the doctor had attended him; not just when he should officially, but at all odd times when he thought he might be of help. And it wasn't because of her then; she wasn't in the picture, he didn't even see her. His one concern was to ease the pain of a man who had worked himself literally to death. He had said since, it had saddened him to the heart to see an effort like George's go for nothing. And then when the funeral was over he had come back and said, 'How are you fixed? What are you going to do, Mrs. Tate?' And she had told him that the bungalow was hers, for George had taken it through an insurance, so she had a roof over her head, but no money. She had told him that she couldn't run the smallholding herself, and anyway she wasn't inclined to gardening to any sort, so she was letting the two cultivated fields to a man who had a smallholding half a mile away. The other two fields she had let for grazing. One of the farmers had been to see her about them already, and the paddock she meant to hold on to, to keep the bungalow a bit private like. As for the rest, she would get a job. It was then he had asked her tentatively if she liked housework, and she had said she didn't know about liking it but she was used to it, as she had done it all her life. So it was on her twenty-sixth birthday that she had seen the inside of Romfield House for the first time, and the doctor's wife and that look in her eyes, which she recognized because its cause was also in her own body. She had also summed her up as being a bit of an upstart, and she guessed that her ah-la voice wasn't her natural one. And this was proved before very long when, off her guard or really annoyed, her mistress's vowels took their natural bent and her Tyneside upbringing came over in her inflection.

Ivy's duties had consisted of doing the housework—and there was quite a bit of it in that twelve-roomed, rambling old place—

43

and occasionally waiting on table. In her very first week she learned a great deal about the members of that small household. She learned it from the condition of their beds. Some mornings the doctor's bedclothes were thrown neatly back; at other times the bedclothes were rumpled and spoke of a disturbed night. In the child's room the bed was merely untidy, but the wife's bed always appeared as if it had been at the centre of a whirlwind.

As time went on and the pain of George's loss eased, the ache of her body increased. She had had this ache before her husband had died, because during that last year of his life he'd had no power to alleviate it. It was when she had been working at the doctor's house for fifteen months she decided to accept Arthur Wheatley's unspoken proposal. Arthur had a small farm near by. He had twenty acres in all and her bit of land was adjacent to his. She did not know whether he wanted her for herself or for the two fields. He wasn't a bad chap, she told herself; a bit quiet, but then that might be an asset. One thing she knew was that no matter how much her body cried out at night he wasn't going to get her without marriage. Once you started that, marriage went up a gum tree, and she'd seen enough of people up gum trees. She wanted marriage and respectability.

And then the doctor went down with a fever. At first they thought he had the 'flu, and then it was decided he had a bug, and the bug kept his temperature at sweating point. It had become evident to Ivy within a very short time that Mrs. Higgins was no nurse; even if she had been in sympathy with the patient, she would have found nursing an irritation. And as Miss Jenny was away on a case, and the stairs taxed Maggie's breath and bulk every time she mounted them, it seemed most natural that she herself, who had nursed her husband, should also help to nurse this man who had been so good to him. Then came the day when he was very low and she was sponging his sweat-drenched body that he said to her, 'You've got kind hands, Ivy.' That's how it had started. In that moment as they had looked at each other they exchanged their need. In the following three weeks the look was repeated again and again, and on the day that the doctor resumed his work she gave her notice in.

She knew Bett Higgins had been both annoyed and surprised. She was well satisfied with her work, she said. Was it because of the extra running up and down stairs over the past few weeks?

No. Then did she want more money? No. In the end she had told her she was going to be married.

She had left on the following Friday, and on the Saturday Paul had come to the house. When she opened the door to him she hadn't been surprised, it was what she wanted. She could see him now as she had that day, this big, burly, attractive man, this man of position, this highly respected doctor, standing with his hat in his hand looking at her and asking quietly, 'Are you going to be married, Ivy?' Without hesitation she had said, 'No.' And he had said, 'You are sure of this?'

'Sure as ever I'll be of anything,' she had answered.

He had come towards her and taken her in his arms, and as naturally as if they had been made for each other from the beginning of time they came together and had satisfied each other; and it had been the same every time it had happened over the last two years. . . . Yet all the while she had worried, worried about what would happen to him if their association ever leaked out. In a town like Fellburn it could mean the finish of him, and with men like old Doctor Beresford and Mr. Parkins he couldn't be too careful. She wondered at times, if he hadn't been in the position of a doctor and hadn't carried on his business in the old house which he loved, whether he would have thrown everything up and taken her away. She wondered . . . often she wondered, but she couldn't give herself the answer.

When the clock in the hall struck the three-quarter chime she ran her fingers through his hair, saying softly, 'Paul, Paul, it's quarter to.'

'Eh? Oh!' He drew in a long shuddering breath and, stretching his legs down the bed, muttered into her flesh, 'You shouldn't let me go to sleep. How long have I been off?'

'Just over ten minutes. Come on.' She shook him gently. 'I'll make you a strong coffee.'

He dragged his head from the warm valley of her and, having pulled himself up in the bed, stretched out his arms to their fullest extent and yawned. Then as he watched her pull on her dressing-gown he said lazily, 'Promise me that one night you'll let me sleep right through, will you?'

'I'll promise you no such thing. Come on now.' She smiled at him, and the smile covered the regret that she would never be able to do as he asked.

When she had left the room he rose from the bed and went to the wash-basin, where he slushed his face with cold water, then got into his clothes. A few minutes later he was standing near the table, fully dressed for outdoors, with a cup of coffee in his hand. She stood close to him, watching him drink, and when the cup was empty she took it from him, and going into his arms she returned his hard, fierce kiss. It seemed that the feeling between them would never be dulled with use. He said to her now, 'Look, I've been thinking. What about a day out? I'm due for a few days....'

'No. No.' She shook her head quickly. 'We've been over all this before; you know yourself it's madness, you know you do. I know why you're saying it, just because of me, but I'm all right. I'm all right. I don't want days out ... jaunts. I've told you.'

'It doesn't seem fair, taking everything and giving nothing.'

She closed her eyes. 'Oh, be quiet. Be quiet.... And look; go on or you'll be late back.'

'Don't come out'—he pulled on his hat—'you'll get cold.' He kissed her again, then turning swiftly from her he went out, and as he passed through the gate he heard her locking the door. He had never said when he would be back and she had never asked. She knew he would come as often as he could.

When he entered the house he heard laughter coming from the drawing-room and he stopped in the act of taking off his coat, trying to distinguish who the company might be. It was now twenty to eleven; she usually got rid of her visitors before this—her young admirers from the Technical College usually came to tea. There had been a succession of them over the past years, one introducing another. They were rarely over twenty, except for that isolated case last year. He didn't want to dwell on that, but still he couldn't forget the ignominy of having to assure the parents that his wife's interest in their twenty-one-year-old son was purely maternal; was she not fifteen years the boy's senior? That business had made him sick, sick to the core. If she wanted a man why didn't she go for a man, not these gangling, pimply-faced youths. Why did she do it? He did not unlock the answer from within him and say because these slim youths were in all ways the opposite to himself. They were not, as yet, heavy of build, their necks weren't short, or their faces large and square. Nor would he say that his wife's obsession with youth was merely perverted sex, a safe outlet for a maddening frustration. When a similar case came before him in his practice he usually had a word with the husband, for nearly always, except if the woman was afraid of sex, the cause lay with him.

As he neared the drawing-room door and a rocketing bellow of mirth came to him he knew who the visitor was, and it was no youth. A frown brought his brows together and his lower lip jutting out—Friend Knowles, and the second visit in a week. Well, at least he was her own age. But he couldn't stand the fellow, and it wasn't because he was jealous, nor because Knowles was the slim, dapper type and the antithesis of himself. Why, he wondered, did you dislike more people than you liked? It was something that few faced up to. Most people, whether religious or not, hid behind the smoke-screen of 'Love thy neighbour', the while hating their guts. Look at himself tonight. Starting with Gray in the surgery; then Mrs. Ratcliffe; followed by Parkins, and, of course, Beresford; and now Knowles.

When he thrust the door open James Knowles and Bett both turned and looked towards him. Then the younger man rose swiftly from the couch where he had been sitting beside Bett, and coming forward with outstretched hand he said heartily, 'Hello again, Paul. Oh, I am glad I've been able to see you before I left; I was just about to go.' He shook Paul's hand as if he were the host and Paul a hesitant visitor.

The handshake over, he stepped back and surveyed Paul, say-ing, 'Hi! You look tired, really fagged. You work too hard. Still'—he poked his head playfully towards him—'just think of all the money you make.'

'Yes, there's that in it.' A flat response, the opposite to what James Knowles expected. It took the wind out of his verbosity for a moment; then coming back on the bounce he cried, 'Tell you what I came round for, Paul. I want you both to come to a dinner on Saturday night. My boss is giving a do up at his private house, Burley Court. You know, the big place that stands back off the top end of the new road. He hasn't been in it long.'

'But we don't happen to know your boss, or he us.' Paul was walking towards the wine cabinet as he spoke.

'Oh, that's all right; he told me I could bring a couple of friends, and immediately I thought of you both.'

'Thanks.' Paul lifted up a bottle of Scotch, where it was already standing on a tray on the top of the cabinet next to some used glasses, and he poured himself out a double knuckle-ful, and he sipped at it before he added, 'I'm afraid I've got a busy day on Saturday. Moreover, I've already made a dinner

47

appointment at the club.'

'I would like to go.' Bett spoke for the first time since he had entered the room, but she did not turn towards him, nor move her position from in front of the fire, and he looked towards the back of her neatly waved head before he said, 'You go then.' He knew she would go in any case; it didn't matter what he said. He also knew that his presence was the last thing that either of them wanted.

'It's a pity, you would have enjoyed it. When our Mr. Calvert Hogan throws his house open, he throws it open, and before the evening's out you can swim through it.'

'I dare say.' Paul drained his glass; then poured out another dose, and with it in his hand he walked towards the fire. And the indication that he was going to stay in the room gave impetus to the visitor's departure, for now, bending over the back of the couch, James Knowles addressed Bett with playful familiarity, saying, 'Well, little-un, I'll have to be on my way, but is it all right for Saturday, eh?' He lifted his gaze from her and looked towards Paul. And for answer Bett rose from the couch and walked towards the drawing-room door, saying casually, 'I'll be ready.'

'Fine. Fine. Well, goodnight, Paul.' Again there was the hearty handshake. 'Sorry about Saturday. Another time, eh?'

'Yes, another time.'

'Oh.' Knowles was half-way across the room when he turned, adding, 'Give my love to Lorna, will you? She was in bed when I arrived. Bye.' He jerked his head. 'You're a lucky chap. She's becoming a stunner. You're going to have some trouble with the boys in that direction, Paul.'

Paul said nothing; there was nothing to say. He just looked straight at the man and watched him turn about and leave the room.

When the lowered mumble of their voices came to him he could almost hear Knowles saying, 'He doesn't change. By God! He is a surly cuss I don't know how you stand it.' Then adding, 'Never mind, little-un, we'll make up for things on Saturday night, eh?' And then he would put his arm round her waist and give her a surreptitious hug.

His thinking urged him towards the cabinet again, where he poured out another measure of whisky, which he drained immediately. He had no room to talk, to criticize, had he? He hadn't a leg to stand on. Yet if he had ten women he could still not condone, even in his mind, her association with a fellow like Knowles. He was a nasty piece of work. It had nothing to do with sex; he was just a nasty piece of work, and it oozed through his veneer. That was, for anyone who had eyes to see.

He felt the best thing to do now would be to get upstairs without coming face to face with her again, at least tonight. He did not want any more words with her, any more rows. He had no desire to pick up where they had left off before Jinny had put in her timely appearance, yet he knew it could happen because he felt irritable, touchy. He had been like this for weeks now. He was tired, very tired. He wanted a rest; most of all a change.

He was still at the cabinet when she entered the room again, and as, without speaking a word, she began her nightly ritual of puffing up the cushions and straightening the chairs he asked, 'Any calls for me?'

She banged a cushion into roundness before she said, 'No; I would have told you, wouldn't I?'

'I don't know so much about that.'

She straightened up and by way of retort stared scornfully at him.

'It wouldn't be the first time, would it?'

'I've never done it deliberately; when that's happened it's because I've forgotten.'

'And forgotten to make a note of the call, too.'

Her lips moved hard, one over the other. Her face took on a pinched look and her body tensed. 'I'm not your receptionist; and in future if you want messages taken you can get somebody in to baby-sit to the phone.'

'You're only asked to do two evenings a week.'

'Two evenings, that's all. Well, it's two too many. And what do I get out of it? Damn all. You wouldn't put me on your books as receptionist, would you? Oh no, I might make a bit of money. Other doctors can employ their wives, but not you. Not the big fellow, the big above-board Doctor Higgins.'

'I told you'—his tone was even, 'I had no intention of dismissing Elsie to satisfy a passing whim—that's all it would have been.'

She stared at him as her face drained of colour; and then she said, 'Damn you! And Elsie. And your Maggie. The both of them are like old moth-eaten nanny-goats running round a dried-up Billy.'

He was holding the empty glass in his hand and he had the fearful desire to toss it straight into her face and see it splinter into fragments. He placed it quickly on the cabinet, turned, and went out of the room.

When he reached his own room he switched on the electric fire, and, sitting on a chair beside it, he placed his elbows on his knees and rested his head on his open palms. Something would have to be done; but what? One thing was certain: they couldn't go on like this, not for years and years. But the only way they could get a divorce, without it impairing his work, would be for her to petition him with cruelty. But she wouldn't do that because professionally it wouldn't harm him. The only way he could get free from her would be if it ruined him, if he was bereft of the work he loved, and through that this house, and his standing in the town. That would be her price for freedom. At least, in this direction, he knew exactly where he stood.

After a few minutes he rose and, going into the bathroom, that led out of his bedroom, he ran the bath, and as he lay in it he heard her come upstairs, pass over the landing and down the long corridor to the room that was hers. He tried to think back to the last time he was in her room; it must be all of five years ago. It was when she had 'flu and he had gone in with John Price when he had visited her, just to make things look normal. He shook his head at the fact that five years ago things weren't normal between them. They had been married sixteen years and for fifteen of those years things hadn't been right. Yet for the first years, because of his parents' presence in the house, he had kept up the pretence, in as much as he shared a room with her, and sometimes, driven through necessity, a bed. He had done this until seven years ago when his mother had died. The day after the funeral he had taken up his abode in this room. It was, looking at it from a doctor's point of view, a terrible thing to do to a woman, to leave her physically alone, to ignore her body, and it was because of this he had made allowances for her attitude towards him. Yet the man in him attached no blame to himself.... He felt justified in this attitude towards her, for no man likes to be made a monkey of.

Later, when he returned to his room, he immediately put the light out, and getting into bed he lay with his hands behind his head waiting for sleep. He'd had three broken nights in a week and he needed sleep. But the longer he lay the further it receded from him. And as this went on he told himself he'd have to have another glass. He'd have the equivalent of three already, besides what he'd had earlier on. The cure, he knew, could be worse than the disease. He was muzzy now, he'd feel like death in the morning. But it was either another drink or lie here staring into nothingness until the dawn, or until the phone rang.

He switched on the light and got out of bed and went to a cupboard in the corner of the room, and taking from it a bottle half-filled with whisky, together with a large glass, he returned to the bed, and, sitting on the edge, poured himself out a stiff drink. After throwing it back in one shuddering gulp he repeated the dose. Then putting the bottle and glass on the bedside table he got into bed again, switched out the light and waited for the cumulated spirit to have its effect. He reckoned that now he'd drank nearly half a bottle since he'd come in. Well, if that didn't do the trick, nothing would. He waited for his muscles to relax, for his mind to become more hazy. But this time the spirit did not drop the curtain of sleep over him and obliterate the day. Instead, he found himself fixed on some half-way mental platform with suppressed irritations floating around him and an aggressiveness striving to escape.

And in this state of mind he imagined himself springing up from the bed, dashing out of the room and down the corridor, kicking open her door and standing over her. He could see the surprise on her face as he gripped her throat and yelled, 'You bitch! You dirty conniving little bitch!' He had always wanted to say that to her: 'You dirty conniving little bitch!' And if he had, perhaps things would have been better, because then she would have said, 'What do you mean? Dirty conniving little bitch?' And he would have told her. Aye, by God he would have told her.

But he had never said it, and the longer he put it off the less able he was to tell her. ... Years ago, when she first became aware that he knew, she had retreated into herself, frightened that he'd expose her, frightened that the good marriage she'd brought off—oh yes, he knew she congratulated herself on the catch she'd made—was going to fall to pieces and she'd be out on her neck. And that's what he should have done if he'd had any sense, finished it right off, thrown her out on her neck. But what had he done? Not a blasted thing. And all because he couldn't bear anybody knowing he had been made a monkey of; especially his father. ... For two pins he'd get up now and go along and beat the living daylights out of her. He should have done that, too, years ago. When he felt his body heaving in the bed he chastised himself aloud, saying, 'Stop it, stop it.' He sat up now, holding his dizzying head. He shouldn't have taken any more of the stuff, not at this hour. Aw, to hell! He'd drink if he wanted to. Yet he'd eased up on it lately; he'd not drunk so much since he'd had Ivy. Aw, Ivy. Oh, if only Ivy were here. He turned on to his side and flung his arm across the pillow. Now if Ivy had been his wife. But they wouldn't have stood for Ivy being his wife. Nobody would have stood for Ivy being his wife, not even his mother. Because why? Because Ivy was an ordinary lass; she was without pretence. Ivy couldn't pretend to be what she wasn't, she couldn't put on the twang, so they wouldn't have stood for Ivy. What! Marry Ivy, who said, WAS YOU and THOSE ARE THEM. Tut! Tut! how shocking. How the doctor had let himself down. Bloody hypocrites. That's what people were. Bloody hypocrites. And he was living with the biggest of them, and she was driving him mad. Only yesterday she had said to him, 'You're going round the bend. YOU should see a doctor. Have your brain seen to.'

Perhaps he should at that. Perhaps he should see a doctor. Aye, he should go to a doctor. He started to laugh quietly.

'Doctor, I'm going round the bend.'

'Are you, Mr. Higgins.'

'Yes, Doctor. Completely round the bend.'

'What's brought this on, do you think, Mr. Higgins?'

'Me nature, Doctor, me nature; it's the way I'm made. Oh, I don't need a psychiatrist, I know all about meself.'

'That's good, Mr. Higgins. That's a very good start. Tell me some more, Mr. Higgins.'

'Well, Doctor, I was taken for a ride. When I was young I was taken for a ride by a clever little puss. Now it wasn't exactly all her fault, oh no. I'm fair.... Fair's fair. Shades of Ramsay. Well, as I said, it's me nature. Doctor, I'm a big fellow, you see, and I'm the protective type—Sir Galahad on a white horse, you know the type. So protective and so galahadish that I tried to keep meself as pure as me white steed. Can you believe that? A bloke like me trying to keep himself pure. It's a fact, Doctor, it's a fact.'

'Are you Irish, Mr. Higgins?'

'Not a bit of it. Begod, what made you think I'm Irish, Doctor? I'm talkin' like this because Maggie Swan talks like this.

52

Maggie's known me since I was knee high to a dobble of spit—that's one of her sayings—and I always talk to meself at night like Maggie does; it's a comfortin' way, there's something warm about it. It was Maggie really who kept me pure. D'you know that, Maggie and hard work. I was always kept busy one way and another. You know, Doctor, there's something in this keeping everybody busy in boarding schools, filling up your time with games, prep, and eating; they make you so damned tired you haven't even any Sir Galahad dreams.... "I pray to our Lady every night of me life for you," Maggie would say, and you know, Doctor, she did. She's the only one in me life who's ever prayed for me because me mother wasn't a praying woman. A fine woman, a broad-minded, grand woman, but no praying woman. So Maggie prayed for me.... Here a minute. Here a minute, Doctor. Now I'll tell you something, an' it's the God's truth. It's just this. I never went with a woman until I was nineteen. It was at medical school; an' you mightn't believe it, but it's God's honest truth, Doctor. I wasn't taken with it, it made me feel a bit cheap like. Honest to God. That's a laugh, isn't it? You must remember, though, I was Sir Galahad, an' begod the first person I thought of—now would you believe it, Doctor—the very first person I thought of when I woke up the next morning was Maggie Swan, for her white steed had turned to grey, and it's rider was black, as black as the coals of hell, and she knew all about the coals of hell.... But I was trying to tell you, Doctor, there I was going along fine. Like yourself I came through on top, an' I walked the wards. Oh, I was a grand figure of a man, everybody said so. It was while walking the wards that I first saw Jinny. She was a young probationer and me eyes were drawn to her because she was the plainest creature I'd ever seen in me life, and she had the biggest neb on her, you could have poked a drain with it, and the thought crossed me mind that God had done a dirty trick dishing out a dial like that to a girl. A man might have got by with it, but not a girl. And then one night, it happened like this. I was on duty and I got talkin' to her and found she was the nicest creature that Himself had ever made. It came over in her voice, and it shone out of those big eyes of hers, whose beauty was lost in the contortion of her face. And, begod, do you know what I found out besides? I found out that she was from this very town. So wasn't it natural like that later when I started up I should bump into her? And wasn't it natural like that she would introduce me to her cousin? And that's how it began. That's how it all began. And as you know, Doctor, her cousin was just a wee, wee thing, an' I was a big hulking fellow with traces of Sir Galahad still clinging to me cloak, and she got hold of those traces, Doctor, the wily little bitch got hold of those traces and she climbed up them, and into me life. You know yourself, Doctor, I never liked little women, and Maggie never liked little women, and she said to me, "Think, boy, think. Don't be rushed, don't let yourself be rushed." But I wanted to be rushed, Doctor, and little Bett wanted to be rushed. By God, aye she did that, an' we galloped like hell towards the church.'

'And what happened then, Mr. Higgins?'

'Aw, what happend then? Well, that's my concern, Doctor. I'm a big fellow, I've got a big head inside and out, an' I've got an opinion of meself, at least I had, and nobody's going to make a monkey out of me and sit on their backside and laugh.'

'Well, shall we talk about it, Mr. Higgins, bring it into the open.... Put it into words? Shall we, Mr. Higgins? Shall we? Shall we follow the advice you gave Mrs. Ratcliffe to ease her nerves? Confiding in someone is a great easer of nerves. You spout that at least once a day, don't you? So what about a small dose of your own medicine?'

'You mind your own bloody business. Do you hear, Doctor? You mind your own bloody business.'

'It would be better for you, Mr. Higgins.'

'I know what's good for me, I don't need to be told. Go on now, get yourself away, go on along to her and ask her to talk about it. Aye, that's where you should be, along of her, she's the one that should do the talking. Go on, have a try....' He swung out his arm and the bottle went flying off the table, but he didn't hear it.

'Doctor, Doctor, do you hear me now? Wake up. Come on, wake up.'

'Aw. Aw. Oh, it's you, Maggie. God!' He turned on to his side and put his hand to his head. 'What time is it?'

'Just turned half-past seven, I've only just got in. Here, drink this cup of tea. You've got to get up, there's a call for you.'

'Aw, God.'

'You been at the bottle I see?'

'Yes, I suppose you could call it that.'

'Aye, well, it's your own look-out.' She thrust the pillow up behind his head. 'An' nobody suffers for it but yourself. But it'll do you no good in the long run, you know that. Well now, shall I get you a couple of tablets?'

'Yes, do that, Maggie.'

When she came from the bathroom with a glass of water and the two tablets in her hand he said to her, 'Who's the call?'

'It's for a Mrs. Ogilby. She's on her time. The husband came to the door just a minute afore I let myself in.'

'Ogilby.' He nodded. 'Well, the district nurse will be there.'

'He seems very anxious for yourself.'

'Huh!' He rubbed his hand through his hair. Ogilby. Ogilby. Aw yes. Yes. He remembered he had promised to be there and he'd better be, too. They should have made a place for her in hospital. But still, she had wanted to have the baby at home.

He swung his legs out of bed, then sat on the edge for a moment screwing up his eyes against the light of day as Maggie drew the curtains. And when she turned from the window she stood looking at him like a mother at an erring son. She appeared a big woman, because of her breadth, for she was below five foot six in height. She had a round face, the skin lying in folds at each side of her mouth. Her lips were thick and pale and held in fullness at the front by four teeth, top and bottom. Her eyes, too, were round and small and dark, and sunk well back in the sockets. They were keen eyes with a youthfulness that belied the rest of the face, for every pore gave evidence of age. Yet emanating from the whole face and body was a suggestion of strength, a protective strength. Again she said, 'You shouldn't do it. It does you no good, serves nothin', an' only puts years on you—you look fifty if a day. Will I run your bath?'

'No, there's not time, I'll have to get going. Look.' He squinted up at her. 'Make me a large, strong coffee, black.'

'Aye, I'll do that.' As she went to pass him she put her hand out and patted his shoulder, and he remembered he had been dreaming about her, or something connected with her. It was all so hazy.

Five minutes later he was downstairs in the kitchen drinking her coffee. She had brought his bag from the surgery, and his coat and hat from the hall, and she stood with the coat in her hand ready for him to get into it.

'How long are you likely to be?'

'God knows. If it's going to be a long job I'll slip back and see

55

Elsie. If not I should be here in time for surgery. Oh, by the way.' For the first time since he had got up, his features moved out of their grimness as he explained. 'I nearly forgot to tell you, Jinny's here.'

'Oh, begod, is she now? When did she come?'

'Last night, after you left.'

'Aw, that's nice. Well, that'll lighten our day.' She nodded at him. 'She's always good to have in the house is Miss Jenny.'

'I'm afraid her stay is going to be short this time. And that reminds me an' all; I'm taking her to Newcastle to catch the twelve o'clock.'

'Aw begod, that's hail and farewell all right. What's sending her off at that speed?'

'Look'—he bent towards her—'she'll tell you all about it. You take her a cup of tea up. Tell her that I haven't told you anything, that I haven't had time, and she'll give you all her news and something that'll surprise you.'

'I'm past surprises, as you know yourself.' She followed him to the door. 'But that won't stop me from goin' up this minute. Button that coat up now, it's an awful mornin', the drizzle goes through to your marrow. I'll cook you something on spec. Take care now.'

As he backed the car from the garage he saw her still standing at the kitchen door, not worrying about the effect of the drizzle on herself. Thank God for Maggie. Yes, indeed, thank God for Maggie. And she threatened to get rid of her. Well, just let her, that was all, then the fireworks would fly. Whoever was leaving Romfield House it wouldn't be Maggie, for Maggie was the only sane, natural being in his life. She had always been there and she always would. At this moment he thought neither of Ivy nor of his daughter . . . nor yet of Jenny.

THREE

JENNY

As the train ran into Fellburn Jenny looked at herself for the last time in the mirror of the first-class compartment. Her heart was thumping against her ribs, but its beat, she knew, was nothing compared with what it would be like when she entered the house.

When the train stopped she opened the door and lifted out on to the dimly lit platform three strikingly new pigskin suitcases. She then beckoned a porter in the distance, and when she saw him coming near and recognized him, she said, 'Hello, Mr. Harris.' At one time she, Bett, and her Aunty May had lived near Mr. Harris.

'Why ... why, hello, Jenny. Why, I didn't know you.' He scanned her face, evidently puzzled. 'You're looking grand.'

'I'm feeling grand, Mr. Harris.'

'You want a taxi?'

'Yes, please.'

'Going to the doctor's?'

'Yes, Mr. Harris.'

'Hooker's outside. That's if he hasn't been snapped up.' He nodded at her. 'He's got a brand-new car, just suit you.'

He moved his head down to her feet, then brought his eyes up to rest for a moment right in the centre of her face. 'Aye, yes. Well, glad to see you looking so well, Jenny. The wife was only talking about you the other day.'

'Yes, Mr. Harris?'

'Aye, she was sayin' she didn't envy you; nursing wasn't everybody's cup of tea.'

'No, I suppose not.' Jenny smiled quietly; she knew why Mrs. Harris didn't envy her, and it wasn't because of nursing.

Mr. Harris's son-in-law was disengaged, and when Mr. Harris had ushered her into the back of the car as if she had suddenly become someone of note—and evidently he thought she had from the size of the tip she gave him—she settled back, telling herself to take advantage of the next few minutes and relax, yet knowing at the same time this was an impossibility.

The taxi-driver deposited her cases at the front door and she stood for a moment before ringing the bell. Within the radius of the street lamp to the left of her she could see people coming and going in the courtyard, which meant that Paul was still taking surgery.

It was Maggie who opened the door to her. 'Yes?' she demanded, peering out from the lighted hall into the darkness.

'Hello, Maggie.'

'In the name of God! Come in. Come away in.'

Maggie lifted a case over the step, and after putting it down by the side of the two which Jenny had brought in, she looked up into the face that for many many years she hadn't really seen, for Maggie, like her master, had never been one to lay any stock on looks. But now she peered into Jenny's face because it was different, the whole long being was different. She put a hand up to her lined mouth and whispered, 'Miss Jenny. Why, Miss Jenny. Mother of God! Who would have believed it.' And now she laid her other hand gently on the lapel of Jenny's coat, and Jenny, as if clutching at support, gripped it and held it pressed tightly to her as she asked in a whisper. 'How do I look, Maggie?'

'Fine, Miss Jenny. Grand. Why saints alive! It's a transfiguration.'

Jenny wanted to let out a howl of laughter, even at her own expense. Transfiguration! Well, that was one up on transformation. 'Oh, thanks, Maggie.' She pressed the hand tighter. 'Where is Mrs. Higgins?' She always gave Bett her correct title when speaking to Maggie.

'Oh, she's in the drawing-room with Miss Lorna. And what...? You'll never guess.' Maggie grinned up at her. 'The child's got a lad, or 'twould be better to say a suitor. A suitor indeed, and a fine-looking one at that. Oh, himself was tickled to death. He caught him hanging round one night a while ago, outside, and he did the right thing; he asked him in. He told him if he wanted to see Miss Lorna then to come openly. An' begod! the young cock's never been off the doorstep since.'

Jenny looked slightly disappointed at this news. She blinked as if wondering what to do, then said hastily, 'Look, Maggie, I'll go into the morning room.' She nodded her head in the direction of the door. 'Would you tell Mrs. Higgins I'm here? Do it on the quiet . . . you know, I'll leave it to you.'

'Aye. Aye, I'll do that. Don't bother with them cases.' She wafted Jenny away. 'I'll see to them afore I go.'

'No, no, they're too heavy for you to hump upstairs; just leave them.'

'Well, never bother now. Away to the mornin' room and I'll get herself to you.'

The morning room was cold and Jenny shivered, and her shivering increased when she heard the drawing-room door open, and as the laughter came to her, together with the sound of Bett's running steps, she knew her cousin was in high spirits, and being girlishly girlish.

When the door was thrust open and Bett cried, 'Why, Jenny!' the name was split, and the last syllable left her mouth hanging agape. Like Mr. Harris, she was staring into the middle of Jenny's face; then her eyes flicked up and down the length of her only to come to rest again at the telling point.

'What—on—earth . . .'

Jenny knew that she was blushing, that the whole of her body was blushing, in fact sweating now.

'We-e-ll!' The word had a tremulous sound. 'So that's it. The big secret.' Bett's voice was strangely flat. 'You've had your nose done.'

'Yes, I've had it done.' Jenny swallowed; then swallowed again. 'That among other things.' She took off her hat.

'And your hair off?'

'And not before time. Nothing's before time, I should say.'

'And you've had it bleached. You've certainly gone the whole hog. Well.' Bett folded her arms across her chest; it was an attitude she took up when she was going to pass judgment, damning judgment, and she said now, 'It isn't you.'

'No, I know it isn't.' There was a touch of sharpness to Jenny's voice and she was trembling no longer. 'I've been stuck with the lot since the day I was born, and now I'm rid of it; well, as much as I can get rid of.'

'And this was all his idea?'

'Yes, it was. But it wasn't the first time I'd thought of it.' Jenny turned her face away from Bett's hard scrutiny. 'Many a time I've thought, if only I had enough money. . . . Well.' She lifted one shoulder and it drew up her bust and brought Bett's gaze to rest on it now; and after a moment Bett raised her eyelids until they seemed to disappear into the sockets, and to the question they asked Jenny said, 'Oh, this part was easy.' She put her hands gently under her breasts. 'I could have worn falsies years ago but they wouldn't have gone with the rest of me.'

Bett's smile was slightly derisive, and she rocked her head from one side to the other as she said, 'I only hope it makes you happy.'

'It will; it has. I've had the best three weeks I've had in my life.'

'And what are you going to do now?'

'I've plans.'

'I bet you have.'

'What do you mean, Bett?' The light in Jenny's face had dimmed.

'Oh, I only mean that if you planned all this and kept it dark then you're bound to have other plans. . . . Where are you going to settle?'

'Here, in Fellburn, I think. I'll have to get a flat. I'll . . . I'll have to have some place to put my clothes seeing as I've three cases full, and a trunk coming on.'

'My, my! We have been busy.' Bett could no longer keep the bitterness from her tone, and turning to the door she said, 'Well, we've got company, but you'd better come in and see Lorna.'

'I'd rather wait until later, until she's by herself.'

'Oh, I thought the new set-up would have given you all the confidence in the world.'

'Are you being nasty, Bett?'

The question was really unnecessary; this is what she had feared all the journey down, Bett's reaction, yet it said something for her new façade that she had dared to voice the question.

'No, of course, I'm not being nasty, only I think it was quite unnecessary to make all this mystery about what you intended to do. And I don't suppose his lordship will be very pleased either; he'll likely get professional pip thinking that you might have said something about the operation . . . because it was an operation, wasn't it?'

'I suppose you could call it that.' Jenny had never thought of Paul being annoyed about her doing this off her own bat, but now the possibility presented itself. Apart from Bett's reactions she had imagined everybody being kind, even pleased. She was under no illusions; her altered nose hadn't made her into a beauty, but it had taken the focal point from people's eyes, and in doing that had literally removed a weight from her body and a burden from her mind. It had also, as Ben had said it would, make her want to dress up. Oh, Ben, Ben. Of all the wise men in the world Ben had been the wisest. Why should she have been so lucky as to meet Ben? If only he had lived; that deep, hidden pain that was always in her would have been soothed, and the dreams to which her mind escaped at night would have faded; they must have done under Ben's kindness. But here she was now, without Ben but as Ben had always seen her. But how would Paul see her? And what if he was annoyed? One thing she did know; it would please Bett if he was.

Jenny did not answer Bett's last remark but said instead, 'I'll go in and see Lorna. I hope she survives the shock.' She laughed nervously and waited for Bett to make some comment, and when she didn't, but continued to appraise her coolly, she became embarrassed. And this increased when Bett swung round and without further words went out into the hall. There was nothing for Jenny to do but follow her, and for the first time in weeks she felt flat, and the feeling didn't lift when she entered the drawing-room.

Jenny had never ceased to be amazed at the mercurial changes Bett could bring about in her attitude, and here again she was witnessing just such a change, for Bett, on pushing open the drawing-room door, assumed an entirely different character. 'Look who we have here,' she cried to Lorna, ushering Jenny in as if she were an exhibit.

'Why, Aunt Jenny.' Lorna turned from the long record-player in the far corner of the room where she was standing near a young man, and flinging her arms wide with youthful gusto she darted across the room, only to come to a sliding stop on the carpet some feet away from Jenny. Her arms dropping slowly to her sides, she gaped for a moment at this smartly dressed woman who was, yet who wasn't, her Aunt Jenny. The face was the same yet different; her nose was gone, the big hooked nose with the wide nostrils, and in its place was a straight affair, still largish but rounded at the end, a nose that was part of the face and no longer protruded from it as if trying to free itself from its base.

'Why, Aunt Jenny!' Lorna's voice was just a whisper, and

61

what else she might have said was checked by the sound of the young man's voice answering her mother, and she remembered they had company, and her arms flinging upwards she embraced Jenny, and Jenny held her tightly.

'Don't be silly, child; leave your aunt alone.' Now Bett's voice separated them and went on, 'This is Brian. Brian Bolton. Brian, my cousin ... Mrs. Hoffman.' She inclined her head deeply towards Jenny as she gave her her married title for the first time.

Jenny shook hands with the tall fair boy, Lorna's first boy, who had looks and undoubtedly charm, perhaps a little too much, Jenny thought, as he said, 'How do you do, Mrs. Hoffman. I feel I know you very well; Lorna is always singing your praises.' Then to her slight annoyance he turned her round and added, 'Do you keep your wings under your coat?'

'Oh, really!' Jenny flicked him away with her hand and walked to where the tea things were still on the trolley to the side of the fireplace. She hadn't much room for slick young men, slick men of any age.

'Go and ask Maggie for a pot of fresh tea, Lorna.'

'O.K., Mammy.' Lorna skipped to the trolley and grabbed up the teapot, and, laughing towards Jenny, darted from the room.

Bett now looked towards the boy where he stood examining some records on the side-table and called in a high voice, as if he was at the other side of the house, 'Put another record on, Brian.'

'A dance one?' He turned his head, his wide grey eyes laughing at her. It was as if he had been coming to the house for years, he seemed so at home.

'Yes, let's have "Twist and Shout" again.' With a few movements of her hips Bett demonstrated the record, and the young man laughed out loud, and she with him.

Jenny, her face unsmiling, stared at Bett. What made her do it? Why must she act like a girl? Granted she was still young, only thirty-six, but she was no longer a teenager, she was a woman with a fifteen-year-old daughter. As the raucous cries from the record burst upon them, Bett, hips, arms, and feet twisting, moved towards the young man, and he, his tall body wriggling with the mobility of a snake, came towards her until they faced each other.

As she watched them Jenny became warm with embarrassment. Yet why? Why? She could do the twist. She guessed that most housewives could do the twist. What woman, listening to Housewives Choice, hadn't done a wriggle? She herself had made Ben laugh until he was sore when she'd had a go. Anybody who could stand could do the twist, so why should she feel so embarrassed now? It was certain that neither of the dancers felt embarrassed. Yet a moment later it became plain to Jenny that Lorna too, when she returned to that room, felt something akin to what she herself was experiencing. She had come in laughing, the teapot balanced on a stand, but by the time she had placed it on the trolley the smile had gone, to return fleetingly as she said, 'Will I pour, Aunt Jenny?'

'No, I'll see to it. You go and have a dance.'

'No, I don't want to. I ... I've been dancing for the last hour.' But as she went to sit down Brian called, 'Come on, Lorna, beat it up.' And immediately the cloud lifted from her face and she was around the couch and facing him. Jenny watched her as she started to dance, her movements slower than her mother's, more flowing, less intense; naturally graceful, nothing forced. As if this fact had made itself evident to Bett, she suddenly stopped her prancing, and coming to the couch she flopped down, helped herself to a cigarette, then lay back panting gently as she blew out the smoke in quick nervous movements.

Without looking at Jenny she said, 'You haven't had any tea.'

'I'll help myself.' Jenny rose to her feet and went to the trolley.

'How long are you going to stay this time?'

'For a week or so if you'll have me; over Christmas, perhaps, until I find a flat.'

'You can stay as long as you like, you know that.'

'Thanks.'

'Have you thought of what you are going to do with yourself?'

'What was that?' Jenny screwed her face up against the heightened noise of the record, and Bett spoke louder, 'I said, have you thought what you are going to do with yourself?'

'Not really.' Jenny returned to the couch with the cup in her hand. 'I feel I'd like to make a home, just a little home, somewhere to come back to after I have a holiday. I'd like to go abroad for a time. But I know that I couldn't live without working; I'll very likely take up nursing again later on.'

'You must be barmy.' Bett slanted her glance towards her. 'I know what I would do if I had it.'

'Yes, so do I, Bett; so it's a good job you haven't, because your place is here.' Jenny had turned her head to meet Bett's gaze, and as she held it she said distinctly and slowly, 'I could give you half of what I've got, and I could do it quite easily because I don't need very much. I know I don't. Just enough to give me a little security—I can always work. But what would happen to you? You'd go mad. I know you, Bett. And what about Lorna and Paul? So ... so I'm not going to give you anything to help you lose what ... what you've got.'

'Who's asking you?' Bett's voice was harsh and rasping. 'It's time enough for you to refuse when I ask you for anything, and that'll be a long time, I'm telling you. As for losing what I've got; you can have it ... anybody can have it.... God, what I've got!'

'I'm sorry, I'm sorry.' Jenny, her voice full of contrition, put her hand on Bett's arm, and Bett, as if suddenly deflated, sat forward on the edge of the couch and dropped her head on to her chest.

'Bett, listen.' She moved closer to her. 'I'm going to get you a little car; you've always wanted a car. Do you hear?'

Bett's head sank lower, and she appeared to be on the point of crying. It was as if she had forgotten the dancers and had become oblivious to the sound of the thumping of the record, but when it stopped she lay back again and composed herself, the only evidence that she was upset showing in the constant nipping of her lips.

Into the silence that followed the noise of the record, Brian's voice, although low, came clearly to them, saying, 'There's a beat session on at the Ricco Club tonight, what about it? The Howlers are topping the bill.' After a short pause Lorna said, 'Oh, I'd love to, but I've got homework.... But'—her voice lightened—'I could do it after. Mammy, can I go out? Brian wants to take me to the Ricco Club?'

Bett pulled sharply on her cigarette. 'You just said you've got homework to do.' Her tone was flat, uninterested. 'Anyway, I don't think your father would like you going there.'

'It's quite all right, Mrs. Higgins.' The boy was facing her now from the hearth rug, bending slightly towards her, a strand of his fair hair drooping across his forehead to his left eye. He looked a mixture of sophistication and gauche youth. 'We just all sit round; there's turns, folk songs, community songs, and "The Howlers" do some of the pops. It's all very nice.' He stressed the last words, speaking like a man who was trying to assure a doubting mother as to the propriety of the club. And then his blue eyes widening, as if the thought had just come to him, he exclaimed, 'Why don't you come along, too? You would love it. It would just be up your street.'

Jenny watched Bett being lifted on to the plane of careless youth by this young man, who hadn't, she thought, much to learn. She watched the eager, hardly submerged girl in her rise to the invitation and grab it with a technique so thin that it was pitiful.

'Oh, you don't want me trailing along with you. Goodness gracious.... And her mother came too!' She made the high infectious sound that she could do so well, it was a cross between a laugh and a giggle.

'Don't be silly.' He bent further towards her. 'You're not like her mother.' He lifted his glance above the couch and smiled at Lorna standing exactly where he had left her in the middle of the room. 'You're not even like sisters, you're more like twins. Come on, what about it, eh?'

It was as if he had thrown both his hands out to her, for she wiggled on the couch and brought herself towards its edge and him, saying again, 'No, no, it can't be done. Anyway, this is one of my nights on; I've got to stay in and receive calls. You see, our cook goes shortly after six and I'm without a maid.' She glanced at Jenny now, a quick questioning glance.

Jenny looked down at her hands, lying slackly, one on top of the other in her lap. She knew that if Bett didn't go to the club then Lorna wouldn't be allowed to, yet she wondered at the same time if it wouldn't be better like that rather than Bett impose her false youth and gaiety into the natural element that was growing between these two young things. Her voice sounded prim as she said, 'I'll not be going out, I'll take the calls.'

'Would you, Jenny? Oh, but it would be an imposition to ask you.'

'Why?' Jenny could not resist making the blunt statement. 'I've done it before, haven't I?'

'Yes, yes, but ... Oh well, I'm not going to look a gift horse in the mouth. Thanks, thanks, Jenny. I'll go and get ready then. What time does it start?' She turned her head back towards

Brian.

'Seven o'clock, but we must get there early if you want a seat; it's generally packed.' He straightened up and pulled at his tie. He looked pleased with himself, as if he had brought something off.

'Give me ten minutes.' As Bett laughed at the tall, smiling youth, Jenny was forced to look away, and her eyes were drawn to Lorna where she was bending over the record-player. Lorna, she noticed, hadn't said anything one way or the other, and when her mother called to her gaily as she went from the room, 'Come on, dear, and get ready,' she replied, 'I am ready. I just need to put my hat and coat on.'

She might have said, Youth is its own dresser, it needs no adornment, for Bett stopped abruptly. Her face straight now, her voice sharp, she said, 'Don't be silly; you can't go out in that get-up.' She indicated with a wave of her hand Lorna's pleated skirt and bulky pullover.

'I'll have my coat on.'

'Oh, well!' She raised her shoulders and her eyebrows together. 'If you want to look a mess that's your business.' Then turning about she closed the door after her.

The boy was looking towards Lorna now, but made no effort to join her, and Jenny looked at him and she didn't know whether she liked him or not. In any case she felt he was a bit too old for Lorna, at least for her first boy. To make conversation she said to him, 'Do you work in Fellburn?'

'Yes, I'm at Boyes, the engineering works, and I do half-time at the college.' He motioned his head in the direction of the Square.

'You're going to be an engineer then?'

'I hope so.'

As they spoke, Lorna came to the fireplace, and lifting her narrow foot on to the raised tilted fender she started to tap it, a sure sign that she was upset. And apparently the boy realized this for now turning to her he said quietly, 'I think you look fine in that.'

Lorna cast a sidelong glance at him. 'I don't really.' Her voice, although holding its natural attractive huskiness, sounded dull.

'It doesn't matter, it suits you. That goldy brown of the sweater is your colour ... isn't it?' He appealed to Jenny, and Jenny said, 'Yes, I think it is, but then Lorna can wear almost anything.'

'Aw, Aunt Jenny.' The set look slipped from Lorna's face and, coming to the couch, she dropped with a plop beside Jenny and added, 'You always say nice things, Aunt Jenny.'

'Me?'

'Yes, you.' Leaning towards Jenny, she dropped her head on to her shoulder and hugged her arm. It was as if she had forgotten Brian's presence for the moment. 'And you look lovely, Aunt Jenny. I meant to say it. And you smell nice. What is it? What's it called. . . . The scent?'

Jenny laughed down at her. 'You'd never guess, not in a month of Sundays. It's called . . . "Snake Charm". Did you ever hear such a name for such a nice smell?'

'Snake Charm! Good Lord! But it's lovely. Was it expensive?'

Jenny closed her eyes and moved her head slowly. 'The earth. Four pounds for a small bottle. I expected to get a cobra with it for that money.'

'Oh, Aunt Jenny.' They were laughing together when Lorna, raising her head from Jenny's shoulder, looked up at Brian and said, 'I told you so, didn't I?' Brian seemed to understand this enigmatic remark, for he smiled down on Jenny; then said, 'Lorna tells me you're going to live here.'

'Oh, not here.' Jenny shook her head. 'Not in the house. I'm thinking of taking a flat, and I want someone with good taste to help me furnish it.' She doubled her fist and pressed it gently against Lorna's nose, and Lorna cried, 'You mean it? You really mean it . . . I could help you choose things?'

'Well, I'll have to have help from someone; I've no artistic sense, although I've got an eye for colour, quiet colours, like flaming red, purple and orange. Oh, I like flaming red, purple and orange, and nicely mixed.'

'Oh, Aunt Jenny, you don't, you don't. Don't believe her.' Lorna shook Jenny as she spoke to Brian, and Brian, playing the gallant, looked Jenny slowly over before saying, 'Your choice of clothes belies that statement.'

The compliment and the way it was said brought a straight look to Jenny's face. No, she didn't like this boy when he was playing the man. She thought again he was much too old for Lorna. She was saved from trying to make any reply to his gallantry by Bett entering the room.

Bett was wearing a grey coat with a broad half-belt at the

back and a high collar, and perched jauntily on her hair was a white fur toque. It was a youthful-looking rig-out, and together with a skilfully made-up face, which gave the impression of no make-up at all, she could have passed for twenty-five or under.

'You're not ready yet.' She looked at Lorna, and Lorna rising slowly from the couch said, 'I told you, Mammy, I've only to put my hat and coat on, they're in the hall. Bye-bye, Aunt Jenny.' She bent and kissed Jenny. 'See you later.'

'Yes, dear.'

'Goodnight, Mrs. Hoffman.' He remembered names.

'Goodnight,' said Jenny.

Then Bett was standing in front of her, pulling on her gloves. 'You don't mind ... you're sure?'

'Of course I'm sure.'

'Bye then.'

'Bye-bye, Oh, what time will I tell Paul you'll be back?'

'You can tell him to expect me when he sees me.'

Jenny turned her head away impatiently, and when she heard the front door bang she rose slowly and walked about the room. She had come home, as she thought of this house, full of her new self, but now it didn't seem to be of the slightest importance. As usual, she felt swamped by the needs of those around her, by Bett's in particular. What was going to be the end of her and this constant warfare with Paul? What was equally bad was her obsession with youth. Didn't she realize even yet she'd get talked about, laughed at? It had happened before. Well, she couldn't do anything about it, she knew that, because although Bett was in no way as mature as herself, she was stronger, for being selfish and self-willed she was less amenable.

But she was glad in a way that Bett had gone out, for this would enable her to meet Paul alone.

She sat down again, and opening her handbag took out her mirror, and for the thousandth time in the past few days she scanned her face. She still couldn't believe she was looking at herself, that this ordinary, normal-looking creature was her.

When she heard the surgery door close she put the mirror quickly back into her bag and snapped it closed. She waited. She paced his steps to Elsie's room. After this she had to wait a further five minutes, and when she next heard his feet crossing the hall she was in such a state of agitation that beads of sweat were resting on her upper lip. The steps came to a halt some way from the drawing-room door and in the silence there came the distant blare of the Salvation Army's band. Being Friday night, and money night, and club night, the army was off to do battle in the centre of Fellburn. The sound was cheery, rousing. She wondered if Paul was standing listening to it. The band or the players never aroused his ire, as it did Bett's. He had been brought up on the sound of it. Such was her agitation that when the drawing-room door eventually opened she gave a start. She hadn't heard him come in.

'Why, Jinny!' His deep rumbling voice was loud, pleased. 'When did you come?' She turned slowly towards him as he rounded the couch.

'About half-an-hour ago, Paul.'

'Jinny! ... Jinny!' His big face seemed to be spreading even wider. His head was moving in small, almost imperceivable little motions.

'Well, Paul?'

'Jin-ny!' He took a slow heavy step towards her; then taking her hands, his eyes still on her face, he said, 'So this was it?'

She gulped and nodded. 'What do you think?'

'I ... I don't know. Honest, I don't know. I ... I liked you as you were, Jinny.'

'Well, I'm still me. But ... but I always wanted to get rid of it and ... and Ben said I must.'

'Ben did?' He jerked his chin to the side, and it gave emphasis to the question.

'Yes; he was the only one I ever spoke to about it. He wanted me to go and have the operation when he was still alive, but I wouldn't. He didn't want me to do it for—for his sake, but for my own.'

Paul's face crinkled now into painful lines, and he said under his breath, 'But, Jinny, I didn't know it worried you so. I could have arranged something, but ... but I would never have thought of putting it to you.'

'No, I understand; it had to come from me. But still'—she leant away from him—'what do you think? Does it make any improvement?' Her lips were apart, there was a beseeching look in her eyes, and he too leant back from her, still holding her hands, and surveyed her from head to foot before saying, 'You're all changed, right from your feet up. Yes, Jinny, I suppose it does. In fact there's no doubt about it. I suppose I should say you look extremely smart, and you do.'

'But ... but you're not really in favour of me having done it,

Paul, are you?'

'Yes, Jinny, yes.' His voice was loud now, like a gentle roar, and he shook her two hands up and down. 'Yes, I am, and it's going to make you happier. Not that I ever thought you were sad, but ... but some time later on, when I get thinking about it, I know I'll be flaming mad with myself for not having proposed it.'

It was in a way as Bett had said, but only in a way, for she could see that he was still flabbergasted at what she had done, at the complete change in her. Well, she was flabbergasted herself.

'Where did you go?'

'To Belling's Clinic.'

'Oh, he's good, he's got a name. You went to the best place. Come on, sit down and tell me about it. I mean the whole thing, all you did.'

So with one hand still in his she told him about the operation, about Doctor Belling himself, about all the contacts she made from the clinic, the beauty specialist, the dress shop with the private room and the two women hovering over her; and she finished with, 'And you know, Paul, altogether I spent five hundred pounds ... five hundred pounds on me.' She thumped her chest.

'You couldn't have spent it on a better person. Good for you, Jinny. And now what are you plans? What are you thinking about doing?'

'Well, I thought of getting a flat, perhaps on Brampton Hill; they're turning the big houses into flats there.'

'Nice; that's nice. I'm glad you'll be near. You're a comfort; you know that, Jinny, don't you? You've always been a comfort.' Letting go her hand now and getting to his feet, he added, 'How is it you're cousins and there's not a spark of you in her? I've looked for it for years; but no, you're poles apart.'

'You're too hard on her, Paul.'

'Huh!' He swung his big body quickly round and his voice was accusing now. 'You mean that? You really think that, Jinny?'

'Yes, I do, Paul.'

'But you know how she goes on, you know she's unbearable.'

'Yes, but...' Jenny shook her head, she couldn't say, It's unbearable for her too, isolated at the end of the corridor. She wished she didn't feel that Bett had a point in her favour; she didn't want to feel any sympathy for Bett. 'It's none of my business,' she went on. 'I don't want to get involved, Paul. What I mean is, I don't want to take one side against the other.'

'I don't understand you . . . at least with regard to Bett, Jinny. I know she's as fond of you as she can be of anyone, yet she's used you at every opportunity; all her life she's used you.'

'Perhaps I wanted to be used, Paul. Free agents, and I'm a free agent, are not often made to do things. If they do them it's because in some part they want to do them. We were brought up together; she and her mother were the only family I had. I suppose that's the explanation really; they were my people. And I've always wanted her to be happy, because in spite of everything, her looks and her gaiety, she's never been happy, not even when she was young.'

He made a sound in his throat, then turned from her as if tired of the conversation, and looking at his watch he said, 'I've got a full evening; I'd better be off.'

'Have you had your meal?'

His mouth twisted in a semblance of a smile as he said, 'No. Anyway, I've never liked eating in the kitchen. You know that, Jinny. And the new order is, the kitchen or the cold dining-room.' He waited for her to make some comment, but when she didn't he went on, 'I could put my foot down and turn every blasted radiator in the house to the top of its bent; I could put every electric fire on, every gadget; but what would that lead to? Anyway,' he wrinkled his nose, 'it's getting to mean less and less. Everything's getting to mean less and less.'

'Oh, Paul; don't sound like that.'

'It's a fact, Jinny. Aw, well, I must be off.' He bent quickly towards her now and, touching her cheek gently, scanned her face for a second before saying, 'Don't change inside, Jinny.'

'There's not much fear of that.'

'Aw, you never know.'

'I'm set in me ways.' She laughed at him.

'I'm glad. Goodnight, Jinny.' He tapped her cheek.

'Goodnight, Paul.'

When he was gone she sat with her chin drawn into her neck, her eyes fixed on her hands gripped together in her lap. And she sat like this until she heard the sound of his car moving out of the yard; then she rose heavily from the couch and went up to her room.

Her new cases were standing by her bed. She did not look at them but walked towards the wardrobe mirror and there, gazing at herself, she asked her reflection, 'And for what?' All the excitement of her transformed being was gone; she felt flatter, more desolate, more alone than she had ever done in her life before. Addressing her new self in the mirror, she said, 'Get yourself out of here as quickly as possible.' And she watched her head nod slowly in answer. . . .

It was around nine o'clock when the front-door bell rang. There had been no calls during the evening, and Jenny knew it wouldn't be them back from the club, because Bett had her key. When she opened the door she expected to find someone from the vicinity, who found it quicker to come to the doctor's house than to phone, but she actually fell back in amazement as Lorna dashed past her into the hall.

'Where are the . . .?' She didn't finish the question but, putting her head out of the door, she looked into the Square. There was no one to be seen; so, closing the door, she hurried after Lorna into the drawing-room.

'What's the matter?'

Lorna was standing in the centre of the room, the fingers of one hand pressed tightly across her mouth.

'What is it, dear?' Jenny approached her slowly and put her arms about her; and Lorna, as if she had been holding her breath for an unimagined time, whipped her hand from her mouth and as her body deflated cried, 'I hate Mammy, Aunt Jenny, I hate her!'

'Oh, Lorna, Lorna. Don't say such a thing. What's upset you?' She drew her to the fire. 'Here, take your coat off and sit down.' She threw her hat and coat to one side and asked again, 'What is it? What's upset you like this?'

'Oh, Aunt Jenny, Aunt Jenny.' Lorna collapsed against her and began to cry noisily.

'There now, there now. Don't go on like that. Come on, come on, dear. Sit down and tell me what it is.'

Slowly the crying ebbed away; and then Lorna, pulling herself upwards, looked through her streaming eyes at Jenny and said quietly, 'I do hate her, Aunt Jenny, I do really.'

'Lorna, you mustn't say things like that.' Jenny's voice was stern. 'Now don't; it's a dreadful thing to say, no matter what she's done. . . . But what has she done?'

Lorna moved slowly from the couch on to the pouffe that was near the fire, and she crouched on it like someone on a rock trying to evade the incoming tide, and with her head hanging

72

she began, 'We couldn't get in at the club, it was full, and there was a dance on at the Borough Hall. She's always looked down her nose at the Borough Hall, yet when Brian said what about it, she went all girlish.' A slight repulsive shiver went through her body. 'She pretended she was going slumming, and Brian met a boy he knew and he joined up with us. And I didn't like him, and he saw I didn't like him, and after the first dance he didn't ask me again. But Mammy'—her head jerked violently—'she didn't give Brian a chance, she danced with him nearly all the time. She made him dance with her. She kept teasing him and laughing and joking, and showing him she could twist better than anybody else ... trying to beat the young girls. I—I felt sick. I couldn't watch her any more so I just walked out.'

The room became very quiet, until Jenny said, 'You know, Lorna, you must realize that your mammy isn't old, she's only thirty-six. It's not old.'

'But she's a mother.' Lorna twisted quickly round on the pouffe and confronted Jenny. 'She's my mother. Queenie Price's mother doesn't act like that, she—she acts properly ... like a doctor's wife should. And Rhona Watson's mother doesn't act like her, and she's pretty. Nor Phyllis Bell's; nor any of the others I know.... She wants Brian, Aunt Jenny.'

'Don't say that, Lorna.' Jenny sounded shocked.

'I will say it; yes, I will say it, Aunt Jenny. I'm no longer a child, I know about things. I read, I read a lot. She's never told me anything that a mother should tell a daughter, and I can't talk to Daddy, not about that. But I've read all about it.' She lowered her eyes. Then lifting her head sharply, and her husky sounding voice coming from deep within her, she said bitterly, 'Mammy wants Brian, and he knows it. He's only been coming to the house for about three weeks and he's changed. I've known him for a long time; he used to meet me on and off coming from school. He had other girls. I know two he went round with. Paula Bradford. She left last year; he used to go with her. And then Mary Weir. But every now and again he would meet me; and then one night he came to the house and waited outside and Daddy saw him and told him to come in. That was the first time she had met him, and she went silly, ab-so-lute-ly silly.... Oh, Aunt Jenny, it makes me feel terrible when I watch her.'

'Come now.' Jenny leant over and pulled her gently from the pouffe, and when she was seated on the couch again she cradled her in her arms and said soothingly, 'You're in love for the first time and everything is larger than life. It's a very nice state to be in, but you tend to exaggerate lots of things when you're like that. Now, have you looked at it this way? Brian is being nice to your mother because he wants her on his side, because he's in love with you.'

'Yes, I thought that at first; but then you see, Aunt Jenny, that's not Mammy's side of it, she'll not see it like that. I tell you she's gone all shot about him.'

Suddenly Jenny pulled her to her feet. 'Come on; you'll see everything clearer in the morning. The time's getting on. You got to bed and I'll bring you a hot drink up, and we'll sit and have a natter. I've got lots of plans for the future, about my flat and everything, and I want someone to listen to me. Go on now.'

As if her light body was held down by weights Lorna went slowly from the room, and Jenny went into the kitchen, and here she stood resting against the edge of the table for a moment. Paul would do something desperate if Bett started that again. Was she mad altogether? Well, not altogether, only a part of her, the part that was starved of physical expression. And who could blame her? You couldn't say to Bett that she should sublimate it. No, that kind of thing was only expected of nurses with big noses. As her thoughts turned bitter she went hastily to the cupboard and, taking out a pan, she warmed some milk.

A few minutes later, when she mounted the stairs with the tray in her hand, she saw Lorna coming out of the bathroom. She was dressed now in her pyjamas and she looked like a slim boy, a beautiful, dark, oriental slim boy, and the sight hurt her, and she wondered if it hurt Paul.

She had been sitting on the edge of Lorna's bed for about ten minutes when she heard the front door open. On the sound she stopped talking, and leaning towards Lorna she said, urgently, 'Now don't be nasty. Just say you came home because you felt tired.'

At this Lorna lowered her lids and pressed her lips together, but said nothing. There was the sound of the drawing-room door banging, then footsteps on the stairs, followed by the bedroom door being thrust open. And there stood Bett, an enraged Bett, no semblance of the girl visible now.

'What do you think you're up to, madam?' She came quickly towards the bed, ignoring Jenny, her eyes fixed hard on her daughter. 'We've searched the place for you. Frightening the life out of me, going off like that.'

'I didn't think you would notice.' Lorna's voice sounded cool.

'What do you mean, you didn't think I'd notice? I went to the trouble of going to that beastly dance hall just so that you could have a dance—you're always on about going to dances—and then what happens? You sit like a stook, and then you just go off without a word to anyone. Well, it won't happen again; I'm not going to waste my time. . . .'

'Oh, stop kidding yourself, Mammy.' Lorna had pulled herself swiftly up in the bed, and now her face was on a level with her mother's.

'How dare you speak to me like that!' Bett's face was scarlet.

'Well, you've asked for it. You are kidding yourself. You kid yourself all the time. . . .'

The force of the slap overbalanced Lorna and knocked her head against the wall. And Bett, leaning over the bed, would have repeated it if Jenny hadn't gripped her by the arms, crying, 'Bett! Bett, stop it! Pull yourself together. What's come over you, woman?'

'I'm not having her speak to me like that. How dare she. How dare she. I won't stand for it.' One arm was flaying the air now. Then all of a sudden it dropped; and Bett's voice dropped, too, and, her small body crumpling, she burst into tears, loud hysterical tears, and tearing herself from Jenny's hold she rushed out of the room.

Jenny didn't follow her, except to close the bedroom door. Then, returning to the bed, she gently drew Lorna to her and held her shivering body tightly in her arms. Yet strangely it was Bett she thought of as she comforted Lorna, Bett who had now lost her daughter, for this thing would always be between them. She wished she hadn't to be sorry for Bett; oh, how she wished that.

2

'Boxing Night. I used to love Christmas at one time, but it's like everything else, it changes. Hand me your glass.'

'No, no. No more for me, Paul.' Jenny laughed up at him while she put her hand over the top of the empty glass. 'I've had three.'

'Come on; give it to me here.' He pulled it from her hand. 'What's three on Boxing Night! And you Poppet?' He turned to Lorna. 'Tonic water? lime? orange?'

'Can I have a sherry, Daddy?'

'No, you can't; you've had one tonight, me lady, and wine with your dinner. My, what's the world coming to ... well?'

Lorna screwed up her face at him. 'Oh, I suppose it'll have to be a tonic water then.'

'Yes, you suppose right.' As Paul went across the room to the wine cabinet, members of a party that was well under way on the television began a Scottish reel, and as the bagpipes' wail filled the room Paul, dropping the glasses on to a table, cried, 'Come on, Jinny. Come on, Lorna. Let's swing our kilts. Come on, we'll show 'em.' Watching the screen, he took the pose of the dancers, right arm cocked high, left arm on his hip, and with surprising agility went into the dance, and with each step he cried 'Foot up; heel, toe, foot up; cross feet, cross feet, a-roll-of-the-body; heel, toe, foot up.... Come on, get on your feet, the pair of you.'

'Oh, Daddy, Daddy.' Lorna was leaning over the side of her chair doubled up with high laughter, and Jenny held herself around the waist to ease the pain of her mirth, until he danced round to her and scooped her up from the couch with a lift of his arm, and then she was spluttering through her laughter, 'Oh, Paul, Paul, I can't.'

'Come on with you. Heel, toe, foot up; heel, toe, foot up.'

When Jenny tried to follow his instructions and all out of time, Lorna threw herself on to the couch and her laughter rose, and as if in agony she cried, 'Oh, stop it, Daddy! Give over, Aunt Jenny. Oh, stop it! You both look ... look ... oh!'

Paul was now leading Jenny in a comic form of the lancers. He would turn from her, bow to an imaginary partner, then gripping her by the waist swing her round. With the change of each figure he would do the bowing act. The music stopped at the same time as they knocked over a small table, and they hung together, panting and laughing. Then Paul, taking her to the couch, bent over Lorna and demanded, 'What's funny about our dancing, eh?'

'Oh, Daddy!' Lorna turned on her back and gazed up at him; her face was streaming, and her mouth wide. 'Oh, I've never laughed like that for ages. Oh, Daddy, you did look funny. And you, too, Aunt Jenny.'

'She's saying we're old, Jinny.' He nodded solemnly at Jenny. 'That's what she's saying. I'll show her.' He reached down and thrusting his hands under her armpits lifted her to her feet, nearly overbalancing them both in the process. 'Look,' he indicated the television, 'they're doing the tango. Now this is my cup of tea. Come on, miss; I'll show you.' Dragging her, still shaking with laughter, into the centre of the room, he now did an exaggerated form of the tango. He was contorting and twisting his big bulk when Lorna brought the exhibition to an end by falling against him, crying, 'Oh, Daddy! Daddy, stop it! Stop it. You're like a big cart-horse.'

'What do you say?' He glared down at her in mock anger. 'I'll have you know, miss, I took the prize for the best tango dancer at the students' ball....'

'Oh, stop it, stop it.' She actually sounded as if she was in pain.

And Paul stopped it. He leant his chin on her head and, looking across to Jenny, said quietly, 'I'm drunk.'

'Well, it's a good job you know it.'

'But....' He now thrust his daughter from him, and shaking her by the shoulders until her head wobbled while she still laughed, he cried in threatening tones. 'But not so drunk, madam, that I can't do the tango. I can do the tango on my head. Watch me.'

When he went down on his hands and knees and tried to hoist his great lumbering body into the air, Lorna once again collapsed. Throwing herself on Jenny she cried, 'Oh, Aunt Jenny, stop him, stop him.'

And Jenny, the tears streaming down her own face, looked to where Paul, violently kicking his great legs backwards, was endeavouring to stand on his head, and she thought, I wouldn't stop him for the world. She'd never seen him act the goat like this for many a long year. In fact she'd only seen him act like this once before. It was the night before he married Bett.

'Aw, to the devil with it.' He straightened his body up and adjusted his coat. 'I used to do that every morning before breakfast.' He went to the fire and flopped into the big chair; then putting his head back and looking up at the clock, he said, 'Good Lord! Quarter past one.'

'Yes, quarter past one,' repeated Jenny. 'It's time I was

77

going.'

'Why don't you stay the night, or what's left of it?'

'Oh no, I must get back, Paul. Don't forget I've got a do tomorrow night and I must be on the spot in the morning to get an early start.'

'Would you like me to come and help you, Aunt Jenny?'

'I would, I would,' said Jenny. 'I've still got umpteen fiddly things to do. You know, I think giving a dinner would have been easier than a buffet affair with all the tit-bits.'

'How many are you expecting?' asked Paul.

'Twenty. It'll be a crush.'

'Oh, I don't know; the rooms are not skinty. You were very lucky to get that flat.'

'Yes, I was.'

'I think I'll go to bed.' Lorna stretched out her arms and pulled herself upwards. 'Goodnight, Daddy.' As she bent forward to kiss him she added, 'Me Highland laddie.' And they laughed again. Then turning to Jenny, she kissed her, saying, 'I'll be along about ten, Aunt Jenny. How's that?'

'Fine. I hope I'm up. Goodnight, dear.'

When Lorna had closed the door behind her, Paul, his eyes still fixed on it, rubbed his hand over his mouth before he said, 'That's the first time I've seen her like herself for weeks. There's something worrying her, Jinny. You any idea what it is?'

Jenny looked away from him. 'No, Paul; not really.'

'Not really? Then you have some idea?'

'Well, she's going with Brian, and it's her first affair. Well, you know what they say, it never runs smoothly.'

'Aye, yes. Do you think she's still seeing him? He hasn't been near the house for over a fortnight. And we're in the middle of Christmas, and no parties.'

'She was at one last week.'

'One! What's one party at Christmas. Even her mother's been to three. Huh!' He dropped his head back against the framework of the chair. 'I wonder if she's enjoying herself?'

'Now, now, Paul, stop it. You know you could have gone with her, you were both invited.'

'. . . And Mr. Knowles?'

After the silence that followed this remark Jenny said briskly, 'Well, Paul, I really must be off. And look'—she rose and stood over him—'it doesn't need me to tell you you're in no condition

78

to drive, so I'll ring for a taxi.'

'A taxi! You damn well won't.' He jumped to his feet. 'No condition to drive! Jinny ... Jinny, I'd have to be very drunk before I couldn't drive my car. Come on, get your coat on and I'll show you.'

With a resigned smile Jenny went upstairs and into the room which she always thought of as hers. It was at the opposite end of the landing from Bett's, and next to Lorna's, and as she stood before the mirror adjusting her hat there came to her the sound of muffled crying, and with her hand still to her head she paused and listened. She wasn't at all surprised to hear Lorna crying; her laughter all evening had been too high, too forced. Again she thought of Bett, but, almost for the first time, without any sympathy. She felt that if she was near her at this moment it would be she who would do the face slapping, and the cause would be more justified.

Bett had gone with James Knowles to a dinner-dance, a special invitation dance, to which the Mayor and Mayoress and their son, Brian, would undoubtedly have been invited. Without ever having seen them together, or any concrete evidence to justify her feelings, Jenny knew that Bett was seeing young Brian Bolton, and the fact made her sick. She also felt sick, but in a different way, for Lorna.

She made no attempt to go into Lorna's room but went straight downstairs, and Paul's voice called to her from the waiting-room door, 'Look at this, Jinny.'

She went out of the smaller hall and into the larger one and saw him standing on the steps of the courtyard. He was pointing to the ground and saying, 'It's like glass; the sleet's frozen; it's a black frost. You're right, I'd better not take the car out in this.' He laughed a thick laugh. 'And you'll get no taxi tonight, either, Jinny, so it'll be shanks's pony.'

'I can manage on my own, Paul, it's only fifteen minutes' walk.'

'Jinny ... Jinny, what do you think I am to let you walk through the town in the dead of night?'

'I've walked through it many times before, Paul, and alone in the dead of night.' She laughed at him.

'Well, this is one time you're not going to do it.'

'But Lorna; she'll be in the house by herself.'

'Oh, she'll be dead asleep by now. And anyway,' he

looked at his watch, 'if the other one's not going to make a night of it she should be back soon.'

'Shall we wait a little longer then?'

'No, no. I don't want to set eyes on her. This is as good a way as any for us to miss each other. You see, Jinny.' He pulled her gently over the step, then locked the door. 'You know I haven't got much control over this temper of mine at the best of times, but when I've knocked off the bottom half of a bottle then I'm not accountable for anything I might say, or do ... to anyone. So come on, Mrs. Hoffman.' He gripped her hand and pulled it through his arm. 'I'm escorting you home. Not because I'm thinking of your safety in the streets but because I want to be looked after during the next hour.' He squeezed her arm. 'The dangerous hours before the dawn, the hours during which you ask yourself questions. Why were you born? Where are you going? And why has this to happen to you? Such daft questions as that. But anyway,' he gave a hick of a laugh, 'it's been a nice night, Jinny. I've enjoyed myself tonight, just the three of us. What about you?'

'Oh, I've enjoyed myself, too, Paul. I've had a grand time.'

'Ups!' Jenny slipped on the icy surface of the path and would have fallen if he hadn't hoisted her upwards. Then they were both slipping, and clinging to each other, and as they laughed aloud the echo came back from the dead Square.

'Let's get into the road. Ah, this is better. You can still feel the grit here.' He kicked at the loose gravel. 'You know what, Jinny. I think everybody should get drunk on a frosty night. How can they say you are drunk and incapable when the road's like glass, eh? Funny thing about people being drunk, Jinny. I've noticed it time and again. Some only need a few whiskies and they trip over their words; but now myself, I've got to be almost blind before I fuddle my tongue. You couldn't tell, could you?' He pulled her arm into his waist. 'You couldn't tell by the way I speak, now I ask you, could you ... could you tell that I've got a load on?'

'No, Paul; nobody would ever tell.'

'And my walk, it isn't bad, is it? Look, I could do a white line.' He let go her arm and demonstrated with one foot before the other.

'Oh, Paul, you're a fool. Come on, come on. If a policeman does come along you'll have a job to talk yourself into being sober.'

'Who's afraid of a pollisman?' He used the northern idiom. 'Who's afraid of anything or anybody?' He had hold of her again. Then his voice changing, he said slowly, 'Aw, this is nice, Jinny. Me and you walking in the night together. A hoar frost around us and the sky studded with stars. I'll remember this night, Jinny.'

He became quiet and she let him be quiet. She had thoughts of her own to think, and she too would remember this night.

When they reached Brampton Hill they found the going more difficult, and a number of times they nearly fell. So when they reached the drive that led to Farley Court, a one-time gentleman's residence which was now turned into four flats, they were laughing again. But as they neared the house Jenny warned, 'Ssh! We'll wake them up.'

'I thought the others weren't in?'

'One lot are, in the upper flat. Not above me; the other side.'

With exaggerated caution Paul now tiptoed into the hall, and when she opened the door of the flat he still tiptoed. He switched on the lights, and he tiptoed across the room, and switched on the imitation log fire set in the strikingly new fireplace; and then he whispered hoarsely, 'Do you think anyone saw us?'

'Not a soul,' she whispered back at him. Then pulling off her hat and coat and holding out her hands she went towards the fire. 'It strikes a bit cold. I think I'll get central heating in—the electric kind, you know.'

Paul was looking about him. 'I like this room. You know, Jinny, I never thought I'd like modern furniture, but you've done something with it. And all these colours. Yet they blend and are restful. I was always under the impression that I wouldn't be able to live with modern furniture, but this looks good; it's nice...' He sighed now.

'There's room for improvement.' She was standing by his side, she, too, looking about her; and her voice dropping, she said, 'You know, Paul, this is my first home, my first real home.'

'I suppose it is, Jinny.' He had turned his head towards her. 'It means a lot to you, doesn't it?'

'Yes, yes, it means a lot to me. You don't know how much. . . . But there.' She brought her face round to his and her tone lightened. 'I suppose I should offer you a drink, but do you think you could carry another one?'

'Madam!' He thrust out his chest. 'You put the plumb line down, an' you'll find there's another three feet afore it touches bottom.'

'Oh, Paul.' She pushed at him with her hand. 'Well, what is it to be? The usual?'

'The usual; I rarely mix my drinks.'

'I have tonight. I've had a little of everything.'

She walked from him towards a cocktail cabinet standing at the side of the fireplace, and added airily, 'And it makes you feel nice; you forget everything for a time.'

It wasn't until she brought the glasses back to the fireplace that he questioned her last remark. 'What have you to forget, Jinny?'

'You'd be surprised.... Is that right?' She handed him the glass of whisky.

'Oh, that's a dose, that's a very good dose. What have you got there?'

'The same.'

'Tut! tut! tut! You are mixing them. Well, here's to you, Jinny.' He raised his glass.

'And to you, Paul.' She drank. And to you, Paul. And to you, Paul. And to you, Paul. The words were dizzying in her head. Everything for you, Paul. Everything for you, Paul. All my life for you, Paul. Nobody else but you, Paul. Here's to you, Paul. Damn Bett. What has she ever done to deserve you? Has she ever given you a day's happiness? And she wants to get rid of you. Why hadn't she ever said to her, 'All right, get rid of him; I'm waiting ... why? Was it just because she had been brought up with her and they were like sisters? Perhaps. Perhaps. But it was more than that; it was the knowledge that Bett needed an anchor; on her own she would go to the dogs. Well, she wasn't on her own and she was still going to the dogs, wasn't she? So to hell with Bett.

'What is it, Jinny? You look so sad all of a sudden. Come on, drink up.' He put his arm round her shoulders, then drained his glass. 'Go on, finish it up and don't look so sad. What is it? What's troubling you, Jinny? Tell me.'

She stared into his big face, into the brown eyes that at this moment looked so kind. He had asked what was troubling her and she gave him the answer. She gave him the answer that she had dreamed of giving him for years and years. The dream had

had no place in her working day; it had been successfully covered by Bett, and loyalty, and long absence. But now it was night again, and her body was warm with a mixture of cherry brandy, sherry, advocat, and whisky, and she fell against him, her arms about him now, her face buried in his neck, crying, 'Oh, Paul! Oh, Paul!' And she pressed her body to his as she did in her dreams, pressed it until she felt the warmth of his flesh.

He was well aware that he was carrying a heavy load, but he had always been able to carry a great amount of whisky, and even when he was very drunk there was always a small section of his mind seemingly immune from the influence of the spirit, and now this section shouted at him, screamed at him. God blast it, man, not with Jinny. No! No! But the shock of the revelation of her feeling for him dulled the voice, yet even while he responded to her it kept crying, 'Give over. Stop it, for Christ's sake, man.' But he held her more tightly. She wants me. Blast it, she's always wanted me. I can see now. She wants loving. She's lonely.... What about Ivy? Oh ... Ivy! Yes, Ivy. But she's lonely. God damn it, she's lonely, an' I didn't know, I never guessed. Thirty-nine, she is, and I'd like to bet me bottom dollar still a virgin.... Stop it, you'll regret it for the rest of your life. Stop it. Her mouth was in his. Stop it. Stop before it's too late, you're both drunk. Isn't Ivy enough? There's the morning, as Maggie says; don't forget there's the morning.

With a thrust he pushed her from him and she staggered back as if indeed she was drunk; and now turning and resting his arms on the mantelpiece and dropping his head on to them he muttered, 'I'm sorry, Jinny, I'm sorry. I shouldn't have done that....' That was the line to take, take the blame. Make it easy for her. It was a dreadful thing to throw a woman off. He had thrown Bett off. Aye, yes, but for a different reason altogether. There was no comparison. He said aloud again, 'Aw, Jinny, I'm sorry, I'm drunk; that's what it is, I'm drunk.' When he received no answer he turned slowly round to see her sitting with her face in her hands, and he went to her and dropping on his knees he said, 'Jinny, Jinny, forgive me. I'm sorry. I'm so blasted drunk I've lost all sense of shame. Look at me, Jinny.'

'Oh, Paul, Paul. It was me, me. ... It was me.'

'What d'you mean ... you? Don't you believe it. Don't you believe it for a minute. I've had it in mind for a long time, even before ... even before you had that done.' He touched her nose with his fingers and her tears ran over his hands. 'You're so good, Jinny, so nice, so nice inside. Will you forgive me and forget it?'

Her head drooped low on to her chest.

'We'll both likely have forgotten it by tomorrow morning, anyway. Your mixing your drinks made your load as big as mine, but I'm more used to it. Come on now, get off to bed and I'll let myself out.' He rose from his knees, then pulled her up to face him. And now he said softly, 'Can I kiss you, Jinny? It'll be the last time, for I'd better not play about with this.'

She gave him no answer, nor did she move when his face loomed nearer, but she shivered when his mouth touched hers. Otherwise she made no response.

'Goodnight, my dear. Try to forget it, eh?'

He left her standing limp in the middle of the room, and when he reached the drive he unbuttoned his great-coat which he had just done up, unloosened his scarf, then slackened his collar and tie. He felt he was about to go up in flames. My God, that was a near thing.... Jinny! Jinny! He'd been a blasted blind fool, hadn't he? But how was he to guess at a thing like that. And she wasn't drunk, not even tipsy. She'd had four drinks since seven o'clock last night. Four drinks in seven hours. It wasn't drink that had made her give way. It was hard, even now, to associate passion with Jinny, yet she had held him as even Ivy had never held him. In those brief moments she had poured herself over him.... Aw, Jinny, Jinny. Well, if he was so sorry for her why hadn't he responded, gone the whole hog, for she had needed him; at least she needed something, someone ... no, not someone, or anyone ... him. Why hadn't he seen it before? All these years she had been handmaiden to Bett. Was it because of him? He saw again the look in her eyes, bare, stark; offering him all she had, all she was; and from Jinny that would be no small thing, even without the passion thrown in ... God! One thing he was thankful for, she had a place of her own. It would have been unbearable if it had happened in the house. Yet somehow he felt that it would never have happened in his house. He wished daylight was here, for when he was sober all this would be blurred and would fade like a dream. But if it didn't, what then? Well, he'd have to keep up the game, the game of shouldering the blame, of being a bit of a skunk, and he'd have to play it well if things were to continue as they had always been between him and Jinny.

As he walked down the slippery hill he realized that he wouldn't have to wait for daylight to sober him up—he felt stark sober now.

FOUR

BETT

It was towards the end of February, on a Monday morning, that Paul, looking at his engagements for the week, decided to visit Ivy that night because there didn't look much chance of him having any free time until the week-end, and he didn't want her to sit at home each evening waiting for him.

Tomorrow night there was a Conservative dinner; on Wednesday he had to go to a medical meeting in Newcastle, which meant him getting back late for surgery and doing his visiting afterwards. He could have got over this by asking John Price to fill in for him, but he didn't like to impose; John was too willing. Of course, being one of a four-way partnership gave him an easier time. Still, that wasn't the point. Then Thursday was clinic day and there wouldn't be a spare minute between getting out of bed until getting into it again.... And Friday. Well, Friday was the day for sweeping up so to speak, getting things tidy for the week-end if he hoped to have a half day clear on Saturday, and he wanted Saturday clear. He wanted the week-end clear so that he could get down to some study, revising. It was only ten days before the Board sat, and he wasn't sure what questions might be thrown at him. He was worried about going before the Board, there was no use hood-winking himself.

By the second post that morning a letter came from Doctor Beresford. Elsie gave it to him when he called in from his rounds to phone the hospital about getting a patient in. It was the first letter he had received from the doctor and it puzzled him, puzzled him greatly. The letter was written in old-world phraseology, and to the effect that Doctor Beresford would like him to call at his house at seven o'clock that evening. The matter for discussion was something that warranted a private meeting, otherwise the letter would not have been written. The whole tone was that of an order, and it both angered him and made him apprehensive, for he linked it with Friday and the selection committee.

During the rest of the morning the letter loomed large in his mind, and one period he almost phoned Beresford; his intention being to say he would be unable to call on him this evening and would he state his business now. But this action, he knew, would be nothing more or less than the outcome of his fear.... But fear of what?

In the afternoon of that particular Monday Betty went to see Jenny.

Over the past weeks Jenny had curtailed her visits to the house. She had made various excuses for her absence and some of them seemed very thin. When she ran out of them altogether she decided that she must do what she should have done weeks ago, get herself away from the agonizing proximity of Paul, for once having dropped the barrier of sisterly affection, try as she might, she couldn't raise it again.

On the day after Boxing Day he had come with the others to her house-warming, and, taking her aside, he had apologized, telling her that everything about last night was a bit hazy, but, having remembered bits here and there, he felt he had overstepped the mark and would she forgive him?

She had wanted to believe that this was really how he had thought it had happened. Oh, how she wanted to believe it to ease the shame; not of what her feelings had led her to, but of what they had not achieved. If only he had loved her, just that once, she would have lived on it for the rest of her life ... or would she? Would it have been the beginning of something unbearable? Because in the light of day it was unbearable that she should have an association with Bett's husband. If only she could have believed him her mind would have been easier, but knowing his innate kindness, she had no proof but that he remembered everything as it happened, and was helping her to shield herself.

And this personal matter was not the only worry she had. She was and always had been very, very fond of Lorna, and she knew there was something wrong with the girl. The boisterous enthusiasm, the heritage of all youth, had fallen from her, leaving her quiet and tired looking, or glum and stubborn, the latter always when in the company of her mother.

And there was Bett. She felt that in some way she had betrayed Bett. In moments of logical thinking she knew that this was ridiculous, more so when she gave thought to the fact of the number of times that Bett must have been unfaithful to Paul. You don't go out often with a man like James Knowles and expect to eat tea and buns, so to speak.

Anyway, she would soon be far away from them all ... although what she was going to do by herself in a hotel in Switzerland she didn't know. She could have taken a holiday in England but she wanted to put distance, long distance, between herself and those nearest to her.

She was actually packing her last case when the doorbell rang, and the sound made her hope it was Paul, then hope it wasn't. But on opening the door and being confronted by Bett, the colour flooded guiltily to her face. She saw at once that her cousin was definitely agitated, worked up to a high pitch about something. It was in her manner, in her walk, and the fact that she didn't come to the point straight away. Also she didn't look well, she looked as if she had a heavy cold. Her face was red and her voice was hoarse as she said, 'Well, if Mohammed won't go to the mountain....'

Jenny followed her into the sitting-room, saying, 'I'm sorry I haven't been round these last few days but I've been so busy. I've had to keep trotting back and forwards to Newcastle about passports and this, that, and the other.'

'You're lucky you can trot back and forwards to Newcastle about this, that, and the other.'

'Aw, Bett, don't keep on. I offered you the car.'

'I didn't want the car, I told you, I wanted the money. But looking back now, I could have taken the car and sold it, couldn't I? I'm a damned fool.'

She turned from Jenny and walking the length of the room looked out on to the tangled garden that surrounded the house before she said, 'You've always done everything in your power to tie me to that house and him, haven't you?'

'Don't talk rot, Bett. I've only thought what was best for Lorna and you, and I didn't want to be the one to give you the chance or egg you on to do something foolish.'

'Foolish! That's funny, that's a ha-ha-ha. Do you know something?' Now she swung round and walked quickly towards Jenny. 'It's the do-gooders of this world that cause all the trouble. If I'd left him years ago we'd both have had some chance of happiness. But no, the respected Doctor Higgins couldn't bear the thought of anyone walking out on him. And then there was you, yarping on all the time, telling me that my place was with him and Lorna. Well, now, as you're going off tomorrow ... it is tomorrow, isn't it?' Jenny didn't answer and Bett went on, 'I thought I'd tell you that your efforts have all been in vain, because very shortly Fellburn will know Doctor Higgins no more; neither will the house. I've always told you that I'd get him where I wanted him, haven't I? Well, the day has come.'

'Don't talk wild, Bett. What's the matter with you?'

'I'm trying to tell you what's the matter with me.' She went and stood by the hearth, and from there, with her head resting almost on her shoulder, she said, 'You were always for the big fellow, weren't you?'

Jenny's heart seemed to stop and she muttered faintly, 'I don't know what you mean.'

'Oh, you know what I mean all right. He could do no wrong in your eyes; even when I was left at the other end of the landing you thought it was no more than I deserved, now didn't you? ... I'd been a naughty girl.'

Jenny drew in a long breath, partly of relief; then slowly and flatly, she said, 'Look, Bett, I've tried for years not to take sides, you know I have. I've tried to be fair.'

'Oh, yes, I know you have.' Bett flicked her fingers in the air. 'Oh, you've been fair.... Yes, and all the time you've been blaming me for the way things were. I was the wrongdoer. Well now, listen to this.... But perhaps'—she moved her head in a sweeping half-circle—'it may not be news to you, you may even be in his confidence.'

Jenny waited, moving one dry lip over the other; she stared at Bett and waited.

'Is it news to you that he's got a woman, that he's been keeping a woman for years, is it?'

The pain went through her like a red-hot blade; she even took a sharp shuddering breath from the impact.

'Well, did you know?'

Jenny made a slight movement with her head; then walking to a chair she sat down.

'And you know who it is?' Bett made a quick grab at another chair and, pulling it forward, sat on the edge and bent towards Jenny. 'Ivy Tate.'

'Ivy! You mean Ivy who was ...?'

'Yes, Ivy who was ... Ivy who was working in my house for three years. What do you think of that? It must have been going on under my nose I ... I'—she squared her lips and showed her small white teeth clenched tight—'I could kill him, I could throttle him. Ivy Tate, a common, cheap, sloppy looking individual, Ivy Tate. But then, when you come to think, would you expect him to choose higher than the likes of her? As I've said before and to his face, he's got his scrap-iron, rag-gathering grandfather in him. Why do you think he wouldn't go to the other end of the town and set up practice? Because he's not at ease with civilized people, that's why. Under the veneer of the doctor he's more at home with the Bogs End crowd, and the likes of Maggie Swan, his dear, dear Maggie. Well, I've told her where she can get off, too. She's going, even before he does. . . . Oh, I'll see to that. . . . Maggie! Maggie Swan. . . .'

'What ... what proof have you?' Jenny's head was lowered now; her words were slow; she felt tired, weary. She also had an odd feeling of being naïve, even stupid. A big virile man like Paul. Of course he would have to have someone; all these years he would have to have someone. She hadn't thought of it that way. Well, she was a nurse and she should have, shouldn't she? She'd been a fool ... all these years he'd been having a woman and yet he'd pushed her away.

'Proof! I've got proof all right. Three times recently I've phoned the club to pass on a call, and each time they said he'd been left some time, and on each of these occasions there were no calls on the surgery board, and yet he never got in until eleven or later. I never thought much about it at first, then something that James said . . .'

'Oh, James! If you're going to believe James Knowles——'

'Yes, I believe James Knowles. I'd believe him before I'd believe the big fellow. But that's no matter; I can believe my own eyes, can't I? You see, I've watched him, I've followed him. What James said was quite innocent. "Paul's got a patient out of town," he said, "Beckley way, up Moor Lane. I've seen him up that way a few times." It was Moor Lane that struck a bell. I'd never been to Moor Lane, or Beckley, but I remembered Ivy Tate lived there and that he used to go visiting her husband. He attended him for over a year, and it was after that that he brought her to the house. Then he must have felt he'd better go careful. It was about the time that he thought of going in for the assistant physician's post and he began to work like stink. So back home she goes supposedly to be married, and from then he visits her. She's on his books—I looked her card up, but there's not an ailment down there. So I watched him; I watched him three nights last week. I waited for his car to come out of the drive. They were cold nights but I wasn't cold; it's a wonder he didn't see me glowing red. I tell you I could kill him.' Her hands were like claws now grabbing at the air.

'What are you going to do?' asked Jenny dully.

'What am I going to do? I'm going to wait and watch the goose being cooked. I lit the fire this very morning. There's one thing he wants more than anything in life, and that's to get that hospital post. Well, I've put paid to that for him.'

'No, no, Bett.' Jenny bounced up. 'You couldn't do anything to harm him in that way.'

'Can't I? Can't I? Just you wait and see.'

'But what do you hope to gain? You'll be cooking your own goose while you're cooking his. Don't you see? If he hasn't got a practice and a house, what's going to happen to you?'

'Do you know he was offered twenty thousand pounds for the house by Pearsons? They want to put up another refrigeration plant. And then the town wants to extend the Technical School, so they're playing against each other. He turned down Pearsons' offer of twenty thousand for that rambling, freezing mausoleum. But he'll reconsider now; oh, he'll reconsider all right.'

'But what is twenty thousand pounds if he hasn't got a job, Bett?'

'He won't only have twenty thousand. He's got ten thousand coming next year from a big insurance his father started for him. Then the old boy left him about fifteen thousand in shares which must have doubled by now. But it isn't only the money I'm after. No, it's to see him stripped, that's what I want. I've promised myself for years I'd see him out of that damned house. I didn't think I'd be able to get him out of the practice though, but after a divorce through another woman, and her a patient ... Well. Not to mention years of cruelty.... I picture him at nights standing before the medical council.... God, with his big head you'd have thought he'd have had that much about him not to take up with a patient. Well, there's one thing I know, he won't be going to his dear Ivy tonight, I've made other arrangements for him.'

'What kind of arrangements?'

'Oh, you just wait and see, as I said.'

'You're mad, Bett. And what about Lorna in all this?'

'What about her?'

'How is she going to react?'

'I wouldn't know, Jenny, and I don't care very much. That shocks you too, doesn't it? She's been on her high horse for weeks....'

'...And you know why she's been on her high horse, you know why, Bett?'

'What do you mean?' Bett's face had had a vicious look, and now of a sudden there was superimposed on it a look of fear.

'You know what I mean, I don't need to go into it. I don't want to make you feel worse than you are now, but for God's sake, Bett, why don't you grow up?'

Bett let out a long, slow breath; then getting up from the chair she took a step backwards before she spoke. 'You know sometimes, Jenny, I hate you more than I do him. Do you know that?'

Jenny shuddered; she shuddered not only at the statement and what it implied but at the tone in which it was said and at the look on her cousin's face.

Bett now turned from her, and as she went to the door she said, 'I hope you have a nice holiday, Jenny. I don't expect to see you at the house again, nor do I expect you to interfere in my affairs. And don't think you can do anything to alter this situation, because the wheels are already in motion. I saw to that before I told you; I wanted you to have something to take away with you.' She turned before she went out of the room and bounced her head once in Jenny's direction, which gave emphasis to her last words. Then she banged the door after her.

Jenny sat down again, groping at the chair as she did so. Dear, dear God. Bett was mad, mad with hate and frustration. What had she done? What was this thing she was going to do which would ruin Paul? She tried to think of all she had said. Platitudes, terrifying platitudes, such as: she had cooked his goose. But what actually had she done? She said she had made sure that he wouldn't get the hospital post, but how had she gone about it? Had she told someone about Ivy, someone in the town who had power? Or was she only bluffing? ... No. No, she wasn't bluffing. And whoever she had told would spring it on Paul.

If he could only be warned. Perhaps he could make a stand of some sort. In her heart she doubted it. What could anyone do against such hate? And Bett had said there was nothing she could do, she was contemptuous of her ... Well, she would see about that; hate was contagious.

The next minute she was running towards the hall where, grabbing up the phone, she dialled the house. When she heard Elsie's precise tones at the other end she said, 'This is Jenny, Elsie. Is the doctor in?'

'No, Jenny, he's out on his rounds.'

'Have you any idea when he'll be back?'

'Oh, not until five.'

'Elsie, listen. I must find him. Can you give me the addresses where he's likely to call this afternoon? And don't let on.... Do you know what I mean?'

'Yes, Jenny, yes. I know what you mean. Just a minute.' After a pause her voice came again, saying, '124 Fowler's Road, a Mr. Smith there. 26 The Avenue, child name of Bailey. Got that? Then 14 Preston Mews, a Mrs. Caldwell. Then there's four calls in Creasy House, Bogs End. The big block of flats, you know. I'll just give you the numbers: 8, 17, 24, and 25. Got that?'

'Yes, thanks, Elsie. And listen.... Don't ... don't let on to anyone I've phoned. But when he comes in ask him if he's seen me. And if he hasn't, tell him to come straight round here, will you? Tell him it's very important.'

'I'll do that, Jenny.'

'Thanks, Elsie. Good-bye.'

Jenny now phoned for a taxi, and when it came she gave the driver the address of 124 Fowler's Road.

It was nearly half-an-hour later when she reached the block of flats. The doctor had been and gone from all the previous addresses, but when she enquired at the first flat she was told he hadn't been yet. Also, that if he didn't get his calls in at the flats in the morning he often didn't come until after evening surgery; that was unless it was urgent.

This last information set Jenny a poser. It was now four o'clock. If he wasn't in the habit of visiting the flats until after surgery where would he go? Not to the club in the afternoon; and he rarely returned home until five, when he would have a cup of tea before starting with the evening patients.... Ivy Tate's. The significance brought her teeth on to her lower lip, and as she stood pondering she became aware that the taxi driver was watching her. Under his stare she considered for another minute. She couldn't go to Ivy's place, she couldn't. To see them even standing together would be a form of torture, for in this she had to agree with Bett, he had let himself down. Yet where would she find him if not there? But one thing was dominant in her mind, pressing everything else aside at the moment: she couldn't tolerate the idea of his exposure being sprung on him. It was going to be dreadful enough in any case, but if he was warned he might be able to put up something of a defence. She had very little hope of the latter, but the important thing was to let him know that the ice was cracking beneath his feet and that all that meant so much to him, his practice and his house, was going to be swamped. There crept in the thought that Ivy Tate might matter too, but this she disregarded. Getting into the taxi again, she said hastily, 'Moor Lane. Do you know where it is?'

'Yes, I know it; it's on the outskirts, near Wheatley's Farm.'

Fifteen minutes later the car bumped its way up the narrow lane, and when abruptly it emerged from the shelter of the bushes on to the wide grass verge she whispered hoarsely, 'Stop! Stop!'

She sat staring out of the window. There was no other car ahead of them, nor to the side of the house, and further on was a dead end, but in the garden beyond the gate Ivy Tate was standing. She had apparently been weeding. Jenny, as if unable to move, watched her open the gate and cross the grass. Then she was standing opposite the open window, facing her. Her face had lost all its high colour; it looked greyish, her eyes were stretched wide and she was visibly trembling as she said, 'Why! Miss—Miss Jenny.... Is anything wrong?'

Jenny now looked at the back of the driver and then to Ivy again before she asked, 'May I come in a minute, I'd like a word with you.'

'Yes, yes.'

As she got out of the car the driver said, 'You want me to wait?'

'Please.'

'O.K.' He nodded at her.

Jenny had hardly entered the bungalow before Ivy, closing the door, turned and whispered under her breath, 'What is it? Something's wrong.... The doctor?'

'I ... I thought he might be here. I have to see him, it's important.'

'You knew a-about him coming here?'

'No ... I mean, not before today.' Jenny watched Ivy put her two hands up to her face and press them against her cheeks, until her mouth formed a button. 'Something's happened. What is it?'

'I've got to find Pa ... the Doctor. Are you expecting him?'

'No. No. At least not yet. But look.' She thrust out her hands now towards Jenny. 'Tell me, tell me what's happened. I'm concerned, aren't I? It's about me? For God's sake tell me, please.'

Jenny looked at this homely, ordinary-looking young woman. In attractiveness she didn't seem to have anything more than she herself had, at least now, except that she was plumpish and a little younger. Yet this was the woman Paul had chosen to come to night after night. For how long? It was two years since she had left the house, and as Bett said it must have started long before that. For years Jenny had known she had been jealous of Bett, but she had never let it get the upper hand; in fact, she had hardly let the emotion breathe. She had told herself it was enough to see Paul now and again, to know that he was fond of her and appreciated her presence in the house. And sanctimoniously she had imagined it was part of her path in life to ease the tension in which he lived. But as she looked at Ivy she knew no such restraint on her feelings, and she cried bitterly within herself: I should have been in your place, I should, I should. And if I'd known as much as I know now I would have been too. As she stared at Ivy there returned to her mind the incident on Boxing Night and she became hot yet again with the shame of his refusal. He had known all right—oh, she was more convinced than ever now that he had known—and he had refused her because he had been faithful to this woman.

'Don't look at me like that, Miss Jenny. I did what I had to do; he needed me and me him. I was lonely, but he was more so. If it hadn't been me it would have been somebody else. I made him happy in a way. Just in a way, the only way I knew. But I also knew that there would be an end to it.' Her voice had lost its tremor and sounded calm now, and she walked towards a chair and, sitting down, she motioned Jenny to a seat opposite. Then she asked, 'How did you find out?'

'She knows; she's been watching.'

'Oh, no.' Ivy groaned out the words, and her head sunk on to her chest.

As Jenny looked at this beaten woman she remembered she had always liked Ivy, she had always got on with her, and she endeavoured now to waive her personal feelings. Leaning towards her, she said hastily, 'She means trouble, Ivy. I don't think she's quite right in her mind where he's concerned. She's going to use her knowledge to stop him getting the hospital post. But what is worse, she'll make a case of it, proving that you're a patient of his, and then his career'll be finished.'

'Oh, my God!' Ivy began to rock herself, her head still down, her body swaying backwards and forwards as if trying to ease a physical agony. Then slowly the rocking stopped and, lifting her head, she looked at Jenny and said, 'She'd have to have proof of that, wouldn't she? I mean legal proof. Has she had us watched, privately?'

'No, no, I don't think so. She just came herself.'

Ivy now straightened her shoulders. 'You have to have proof in these things, eye-witness accounts so to speak. I could say he had been attending me for my allergy ... I've got an allergy. Certain foods I eat bring me out in great weals and I feel off colour.' She stared at Jenny for a moment in silence before saying, quietly, 'It may not be too late; there is something I can do. Would you wait a few minutes more?'

Jenny inclined her head, and Ivy turned slowly away and went into the bedroom, closing the door after her.

Jenny looked about the room. The furniture was cheap and ordinary, there was not a vestige of taste in anything; the only comfortable thing in the room was the couch. It would be. Her mind tried to move away from the couch and its comfort but failed. Even when she had been running helter-skelter round the town trying to find him, there had been in her a feeling that the whole thing was nasty, that he had let himself down. Ivy Tate, who had been a servant in his house. She knew these things happened and always would. It was more prevalent today than ever, but she hadn't associated Paul with promiscuity, and if she had she would have imagined him picking someone in his own class. Yet had he taken a wife out of his own class? Bett liked to think of herself as having been brought up superior, but the truth was she had been an ordinary working girl, a typist, not old enough when she met Paul to have reached the post of secretary. And then, when she came to think of it, had he, in taking Ivy, stepped so far out of his own class when only two generations ago his grandfather had been a man of Bogs End?

96

There was a lot of truth in what Bett said, and his association with Ivy Tate proved it.

She began to walk round the room as if to get away from her critical thinking. She didn't want to think like this about him. It was as if she hated him too, and she had to admit that the relationship between him and this woman wasn't as nasty as she would like to think. There was really nothing nasty about Ivy Tate. In the local idiom, she was a nice lass; you could see it in her face.

When the door opened and Ivy came out of the bedroom she expected to see signs of her crying, but her face wasn't wet, nor were her eyes red, but there was in her expression a look of painful resignation, and it touched Jenny more than anything else could have done.

'Will you give him this yourself?' She held out a letter. 'And if he should still try to come, stop him, will you? Because it'll be no use. An' the less he's seen coming here the better.'

'I ... I doubt if I'll be able to stop him coming, Ivy; he'll want to see you.'

'I've ... I've explained it all in the letter. I won't be here. An' when I do come back things'll be different. It ... it won't be any use him coming then. It's all in there.' She pointed to the letter Jenny was holding.

The two women looked at each other; then Jenny said softly, 'I'm sorry, Ivy.' And she was sorry, really sorry.

'So am I.' Ivy's lids blinked rapidly. 'But I'm not surprised at this, I'm only surprised it went on so long.' She moved closer to Jenny until she had to look up at her, and her slow words expressed the pain she was feeling. 'I'd sooner die than anything should happen to him, anything, and through me.'

Jenny at this moment felt very small. She had imagined that in hiding her love for Paul all these years she had been doing something noble. She had imagined there were only two people in the world who really knew Paul, and loved him: one was herself, and the other, Maggie Swan. Lorna's love she didn't count; it was that of a child for its father. But this ordinary woman's love, she saw, was something big. It was an utterly unselfish love. And this was borne out as Ivy said softly, 'He's ... he's very fond of you. Will you do what you can for him? He'll need somebody calm like, for if he loses his temper with her God knows what'll happen.'

Calm like. She was very far from being calm like. When Ivy

turned towards the door she followed her, and she paused in front of her on the step and said, 'I'll do my best, Ivy. Good-bye.'

'Good-bye, Jenny.' Ivy now omitted the 'Miss'.

Jenny was aware that the door closed immediately behind her, and as she went towards the waiting car she had the impression that Ivy was standing with her face pressed tight against it.

In a few minutes they were on the main road again. 'Where to now?' asked the driver laconically.

'Romfield House,' she said. Bett had told her in plain words that she wouldn't be expected there again, but she was going.

It was a quarter to five when she reached the house, and even as she stood on the pavement paying off the driver the sound of the raised voices penetrated the thick walls. She did not ring the front-door bell but went into the courtyard, and there, im-mediately, Bett's high screaming tone met her, answered by Maggie's thick, loud, coarse twang. When she passed the kit-chen window she saw Paul's back blotting out the room and its occupants. She let herself in through the waiting-room door. There was no one about—Elsie had two hours off in the after-noon and wouldn't be in until five when the patients started to arrive. Quickly crossing the waiting-room, she went into the private hall, and here the voices filled the house, seeming to make it vibrate with their anger.

'Quiet, woman! Quiet! Do you hear me?'

'Don't tell me to be quiet. I've told you, she's going, and now, this very minute.'

'And how many more times have I to tell you she'll go when I say, and not before. And that won't be as long as I'm in this house.'

'Ha! Ha! Ha! God Almighty man makes big joke.... As long as you're in this house! Well, let me tell you, big fellow, your time's running out, and fast.'

'You're crazy, woman. There's been times in the past when I've doubted your sanity, but now....'

'Crazy, am I? Well, we'll see who's the craziest before the next twenty-four hours is over. But the point in question at the moment, doc-tor, is that I'm dismissing my cook. I'M DIS-MISSING HER HERE AND NOW. Get that into your thick skull. And you, or no one else, is going to stop me. Her time, like yours, is short anyway, but I'm going to have the pleasure of seeing her going through that door, her bust flat. And it'll be the first and last time, won't it, Maggie, for you've got the most fluctuating bust in the human race, haven't you?'

'I know what you're after suggestin', Madam, but I've told you afore I take nothin' away up me jumper. But if I did it wouldn't be yours I was takin', an' that I've told you afore an' all. An' I'll tell you this, I'll come back to the door each mornin' and himself will let me in, an' I won't stop comin' till he says with his own lips that I've got to. Not that it's any pleasure workin' in this house. Sheer hell it's been for years now, for you're no more fit to be a doctor's wife and have a place like this than any slut from Bogs End. But then you were born and bred not a kick in the backside from the place itself, an' you went to what was in my day the council school, an' you stand there darin' to put on your airs to me....'

At the sound of splintering china Jenny was impelled into the kitchen, there to see Maggie pressed against the fridge door and to her side the shattered remains of a heavy glass water jug which had fortunately missed her and hit the wall.

At the centre of the kitchen Paul stood holding Bett. He was gripping her shoulder with one hand, while with the other he slapped her face.

Jenny herself screamed as she ran in between them, and when she caught the deflected blow from his open palm he stopped, but still held Bett, who, her face now scarlet with inward rage and the slapping, continued to kick out at him and claw his jacket—which was as far as she could reach the way he was holding her—as if bent on tearing him to shreds. Like an enraged bull he swung her about and, gripping her around the waist, hauled her ignominiously from the room, across the hall and into the drawing-room. There, throwing her bodily on to the couch, he stood over her, glaring down at her as he panted for breath.

Bett lay still now, rigidly still. Her eyes and lips looked colourless and stood out from the rest of her face, and the hate that was in her came up like vapour and enveloped him.

When he could speak he said, 'This is the finish, do you hear me? It's the finish. I'm divorcing you.'

Jenny, standing with her back to the closed door of the drawing-room, could not see Bett's face but she heard the strange noise she made. It was an unreal, inhuman sound. Then she saw her head slowly appear as she pulled herself upright on the couch.

Bett hadn't taken her eyes from Paul, and now they bored into him, seeming to screw each word home. And they were more impressive because they were spoken quietly. 'You! You are going to divorce me? Oh, no. No, you've got it wrong. It's me whose going to divorce you. I'm not only going to divorce you, I'm going to ruin you. I always said I would and that's just what I'm going to do. The wheels are already moving and you can do nothing to stop them. This is final, final, big fellow, do you hear? Oh, you've got something coming to you, and I won't spoil it by telling you.'

Glaring back at her he wondered if she really had become unbalanced. He imagined that if she'd had any real evidence on which she could get a divorce, such as knowledge of Ivy, she would have spurted it out. He didn't give her credit for enough hate to make her diabolically cunning. All this was an act coupled with wishful thinking. But there was one thing clear in his mind: he couldn't go on. A little more of this and he might do her an injury. He said now, 'Who divorces who doesn't matter as long as it comes about.'

'You think so? Oh, but I see it differently. As I told you, you're going to learn a lot within the next few hours. And in a very short space of time I'll see that you own just what you stand up in. You'll be so fleeced you'll feel the wind through your clothes. And you'll have no chance to earn more.'

No chance to earn more? What was she up to? Unblinking, he returned her glare before he said, 'Well, you must remember that if I have no practice I have no money.' He sounded tired now.

'You'll have what this house brings and all your other odds and ends. Oh, I've got it all worked out. It'll be enough to keep Lorna and me going for a while.'

'Lorna?' It was a question.

'Yes, Lorna. You'd forgotten about her, hadn't you? Lorna will be going with me, for you've no claim on her, have you? You won't, like an ordinary father, be able to claim her for part of the time.'

'Shut up!' He bent nearer to her, and she, thrusting her face towards him, cried, 'No, I'm not going to shut up, I'm going to bring it into the open, air it at last. Say it, YELL IT, SCREAM IT ... Lorna isn't yours.... That's what's tormented your load of flesh, isn't it? It's been like sandpaper under your vest for years, never letting you rest.... She isn't yours. You were a bit

100

puzzled by the look of her from when she was born, weren't you? And, of course, she was a premature baby, she had to be. And then the day when Arthur Dressell came looking for me and you saw him holding her, you knew then, didn't you? Arthur's mother's maiden name was Haiyakawa. Very Japanese, don't you think? Anyway, he gave me a baby, and that was something you couldn't do; for all your brawn you're as ineffectual as a——'

As his hands gripped her throat Jenny reached him. Silently now she pulled and tore at him, and when at last she got his hands free they both staggered back, and she fell lopsidedly into the armchair. Remaining where she had fallen, she watched him with his hands held out before him, as if they had been burnt in some way, walking across the room.

When she saw the door close she looked at Bett. She was lying with her hands on her neck gasping at the air. Slowly Jenny got up and went to her. Her body was trembling, so she could hardly stand. As if she herself had almost been choked she gasped, 'Why ... why did you have to——?'

'Don't ... you ... start. You....' Bett suddenly closed her eyes and put her hand across her stomach. Leaning forward she said feebly, 'I'm going to be sick.'

Without a word Jenny hastily helped her from the couch and out of the room and up the stairs into the bathroom, and there she held her head while she vomited.

A few minutes later, when they were in the bedroom, Jenny said, 'Come on, get your things off and get into bed, and I'll get you a drink.'

'Leave me alone.' Bett pushed her to one side. 'I told you you weren't wanted, didn't I?'

For answer Jenny said, 'You'll feel better lying down.'

Bett slapped her hands away. 'I can take my own clothes off, just leave me alone. For God's sake! I'm all right. Don't you worry about me.' She wagged her head airily now.

Jenny looked down on her, and her voice held a perplexed note as she said, 'I wonder why I always have, and still do, because you're not worth it.' On this she turned quickly away and went out of the room.

When she went into the kitchen Maggie was sitting at the table, her head resting on her hand, and she looked slowly up, and after a moment said, 'I never thought I'd see this day. He's broken, broken entirely.'

Jenny didn't know how much Maggie had heard, but very likely she knew it all. Maggie, like many a privileged servant, gave herself the licence to hover outside doors.

'I'm worried. I'm worried to the soul of me. An' I would leave this minute if I thought it would do any good, but who will he have with me gone? And then there's yourself off the morrow. Oh, I wish you weren't goin'.' She moved her head in wide sweeps. 'I wish to God you weren't goin'. I've a feeling on me that always spells trouble. I'm worried, Miss Jenny, I'm worried.'

'Where is he, Maggie?'

'In his surgery. He wouldn't let me near him. He's not fit to work the night.'

'Would you mind making me a pot of tea, Maggie?'

Maggie didn't ask who the tea was for; she simply answered flatly, 'I'll do that.'

As Jenny went into the waiting-room she saw Elsie behind the partition at the far side of the room, where the patients' filing cabinets were kept. Already there were four people standing in a queue waiting for the numbered round discs that would ensure them their correct turn.

When she knocked on the surgery door and received no answer she opened it slowly, to see Paul sitting behind the desk. His hands were resting on the arms of the chair, the fingers hanging limply over the edge. She had always thought that he carried his age well, not looking anything near his forty-three years, but at this moment he looked fifty and over. She came slowly forward and sat in the patient's chair. Except for her hat, which had been knocked off when Paul accidentally struck her in the kitchen, she was still in her outdoor clothes. Her handbag was again in her hand, and inside of it was the letter, but how, she asked herself, could she give it to him after what had happened. Yet perhaps this was the best time; let it all come together. One shock might cancel out the other, at least in part. She said softly, 'Can't you get out of surgery tonight? Maggie could tell them you've been called away. Or why not phone Doctor Price?'

He stared at her for a full minute, and then asked, 'Did you know about Lorna, Jenny?'

She dropped her gaze from his.

'All the time?'

Her head moved lower still.

'You made a monkey out of me, too?'

'No, Paul. No.' Her head was up. 'I couldn't do anything, it was too late. I didn't know before you were married, but afterwards I remembered she had been friendly with Arthur Dressell when he was a student, and when he went back to France, where his people were, she was in a state. Then almost immediately . . . there was you and . . . and she . . .'

'And she chased me. Say it, Jinny. Huh! How that girl chased me. . . . Did she ever mention it to you that she knew I was on to her when Lorna came early?'

'No.'

'I love Lorna, Jinny. Do you think that strange?'

'No, Paul, no.'

'It's funny but I couldn't bear the sight of her after I saw Dressell. Then one day, she was about two at the time, she cried when I pushed her away, and after that, well. . . .' He brought his limp fingers into the palms of his hands but seemed to have no strength to clench them. 'What will happen when she tells her, Jinny?'

'She'll still love you. She'll always love you.' She did not say she hates her mother. 'And you'll be able to see her. She can't stop you from seeing her, no matter what she says.'

He rose heavily from the seat, and, standing with his hand on the corner of the desk, he said, 'First thing tomorrow I'll see Parkins and get the proceedings started.'

'Paul!' She glanced up at him. 'Bett knows.'

'Knows?' He screwed up his tired face at her. 'Knows what?'

Jenny could not continue to look at him as she said under her breath, 'About Ivy.'

From the level of her lowered gaze she saw him seat himself again. His hand on the desk, his body bent towards her, he whispered, 'She knows? She can't; she would have said; she would have hit me with everything she's got.'

'She's already done that.'

'What do you mean?'

'I don't really know, but she's done something, and the result, when it comes about, will mean your ruin. Your practice and everything, but I don't know what it is.'

He drooped his head forward, his eyes moving over the desk, darting from one thing to another, as if trying to read an explanation somewhere. And then his head jerked upwards again and he said, 'How did you come to know, Jinny?'

'She told me this afternoon.'

He shook his head violently now as a swimmer does when breaking the surface of the water. He couldn't make it out, her knowing, and not saying a word about it. It wasn't her type of reaction. He had imagined that should she ever find out she would pounce on him with it.

'How long has she known?'

'I don't know, Paul, but she's followed you a number of times.'

'God almighty!' He strained his lip through his teeth. 'Ivy....'

'Paul,' Jenny leant towards him. 'I tried to find you this afternoon. I went all round the town, and ... and when I couldn't get you I—I went out to Ivy's.'

'Jinny!'

'I—I told Ivy. I had to, because at the sight of me she guessed something was wrong. She thought something had happened to you. She—she gave me a letter for you, Paul.' She opened her bag and slowly handed him the letter. And slowly he took it from her hand, and more slowly still he picked up a paper knife and slit it open. After taking the folded sheet from the envelope he held it for a moment and looked again at Jenny before unfolding it.

The change was so sudden that it startled her, making her body jerk and causing the chair to scrape backwards on the polished tiles. He was standing before her, his body stiff, seeming broader and taller than he already was. There was anger in his face, but of a different kind from that which had been brought there by Bett, and through gritted teeth he spoke to her as he had never done since the first day they met. 'You shouldn't have done this, Jinny. You should have minded your own business. This is my business, and my business alone. You know what you have done?' He bent nearer. 'Do you? You've spoilt a good woman's life and Ivy's a good woman.' He threw the letter on the desk. 'You've made her sacrifice herself when there wasn't a damn bit of need. What's the practice and any other damn thing compared to peace and happiness? And Ivy gave me peace, and I made her happy.... Oh, Jinny.' He ran his hand over the top of his head and round to the back of his neck, and he held it there, pressing his head forward as he still stared at her.

She could say nothing; she felt as if he had hit her, blow after

104

blow. And not the least painful was the knowledge that if it came to the push and he had to decide between his practice and Ivy, he would pick Ivy. He would do in this matter what he had thought right, right to Ivy. A good woman. You could go on all your life doing good and you got no thanks, but you could become a man's mistress and through that you claimed the title of a good woman. There was a bitterness in her that was new.

As she pushed the chair further away from him so that she could rise he grabbed at her limp hands. 'Jinny, Jinny. I know you did it for the best . . . you did it for me, but oh! Oh! how I wish you hadn't. Believe me, I'm not thinking of myself so much in this, but of her. I'll miss her, God knows, but I'm not so besotted that I don't realize that I'll get over it in time; but for her, it's her whole life. . . . You see she's—she's going to marry Wheatley. He's a farmer. I've closed my eyes to it for a long time but I knew he was after her, and not as she always said, because she's got a bit of land.' He turned his head towards the desk where the letter was lying, then asked, 'Do you think there's any chance of stopping her, or is it already too late?'

Jenny pulled her hands from his and her voice cracked as she said, 'Don't ask me. Don't ask me any more.'

'Oh, I'm sorry, Jinny. I'm sorry I've upset you.'

As she moved towards the door he said softly, 'Don't go like that. I'm at my wit's end. Don't you take the pip at me, Jinny . . . please.'

She looked at him over her shoulder. 'I'm not taking the pip at you. Anyway, I'll be off tomorrow and . . .'

'Aw, yes.' He stepped hastily towards her. 'I'd forgotten. Your holiday. Oh, Jinny.' He only just prevented himself from adding, 'Don't go.' He needed her at this time, needed her balancing influence. 'I hope you have a good time; you deserve it.' Again he took her hand, but this time she didn't allow him to hold it. Instead, withdrawing it quickly, she said, 'We rarely get what we deserve. I'll be seeing you, Paul.'

She went out into the waiting-room that was now half-filled with people and made her way to the kitchen. Maggie was at the stove and she jerked her head towards a tray on the table which held a teapot covered with a cosy, milk jug, and a cup and saucer. 'It's ready.'

'Thanks, Maggie.'

Jenny picked up the tray and went upstairs. Bett was half sitting up, leaning against the bed head. She had her hand to

105

her throat, and Jenny, after putting the tray on the table, asked quietly, and somewhat stiffly, 'Does it hurt?'

'Yes, it hurts.' Bett went on stroking her neck. 'And inside too. I've had a throat for days, and nearly being throttled to death hasn't helped in any way.'

Jenny, her own nerves frayed and still harbouring a feeling of bitterness, wanted to say, 'You only got what you asked for,' but Bett, she saw, was in no condition for home truths; she looked shaken, even ill; and she was trembling so much she could hardly take the cup of tea Jenny offered her.

'Are you cold?'

'Yes, I feel shivery.'

'I'll switch the blanket on.'

'Jenny.' Bett put out her hand and gripped Jenny's wrist as she went to move away from the bed, and her tone softening now, she said somewhat grudgingly, 'I'm sorry.' Then she asked, 'Are you going tomorrow?'

'Well yes, I told you all my arrangements are made.'

Bett closed her eyes and a shudder passed over her body, communicating itself to Jenny through their joined hands. When the cup in her other hand began to rattle on the saucer, Jenny took it from her and put it on the table.

Bett was now gripping the front of her nightdress, and to Jenny's astonishment she began to whisper, 'Don't go, Jenny. Don't leave me, I need you.'

Never, in her long acquaintance with Bett, had she heard her speak as she was doing now, nor had she seen her look like this. She had seen many facets of her cousin's character but never had she seen her looking really frightened and her whole body shaking as if with fear. She said gently, 'It'll be all right. You can make it all right with him if you go the proper way about it. Everything could be . . .'

'Oh, him! It isn't him. . . . It isn't that.' Her voice had again assumed the tone she always used when speaking of Paul. 'It's——' She stared up into Jenny's face. Then her head drooping slowly, she screwed her eyes up until they were lost in their sockets.

'Oh, my God! Bett. Bett, look at me. You're . . . you're not pregnant?'

Bett opened her eyes, but with her head still hanging she said slowly, 'No, I'm not pregnant. It's funny'—her face moved into a twisted smile—'people always think that's the worst that can

106

happen to a woman ... for her to be pregnant.' She turned her face away, and then her body, and fell heavily on to her side.

'Well, tell me what it is.' Jenny leant over her.

'It doesn't matter, it doesn't matter. Forget it.' She had stopped trembling and her voice was controlled now. 'And forget that I asked you. You go tomorrow. It's this cold; it keeps hanging about, it's making me lose my grip. Go on, leave me alone; I'll likely go to sleep.'

Jenny stood looking down on the small, huddled body. She had never seen Bett like this. 'Will I send Lorna up to sit with you for a while?'

'No, no.' The answer came quickly, jerking her body into a different position. 'I don't want anyone; I just want to be left alone.'

'Drink your tea while it's hot then.'

'I will in a moment. ... Go on.'

Jenny went slowly from the room; then stood on the landing. There was something wrong with her. What was she frightened of if she wasn't pregnant? It certainly wasn't what she had done to Paul or what she was going to do to him; there was not a vestige of remorse in her on that score. Her mind lifted to James Knowles. But if she wasn't pregnant what had she to fear from him, or anyone else? But one thing was certain: she was afraid of something. If she knew her cousin, she was very much afraid of something.

She found herself walking towards what had been her room and passing it and knocking on Lorna's door. Lorna was in the habit of shutting herself away when her parents battled in the open. She had never been able to stand them rowing.

There was no response to Jenny's knock, and she pushed the door open to find the room empty. She stood with her hand on the door knob gazing about her. Then turning, she ran down the stairs and in and out of the rooms on the ground floor. She was still running when she entered the kitchen again.

Maggie hadn't seen Lorna. Not since she came from school, she said. She wiped her hands on her apron. 'What is it?'

'She's not in the house. Has she been in?'

'Aye. Yes, I've told you. She came in at quarter past four as usual an' had a cup of tea an' a cake. She took it out with her; she often takes it up to her room an' gets on with her homework right away. What about the playroom? Have you looked there?

She's got a lot of books stacked up there. Her ... her mother won't have them in the bedroom.'

'I've been in the playroom. Perhaps Elsie's seen her. She may even be with her.'

She forced herself to a walk as she entered the waiting-room. It was full now, with some people standing. She passed through them and into Elsie's office. 'Have you seen Lorna, Elsie?'

'Yes, she went out just a moment or so after I came in. Just before you went in with the doctor. Why, what's the matter?'

'Nothing, nothing. Did you speak to her?'

'No. I didn't get the chance; she was running, kind of helter-skelter.'

Kind of helter-skelter. Yes, she would have run helter-skelter if she had heard the conversation in the drawing-room. She was likely still running now. She hurried from Elsie and into the kitchen again. Maggie seemed to be waiting for her.

'Where were you, Maggie, when all that was going on in the drawing-room?'

Maggie jerked her chin as if trying to remember, and she said, as if to herself, 'Now where was I?'

'Maggie, were you in the hall when they were going at it?'

Maggie now looked her straight in the face. 'I was.'

'Did you hear all that was said?'

'I did. I did, and God forgive her because I never will, even if himself does.'

'Did you see anything of Lorna at that time?'

'The child? No. An' would I have let her stay there an' that goin' on? You know me better than that, Miss Jenny. But why do you ask?'

Jenny put her hand to her brow. 'Elsie says she went dashing out of the house just after that. I believe she must have heard. I feel sure of it.'

'She couldn't have; there was no other place for her to be downstairs unless ... unless she was in the mornin' room. But then she never goes into the mornin' room; it's as cold as charity in there, as you know, even on the best of days.'

'But if she was in there, Maggie, she could have heard every word, because there's only a wooden partition filling the archway that used to divide the room.'

'Don't say that.' Maggie put her hand behind behind her and dragged at one of the stools from under the table and sitting down she mopped her face with her apron. 'That child adores the ground he walks on. He's all she's got, an' she's always known it. She's always known that her mother had no time or feelin' for her.'

'Maggie!'

'It's no use; you can't stop me tongue from sayin' the truth. She's had no love for the child from the day she was born, an' it's all clear now why. She jumped into the marriage to save her face, and she hated the cause of it and the cause of it was the child. An' she also hated the face-saver, himself. Aw, how she's hated him. There's lots of things clear now, though it isn't to say I hadn't me doubts from the beginning. But I smothered them because I couldn't bear the thought of himself being taken for a ride by the likes of her. An' now this. . . . I'm tellin' you, if that child knows he's not her father she'll be lost entirely.'

'But after this she would have known sooner or later, Maggie. You've got to look at it that way. What I'm afraid of is the way she's learned it.'

'What are you going to do?'

'I don't know.'

'Should you tell himself?'

'Not for a while. Let him get his surgery finished; she might be back by then. She might walk it off, although something makes me doubt it.'

'And me too. Anyway, I'll not budge till I see her home. . . . Did you have a drop of tea?'

'No, Maggie.'

'I'll make you a cup then and bring it in to you.'

'Do you mind if I sit in here?'

'Do I mind?' Maggie stopped in her journey across the kitchen. 'I'll be only too glad of your company. I never mind pleasures, and they are few and far between in this house.'

There was hardly a word exchanged between them while they waited for Paul to finish the surgery. And it was turned half-past six when the sound of a car starting up in the courtyard took Maggie to the window, and as she peered through the fading twilight she exclaimed: 'He's off!' She swung her head round to Jenny, and Jenny, behind her now, knocked sharply on the window, but the noise of the car must have drowned the sound for he did not turn his eyes in the direction of the kitchen.

'Well, what are we going to do now?' Maggie spread out her

hands, palms upwards.

'I'll go and ask Elsie where he's visiting.'

'He had no visits,' said Elsie. 'He had got them all in during the afternoon. Yes, even the flats.'

'Do you know where he's gone, then?' asked Jenny.

'I haven't a clue. He generally tells me when he brings the cards across, but he didn't bring them tonight. He just went straight out after he'd finished the last patient. . . . What's up, Jenny?'

'Oh.' She shook her head. 'There's a bit of trouble in the house.' It was no use trying to hoodwink Elsie.

'Bad for the doctor?'

'It could be, but I hope not.'

'So do I. Has no one in there any idea where he's likely to have gone . . . the missis or Maggie?'

'No, I don't think so. . . . I'll be seeing you, Elsie.'

Jenny turned away. No, they mightn't have any idea, but she had. She could see him speeding to Moor Lane.

2

The bungalow was in darkness. Both the front door and the back door were locked and there was no key on the shelf among the paint tins inside the shed. Ivy had done what she had said she was going to do in the letter. He knew she would have done it but he'd had to come. He didn't know how far away she was, whether she was over at Wheatley's, or miles out of town, but he knew for a certainty that she had gone from him for good and all. He felt the loss of her weighing on him as if she were dead. It was impossible to think that he would never hold her in his arms again, feel the warmth and response of her kind body, and have those moments of oblivion and perfect rest with his head between her breasts. . . . But it was over.

On the main road once again, and driving towards Fellburn, it came to him that although his association with Ivy was finished the consequences were only about to begin. When he had received Beresford's letter this morning it had puzzled him, but now it puzzled him no longer. It had come to him during surgery that Beresford was Bett's secret weapon. Working through Beresford she would, as she had said, see him where she had always wanted to see him, outside the medical profession, outside of Romfield House. And it went without saying . . . you couldn't be a consultant if you were no longer a doctor. Yet somehow at this point of emptiness the vital issue of his livelihood didn't seem so important. He was a little tired of medicine, National Health medicine, jumping like a frog from one human being to another; he had been tired of this way of practising for a long while; this was why he had laid so much stress on getting the assistant's post and so specializing a bit. Now he was in danger of losing the lot. Yet nothing would have mattered all that much, he supposed, if Ivy had been waiting for him and they could have disappeared into some backwater, and there lived out their existence together. . . .

He swung the wheel violently about and turned into Melbourne Road. Why was he kidding himself like this? He would have gone into no backwater with Ivy, nor would she have wanted him to; she would have wanted him to fight, fight to keep the place he had won through hard work. And hadn't she given him the chance to fight? He had said to Jenny that Ivy had sacrificed herself, and she had done just that. Well, he would take it from there. If he sank, he sank, but he wouldn't go down without first trying to swim.

Mrs. Beresford opened the door to him, and as he looked at her he was struck yet again by the fact that happily married couples grew more alike as the years gathered on them. Mrs. Beresford was sparse-framed, prim behind her smiling façade, and swathed in invisible garments of moral righteousness. The Beresfords were church-going people. And so were many other doctors in the town, but the Beresfords were pie and sanctimonious, of the type that got under his collar and made him sweat. The Beresfords had found each other early in life. Each had what the other required; the marriage had been perfect, as perfect as marriages can be after forty-one years. They had three children, of whom they were proud. The eldest son was a medical missionary; the youngest son was a schoolmaster in a public school; and their only daughter was headmistress of a girls' school. None of them was married except to their vocations. Doctor Beresford and his wife knew that they had been blessed with such a family only because of their own good living and example.

Mrs. Beresford, still smiling, ushered Paul into her husband's study, saying, 'Doctor Higgins, George,' and left them immediately.

The atmosphere of the room was foisty as if the windows

111

hadn't been open for years. Like the old fellow's mind, Paul thought.

Doctor Beresford was sitting behind a long mahogany desk which was covered with letter holders and papers of various sizes, together with a number of books, two heavy brass inkwells, and a totem-pole paperweight. He did not rise to his feet nor offer his hand, but inclined his head and said, 'Good evening.'

'Good evening.' Neither of them had named the other; it was like a declaration of war. But this war was old, Paul knew, and dated back to his father.

Doctor Beresford now indicated a chair with a wave of his hand.

'Thank you.' Paul made his tone light; he refused to be put in the position of a boy in the headmaster's study, which was the attitude his colleague was taking up.

'You received my letter?' Doctor Beresford had his elbows on his arms of his chair now, his finger-tips tapping slowly together. It was a position that some actors adopted when playing the doctor, and it looked just as much out of character in this instance.

'I'm here, aren't I?' It was impossible to maintain the light tone.

'Yes, yes, of course.' The head bounced in time with the tapping fingers. 'It was merely an opening, merely an opening. In a business like this one has to start some place.' His eyes had been roaming over his desk as he spoke, but now they seemed to jump on Paul as he demanded, 'You follow me?'

'I'm afraid I don't.'

'I've never considered you a stupid man, Doctor.'

'Thank you.' It took all his willpower not to add, 'I cannot return the compliment.'

'So we will stop fencing, eh?'

Paul, deliberately now, put his elbow on the desk and leaning just the slightest bit towards Doctor Beresford said slowly, 'I'm afraid you'll have to be more explicit. I really don't follow you.'

'You're making this very awkward for me, Doctor, so don't blame me if I speak openly. I'm a doctor and also a man of the world. . . .'

'Your own particular world.' He shouldn't have said that.

'What do you mean to infer by that?'

'Just that the phrase is rather outdated; men no longer make the grand tour to become men of the world. We're all men of the world now, particularly, as I said, of our own small worlds.'

Doctor Beresford closed his eyes for a moment, wetted his thin lips and said, 'We're fencing again, Doctor.'

'Then it's up to you to come into the open at once, which will do away with the need for further fencing, won't it?'

Doctor Beresford sighed patiently. 'I sent for you, Doctor, in the hope that I would be able to help you.'

You did like hell. Again it was difficult not to put the thought into words.

'This is a delicate matter, and it has always been my opinion that men of our profession should be men of integrity; however, there is always the odd one who runs amok and besmirches the nobility of our calling. . . .'

God in heaven!

'. . . When this happens I feel that our dirty linen should be washed in private; that is, as much as possible. . . .'

'Doctor Beresford, what are you accusing me of?'

'I am not accusing you of anything, Doctor Higgins. I am merely going to bring to your notice the penalty attached to having a liaison with a patient.'

The two men stared at each other.

'I hope you know that you are laying yourself open to an action for slander, Doctor Beresford.'

'Now, now, Doctor, don't get high-handed. I've told you, I'm trying to help you.'

'Like hell you are.' It was impossible not to say it.

'Control yourself, Doctor.'

'Oh, for God's sake, Beresford, stop this cat-and-mouse game and come into the open . . . or should I get straight on to Parkins. . . . Yes'—he nodded—'I think that would be a very good idea. Parkins is my solicitor. Is he yours?' He watched the thin nostrils draw inwards, the eyelids waver. For the first time the old man was wondering if he had been put on the wrong track.

Doctor Beresford's altered tone conveyed his feelings as he said, 'Now, look, Doctor, don't get heated. I've done this in good faith. I received certain information which left me no alternative but to follow it up, yet I didn't do so; I thought it only fair to see you first.'

'You thought it only fair to see me first! You knew if you followed any such information up where it would land you if you were wrong, and your implication is going to land you in exactly the same place.... Court, because I'm not going to let this pass, Beresford; this is serious. You know what you're doing, don't you, what you're insinuating? This is my career....'

Doctor Beresford brought his fist gently into the palm of his other hand and wagged them for a moment under his chin. Then grabbing at a letter to the side of him, he demanded, 'Look. What am I to do when I get a thing like this? Send it to the authorities?' He thrust the letter at Paul. 'That is what I could have done; but no, as I said I wanted to help you.... Read it.'

Paul's hand was steady as he took the letter, but as he saw the writing he had to hold it in both hands to stop the paper from fluttering. Although it only confirmed what he already knew it still came as a shock to him.

'Dear Doctor Beresford,

Knowing you as a man of integrity I feel bound to bring before your notice the unprofessional conduct of one of your colleagues. This doctor has for a number of years been having an affair with one of his patients, a woman named Ivy Tate, of Moor Lane. She also worked as a maid in his house for three years. He is in the habit of visiting her in the evenings two or three times a week, and on Thursday evening of last week entered her house at half-past seven and did not leave until eleven o'clock.

As I understand that this doctor is applying for the post of Assistant Physician in the local hospital I think it only fair that the Regional Board should be made aware of the circumstances. I have no need to draw to your notice, Doctor Beresford, that this man has already got a wife and daughter.

I know you will act according to your conscience.'

The letter ended here.
The bitch! The vicious, vicious bitch!
He drew in, through his teeth, a long filtered breath, and over the top of the sheet of paper he met Doctor Beresford's eye. 'Do you believe it?'

'Now what do you expect me to say to that? I can only ask you, is it true?'

'It's true that I know Mrs. Tate, and I knew her husband

114

before he died. I attended him for a long while. And as this states'—he flicked the letter disdainfully—'she worked in my house; I gave her the work to help her. It's also true that I have visited her on many occasions.' And now leaning well over the table until his face was only a foot from the old man's he went on, 'It's also true, Doctor, that she's about to be married.'

They were staring hard at each other, eyes unblinking, and Paul kept the situation like that for some seconds before he went on. 'I don't usually visit her three times in one week, but there was a lot to talk about last week. She was very excited'—God forgive him—'for I suppose you could say she's making quite a good match. You see, she's marrying well-to-do farmer.' Slowly he straightened his heavy back, and it was heavy, heavy as Judas's. It didn't lighten the weight to know that this was how Ivy would have wanted him to tackle it. He finished with, 'A little knowledge, Doctor. The old adage is right once again.'

There was a slight pink tinge to Doctor Beresford's sallow complexion and it was a full minute before he said, 'In my place what would you have done? And a further question.' He picked up the letter from where Paul had thrown it on to the table. 'What would you do now?'

'I'll leave that to you, Doctor. As it says, whatever your conscience dictates. But I'll tell you what I'm going to do, I'm going to get in touch with Parkins first thing in the morning.... Take that and present it to the Board by all means, but understand'—here his voice dropped to a growl—'I'll defend my name and not only before a medical council but, Doctor Beresford, in a public court. Goodnight to you.'

'Now just a moment, just a moment.' The old man pulled himself upwards, his hand extended across the desk, and Paul, now at the door, turned his head over his shoulder, not sufficiently far enough to look at the old man, but just enough to indicate his contempt. And again he said, 'Goodnight, Doctor.'

On leaving the house the cold night air hit him and made him conscious that his whole body was bathed in a lather of sweat. As he drove the car towards home the sweat ran into his eyes, and once he actually pulled up to mop his face. As he alighted from the car in the courtyard he saw that the curtains of the kitchen window were drawn aside. That meant Maggie was still there. But he didn't want to see Maggie, or anyone else; he wanted to be by himself and think. The bluff he had used on Beresford would only get him over a short space of time, for if Bett named

Ivy as co-respondent that would be that. Ivy's marriage would do little to save him except perhaps stop Bett from proving her case. But the smear would stick, and he'd be lucky, damned lucky, if he kept his practice.

As he crossed the waiting-room towards the surgery Jenny came hurrying through the house door.

'Paul! Just a minute.'

He kept his eyes turned from her. 'I'm going to be busy.'

He had the surgery door open and she was close behind him. 'Paul; you must listen a moment; it's important.'

He continued into the room, his back still towards her.

'It's about Lorna.'

'What about her?'

'I—I think she must have heard you and Bett ... in the drawing-room. She ran out of the house after that. Elsie says she saw her running through the waiting-room here. She—she hasn't come back.'

He stopped. 'But she was up in her room. She always dives up there if we have——'

'She must have been in the morning room.'

He rubbed his hand round his face leaving traces of moisture along the edges of the pressure, then walked to his desk, round it, and came to confront her, saying flatly, 'Anyway, she would have known sooner or later. It would have only been a matter of hours before her mother let her have the full story, if only as a means of taking another shot at me.... By the way, Jinny.' He pulled his nose between his finger and thumb. 'I've just come from Beresford; she'd written to him.'

'Oh, no!'

'Oh, it doesn't matter. She's out to destroy me, but she'll likely destroy herself in the effort. It wouldn't surprise me if the woman doesn't go mad. She's been neurotic for years.... But enough of her.' He jerked his head backwards as if throwing Bett and all her works away. 'Where do you think Lorna's got to? Couldn't she be with some of her friends?'

'I phoned the Watsons first, then the Bells, and then Doctor Price's house. Queenie said she hadn't been there, but as I was talking to her the doctor came on to the phone. He asked what time Lorna had gone out and I told him. He said it was most odd, but when he was coming along Sunderland Road at yon end, about four miles out, he picked up a girl in his headlights. She was walking on the grass verge and he was so sure it was

116

Lorna that he pulled up: but when he called to her she took to her heels and ran on to the waste land. He—he said it puzzled him for a bit but he could understand the girl running away if it wasn't Lorna. He said if she wasn't back shortly, to contact him again.'

Before Jenny finished speaking he had picked up the phone and dialled a number. 'Hello. That you, John?'

'Yes. Yes, Paul. Has Lorna turned up?'

'No ... I'm worried. About this girl you saw. Where abouts exactly?'

'Well, you know the waste land near Braithwaite's factory. Just there.'

'You think it was Lorna?'

'Paul, I'm sure of it now. I was sure of it then, but when she ran ... well, you understand.'

'How long ago, John, exactly?'

'Oh, an hour and a quarter to an hour and a half I should say.'

'She could be anywhere by now.'

'Was there any trouble?'

'Yes ... yes.'

'What are you going to do?'

'At the moment, I don't know. She might turn up, but on the other hand if she was that far out who knows, she might be going straight on. I think my best bet would be to inform the police. What do you think?'

'Mine, too. Look, I'll come straight over.'

'Thanks, John.' He put the phone down, held his hand on it for a minute, while he looked at Jenny, then dialled the police station and asked if Sergeant Cooper was on duty.

The sergeant came on the phone and his voice was more than affable. 'Anything I can do for you, Doctor?'

Paul told him what had happened, finishing with, 'It might be nothing; I might be making a mountain out of a molehill and I'll feel a bit silly if she walks in within the next few minutes but ... but, you see, she was in a bit of a temper when she went out.'

'I understand, Doctor, I understand; I have three of my own. Leave it to me. I'll get things moving right away and I'll keep you informed.'

'Thanks, Sergeant.... By the way, I'm going out to have a look round myself, I'm just waiting for Doctor Price to join me.'

'There'll be someone in the house?'

'Yes ... yes.' Paul cast a sideways enquiring glance towards Jenny.

'Very good, Doctor. I hope I have news for you shortly. Don't worry. She couldn't have got very far, unless of course she took a lift. But ... but likely somebody will have seen her. Don't you worry, sir.'

Paul put the phone down and resting his two hands on the desk repeated, 'Don't you worry, sir.' Then glancing sideways at Jenny he said again, 'Don't you worry. I feel I'm going mad with one thing and another and I'm told not to worry.... How often I dish out that advice myself.' He turned round and leant his buttocks against the edge of the desk and asked her, 'Will you get me a drink, Jinny?' But as she turned away he said quickly, 'No, no, better not; I'd better keep my head clear.' As he glanced at his watch she looked at him and said tentatively, 'Paul,' and her tone brought his head round to her.

'Yes?'

'There's something else I—I think you should know. I've just come down from Bett. She isn't well, she's running a high temperature....'

'Jinny.' His big body reared upward away from the support of the desk and he seemed to expand as he growled at her. 'Don't you expect me to show the slightest concern about my wife's condition. I don't care if she's got a fever so high it melts her bones. At this minute Bett could be lying dead at my feet and I would step over her and walk out....'

The colour drained from her face. He had every reason to be wildly angry, but it seemed that he was also blaming her; this was the second time he had gone for her in a matter of hours. The Paul of her acquaintance was an impatient, sharp-tempered, slightly arrogant individual, but at all times so very human; not so the man facing her.

'...And don't mention Bett to me again, not for a long, long time. Tomorrow we part company, and if she doesn't go off of her own bat, I'll put her out. She'll drain me dry when it comes to a settlement, and if my throwing her out goes in her favour, so be it, but out she goes....'

Not a little to her own surprise, Jenny found her anger rising swiftly against him. There wasn't another soul in the world she really cared two hoots about, except perhaps Lorna, and it didn't seem possible that she could go against him in anything, but now she cried at him and her voice wasn't low, 'All right! all right! You needn't go on. But when you can forget your personal feelings remember you're still a doctor. And don't forget also that I'm a nurse, and as such I know she's in need of help. Her throat is infected, and this hasn't just started today. She must have been feeling off colour for some time. Now if you don't want to give the order perhaps you'd have no objection to me asking Doctor Price to look at her?'

He had been glaring at her as she went for him, but now his face relaxed just the slightest, and in a semblance of his ordinary tone, he said, 'You know you could have been sisters, you and her, Jinny, for when it comes to a balance between us you always tip the scales to her side.... Well, you do what you like, only don't tell me about it.... There's John, now. Look.' He turned back to her. 'I suppose it's a kind of nerve to ask you after that to stay on until I get back....'

'Aw, don't be ridiculous.' She blinked her eyes and jerked her head away from him. 'Go on.' Her voice softened. 'And for God's sake find her.'

As he went across the hall to the front door he saw Maggie standing just within the kitchen door as if she was waiting for him, but all he did was to pause slightly and exchange a glance with her.

John Price was a tall, thin man, a few years older than Paul, and the father of two daughters and two sons. He had been friends with Paul for many years, even before he had been asked to attend Bett, but he knew as little, or as much, about either of them as did any outsider. He knew, for instance, that they had separate rooms, but so did a number of people, because the daily helps and maids had been numerous over the years. And then it wasn't anything new for a couple to have separate rooms, particularly a doctor who was liable to be disturbed any hour of the night. Who knew; it might be out of consideration that he had a separate room; yet in this particular case John Price had his own opinion. The only thing he knew that was perhaps not public knowledge was the situation between the Higginses had been tense for many years, and he was sorry for them both because he liked Paul and in a way he was fond of Bett. When defending her to his wife he had often said, 'She's never really grown up, and whatever you say, you've got to admit she's always cheerful.' His wife had had varying answers to this kind of comment, but they all suggested that Bett was only cheerful in the company of men. And she had now and again commented on Lorna's strange oriental look; she hadn't much use for the theory of throwbacks.

But he was worried about this business of Lorna. He could still see the frightened face of the young girl in the headlights. He blamed himself now for not giving chase, but if he had been wrong he could have scared the girl to death.

He said on greeting, 'Hello, there. Any news?' What was the trouble, anyway? Queenie said she was all right when she left her after school.'

'Aw.' Paul put his hat on and tugged on the brim before saying, 'We had a few words.' He did not mention Bett.

'Oh, well, I can understand that upsetting her. I could never imagine you and her having words. It's funny, but whenever Queenie and her used to fall out Queenie used to do a mime of her talking about you. The little devil used to call you Lorna's Big Chief Daddy Doctor.'

Paul jerked his chin. It was meant as a light movement, in place of a laugh.

'Where do you intend to look?'

'Well, I think it would be a good idea if we went along to where you saw her and we worked from there. She might be miles away; on the other hand she might be hiding among the buildings around there. But I think I'd better call at the station first and tell the police where we are going.'

Before John Price got into his car he turned to Paul and asked, 'How's Bett taking this?'

Paul was pushing his bag and some files along the seat; his body was bent and his voice came muffled in reply, 'She's under the weather. A bit of a cold, I think. She's in bed.'

'Oh, I'm sorry to hear that; I'll look in on her later.'

Paul's car door banged shut behind him. Then Doctor Price's door followed suit, and the two cars moved swiftly out of the Square.

3

Maggie sat with her slippered feet pressed close to the bottom of the Aga cooker, while her hands gripped the towel rail. She had a feeling on her of impending doom. If anything happened to the child it would be the finish of him, seeing that it had come about because of the two of them warring. She had known all along right in her bowels that the child was no blood of his. She remembered the slant-eyed little fellow coming to the house and the tizzie herself had got into. She had known then all there was to know, and the old doctor had known, and the mistress, too. Ah, yes, she had known.... And then himself.... It was from that day that that look had come on to his face. Aye, they had all known, yet nobody had said a word because it was a thing best left buried. And the little snipe had played it off with a high hand, defying the lot of them, saying as plain as if she had bawled in their faces, 'You prove it. Go on, prove it.' Well, there was one thing to be glad of: it had burst into the open at last. They couldn't have gone on much longer as they had been doing these past years, with the hate growing atween them so thick you could cut it with a knife.

Then look how the little upstart had treated her, like so much muck beneath her feet. Before the mistress had died young mistress Higgins had minded her p's and q's, but from the day the mistress had been carried out of the house she had done her best to get rid of her. And begod! two seconds she wouldn't have stayed if it hadn't been for himself. No, she wouldn't that. But there was nothing she wouldn't put up with for him, for he was to her like a son; in fact if there was anything closer than the flesh of your flesh then he was that. Never had she had the same regard for her own boy, and let's face it, he hadn't it for her, for at no time in his life had he shown her half the consideration that young Paul had. The mistress had given birth to her only son six weeks after her own Monica had been born, and from when her daughter was six weeks old she had lain during the day in a clothes basket in the corner there while she herself had gone about her duties, and later on wasn't it natural, when the mistress wasn't feeling too good that she should nurse them both on her knees and that they should often drink from the same font. Perhaps that was why she loved him so, for she had suckled him like a mother. He was supposed to have been bottle fed and everybody exclaimed at his thriving and the wonders of the patent food, and she had smiled quietly to herself and went on giving him the mixture as before, and in after years as she saw him broaden and grow she had taken credit to herself. She knew in this moment that if her three children, who had gone from her, should die altogether from one blast she wouldn't feel it half as much as if anything should happen to himself. She sometimes felt that she hadn't very much to live for. When she left this kitchen at night and went back to her empty house, all she thought about was getting her feet up and getting her rest to enable her to carry on another day. She knew that in ordinary circumstances she would have given up work long ago, for she was past it; she was old—how old only herself knew. Most people when they guessed her age were out by ten years or more. But for the remainder of her time she was determined to spend it near him, for she knew that if during some part of the day she didn't see him then it wouldn't be much use her going on.

When the kitchen door opened and Jenny appeared, she turned her head slowly towards her and said, 'If that phone doesn't ring soon they'll have to cart me away. Another night it would be deafenin' you. I've never known it so silent. Isn't it just like the thing?'

Jenny came slowly towards the stove. 'Well, in one way it's a good job it isn't ringing, for he wouldn't be able to see to anyone tonight.'

'No, you're right there; he wants no calls the night. With one thing and another he's had his bellyfull the day, and I've a feelin' inside me it isn't finished yet.'

'Oh, Maggie, don't say that.'

'Aw, Miss Jenny, I come from a race that can smell disaster from afar off, an' I wish to God you weren't goin' the morrow.'

'At the present moment I can't see myself going tomorrow, Maggie.'

'Have you told her'—Maggie jerked her head upwards—'that the child's gone?'

'No, no, I haven't, Maggie, she's in no fit state to be told. She's partly hysterical as it is.'

'Well, she hasn't far to look for the cause of her trouble. She deserves all she's got an' more. Not that I'm holdin' it against her for tryin' to brain me with the water jug. No, no; that's a natural sort of response, an' it's many the time I've done the same meself, let fly at my Frank with what came to me hand when he came in bottled, God rest him. No, I'm not holdin' that against her.... Has that clock stopped? It must be more than quarter to ten.'

Jenny looked at the wall clock, then at her watch. 'It might be a minute or two out, but that's all; the time hangs heavy.'

'Aw, well, I wish to God somebody would use that phone. That's all I ask.'

As if in answer to Maggie's plea the phone shrilled from the hall and Jenny, darting out of the kitchen, picked up the receiver.

'Is Doctor Higgins in?'

'No, but can I take a message?'

'Yes. This is a report to tell him that a girl who answers the description of his daughter has been picked up in Newcastle. She is being held at Pilgrim Street Police Station. But she won't give her name. Will you ask him to go there?'

'Oh, yes, yes. Thank you. Thank you very much. As soon as I hear from him—he's out searching—I'll tell him. Thank you; thank you very much.' Jenny's hand remained gripping the phone after she had replaced it on the rest, and for a moment she rested against the wall by the side of the table, her whole body slumped.

'Maggie, Maggie.' She burst into the kitchen now. 'They've got her. At least, someone of her description. But there's not two Lornas.'

'Aw, thanks be to God.' Maggie was standing holding on to her chair, and she crossed herself. Then drawing in her thick wrinkled lips she sucked at them for a moment before saying, 'I'll make a cup of tea.'

Jenny began to pace the floor, talking all the while. 'It must be an hour since he rang; he could be miles away. Oh, if only he'd call. But anyway she's safe.'

'There it goes.' As the phone rang again, Maggie's voice almost drowned it....

'Hello. Oh, Paul. Paul, listen. They've found her. She's at Pilgrim Street Police Station, Newcastle.... Paul, are you there?'

'Yes, yes.'

'But where are you?'

'We're in Low Fell. John and I arranged to meet here. We'll ... we'll get off now, Jinny. Thanks. Thanks.'

The phone clicked and she put the receiver down, then she stood looking across the hall and up the stairs.

She should now be able to think. Well, that's that. I can leave tomorrow as arranged, but in her mind she was looking along the upper landing and to the end of the corridor, to where Bett lay tossing and turning in distress, both mental and physical. What would happen to her if she was left with Paul and Maggie? Paul who wouldn't go near her, and Maggie who hated the sight of her, while the fact of being visited by either of them

123

would, Jenny knew, increase her mental distress. And then there was Lorna. The gulf between them would be greater than ever now. Why, she asked herself, as she returned slowly to the kitchen, was she pulled from all sides by the emotions that filled this house.

'It was himself?'

'Yes, Maggie; he's going straight there.'

'Thanks be to God. An' sit yourself down an' have this cup of tea; you look as white as a sheet. And you'll have to content yourself to wait, for it'll be an hour afore they are back. So sit down, sit down.'

4

It was nearer two hours before they came. The sound of the car coming into the courtyard brought Jenny to the door, while Maggie busied herself at the stove, knowing that it was better at moments like this not to make too much of them.

From the light of the kitchen door Jenny saw Lorna and Paul standing beside the car. Then from the street came Doctor Price. Like Maggie, she told herself to act calmly and make no fuss, and so she waited. At least for a short time until she heard Paul's voice curt, commanding, saying, 'Now stop this, Lorna, and come inside.'

'Come on, Lorna, that's a good girl.' Doctor Price's tone was low and persuasive.

'I—I don't want to. I'm not going in.'

'Lorna!' Paul was shouting.

'I'll go to Aunt Jenny's.'

'I've told you your Aunt Jenny's here. Look, there she is.' He twisted her round and pointed towards the light of the doorway. Jenny came forward. She held out her hand, saying, 'Come on. Come on inside.' But Lorna remained stubbornly firm, pressing her back now against the car. 'I want to go to your place, Aunt Jenny.'

'All right, you can in a minute, but come inside first or we'll all be frozen.'

'Will you let me stay with you, Aunt Jenny?'

Jenny did not look towards Paul but she paused a moment before saying, 'Yes, yes, of course you can. You know you can.'

'Well,' Lorna jerked her chin to the side, turning her head full away from Paul, 'I'm only coming in for a minute, so

124

there.' She sounded different, older, brittle. It was as if she had been away for years.

In the bright light of the kitchen she stood with her head down, and Maggie, coming from the table with a cup in her hand, said, 'Sit yourself down a minute an' drink this cup of chocolate; it's just how you like it.' She spoke as if everything was ordinary, but Lorna exploded the myth by saying loudly, 'I don't want any chocolate, Maggie; I want nothing, nothing.' Her throaty voice was high, cracking.

'Jinny.' Paul sounded tired. 'Take the doctor into the drawing-room and give him a drink, will you?' He glanced at John Price now and added, 'I'll be with you in a minute.'

When they had gone he stood looking at Lorna, but she wouldn't look at him; her head was still hanging when he reached out and firmly taking hold of her hand drew her forward, saying, 'Come with me.'

As she pulled against him he said, 'Just for a minute, come along.'

She resisted him all the way to the surgery, but when he had closed the door behind them she flopped down on the edge of the patient's chair and, her head bowed again, she waited.

Bending over the ruffled black shiny head, he said softly, 'Lorna, look at me.'

For answer she jerked her body away from him.

'It's no use evading this, Lorna; we've got to talk about it ... clear it up.'

He was slightly startled when she swung quickly round and looked up into his face as she demanded, 'Is there any way we can clear it up, Da ...? You see, that's the point; I was going to say Daddy, and you're not, are you? You're no relation. She said you were no relation....'

'But that's where you're mistaken.' He dropped on his hunkers before her and, gripping her hands, went on hoarsely, 'I'm your father in the real sense of the word, in the only sense of the word I'm your father. I love you ... I love you, Lorna.'

'When you knew you weren't my father did you love me then?'

Her eyes bright and dark were looking straight into his, demanding the truth, and he gave it. 'No, not at first. At first I was wildly angry and hurt and ... and I pushed you aside, literally pushed you aside, till one day when I did that you cried, and we looked at each other, very much like we're doing

125

now, and it was done. I knew you were mine in all that mattered, I knew then that I would never have a child by your mother and you were the only child I wanted. I loved you then, Lorna, and that feeling has increased with the years.'

'But you're not my father.'

He gulped in his throat, and as he searched for words he watched slow painful tears fall over the dark line of her lower lids, and when, haltingly, she began to voice something of the agony of mind he himself had carried for years he felt he couldn't bear it.

'My father was a Japanese wasn't he? Wasn't he? ... Years ago a girl at school said I looked a bit Chinese and I hated her for it. But ... but of the two I'd rather be Chinese than Japanese. I—I think they're filthy.' Her face became awash with tears, and her head bounced up and down as she pulled her hands from his.

Dropping on to his knees, he took her in his arms and soothed her for a moment before saying softly, 'Your father wasn't all Japanese, just one of his parents. And they're a very talented race; there's nothing to be ashamed of being Japanese.... What?' He put his ear closer to her to catch her spluttering words. 'In the war ... in the war people said ... they were terrible.'

'Every nation was terrible in the war. And, Lorna, listen to me.' He lifted her face to his. 'Your father looked a nice man. I—I only saw him the once, but I remember thinking how good looking he was. And you have his looks. I—I think that's been the hardest thing for me to bear over the years, you being so beautiful——' When she dropped her head on to his shoulder he pressed her more tightly to him and went on: 'Because if you had looked like us, what I mean is a combination of me and your mother, it wouldn't have made for beauty, I know that.'

'Oh, Daddy! Daddy!'

On the sound of his name coming easily to her lips again he took in a long, slow breath. After a moment she raised her head and between gulps she asked, 'What am I going to do?'

'Do?' His brows went up slightly.

'I can't stay here. I can't, I can't. I couldn't look at Mummy, I just couldn't.'

'Would you like to go away to school, or some place?'

'Perhaps.' She thought for a moment. 'Perhaps. Yes, later on, but in the meantime can I stay with Aunt Jenny, please? Please,

126

Daddy.'

'But your Aunt Jenny is leaving tomorrow; she's going on holiday.'

She put out her hand and picked at the lapel of his coat, and she kept her eyes on her jerking fingers as she said, 'Would you ask her to take me with her?'

'Oh, but, Lorna...'

'Please, Daddy, please. I'll have to go some place. I can't ... I can't stay with Mummy. It isn't only about tonight's, it's ... Oh!' She twisted her body from side to side.

'What is it? Tell me?'

'No. No. Only I want to get away. Go and ask Aunt Jenny. Just ask her. Please, Daddy, please.'

'Very well.' He pulled himself up. 'Come into the kitchen with Maggie and have your drink and I'll have a talk with your Aunt Jenny.'

At the kitchen door he pushed her gently inside and nodded over her head towards Maggie; then went to the drawing-room, there to find Jenny alone. She was standing looking down into the fire, and she turned her head swiftly towards him.

'Where's ... where's John? Has he gone?'

'No.' She looked away from him. 'I asked him to have a look at Bett.'

When she finished speaking he went towards the wine cabinet, and as he poured himself out a drink he said, 'Jinny, can I ask you to take Lorna with you?'

'What do you mean? Home, tonight?'

He came towards her, the glass in his hand. 'No, to Switzerland. There'll only be trouble if she stays here. In fact, I don't think she will stay. I think she'll repeat tonight's performance again, I'm sure of it.'

'Yes, of course I'll take her.'

'You won't really mind? Oh, I say, you won't really mind, when I know it's a bit thick, in fact it's an imposition.'

'But I don't mind taking her; you know how fond I am of her. But there's another point. I'm wondering whether I should go at all ... I've got to speak to you about this, Paul, whether you like it or not. Bett is ill, and if she's left with you and Maggie who's to see to her?'

'Jinny.' He lifted his glass and drank most of its contents before he went on. 'Who I'm concerned about at the present moment is Lorna. She's had a shock tonight and if we don't

127

want repercussions later on she's got to get away.' Again he lifted his glass, and drained it and placed it on the table before he said, 'I'll get a nurse in if she's bad enough. And I'll go and see about getting more help for the house tomorrow. But, Jinny'—he walked up to her—'you'll do me the biggest favour of my life if you'll take Lorna away, and now. Let the scales weigh in my favour this time ... please, Jinny.'

She stared at him without speaking; then turning from him, she said, 'All right.'

'Thanks. Thanks, Jinny.' His hand went out and gripped her arm, but she did not turn towards him again, not even when the pressure deepened. When he let her loose she went down the length of the drawing-room, saying, 'We'd better go now; I can get her things tomorrow.'

They were crossing the hall when John Price came down the stairs. He came down slowly and they both stopped and watched him, and when he reached the foot Jenny went towards him and asked, 'What is it?' She was a nurse and the countenances of doctors weren't inscrutable to her. She saw that something was amiss and again she said, 'What is it?'

'I'm not quite sure yet, Nurse.' Although John Price had known Jenny for years he had always addressed her as nurse, and she had addressed him as doctor. He turned to Paul. 'I'd like a word with you.'

There was a short silence before Paul said, 'Lorna's spending the night with Jinny. I'm just going to run them over.'

'Oh, well.' John Price nodded his head. 'Go ahead. Go ahead.'

'Do you mind waiting?'

'Not in the least. Go on, go on. But I'd like a sedative for her. If you'll give me your keys I'll see to it.'

'They are in the desk in the surgery.'

'I won't be a minute.' Jenny glanced at Paul. 'I'll just pop up and see her before I go.'

It was Doctor Price who answered her. 'I wouldn't, if I were you, Nurse; I'd leave her as she is for tonight.'

Jenny, her eyes on the doctor, wanted to remind him that first and foremost she was a nurse, but she didn't. She went towards the kitchen, leaving the two men again looking at each other. It was John Price who turned away first, and Paul stared after him as he went out of the hall and into the waiting-room towards the surgery.

What now? In God's name what now? John looked shaken. Was she really ill? Something serious? He hoped to God not. He wanted this business over, no delay. He knew that he was quite prepared to lose his livelihood rather than continue life with Bett.

In the kitchen he put his arm around Lorna's shoulders and led her towards the door where Jenny was already waiting, saying, 'Have you said goodnight to Maggie?'

Lorna turned and, looking back at Maggie, said, 'Yes, and good-bye; she knows I'm going with Aunt Jenny.'

'It isn't good-bye, me bairn. You go and have a good holiday, have the time of your life. Go on now.'

'Bye-bye, Maggie.'

'Bye-bye, hinny.' Maggie shuffled forward, saying, 'An' good-bye again, Miss Jenny. An' you enjoy yourself an' all. Have a fling. Go on, have a fling.'

Jenny gave the old woman a weak smile. 'You'll be seeing me again, Maggie, I'll be round in the morning,' she said.

'Stay where you are till I come back, Maggie, and I'll run you home,' Paul called from the yard, and she answered, 'Aw, never you bother, I'll be in me bed by the time you get back.'

'Now look.' He came back to the doorway. 'I've told you. Stay put; I'll not be more than a quarter of an hour.'

'All right. Have it your own way.'

Not until the car had left the yard did Maggie close the door. Then, as she went to sit down, she heard the distant sound of a man's cough, and she remembered that Doctor Price was still in the house and was likely waiting for himself coming back, so she decided to make a pot of coffee. This done, she took the tray into the drawing-room.

The room was empty, and when she returned to the hall she glanced towards the stairs. Then her eyes were drawn towards the morning-room door which was open. What made her go towards it was the reflection of a glow in its dark panelling. The fire had been left on. The child had evidently switched it on when she was in there, and in her flight and shock had forgotten to switch it off again. If milady had been about it wouldn't have been left on. Oh, no. You could freeze to death to save a shilling or two. She stood looking about her. She had never felt the room as warm as this for years. It was a nice room and she would have liked it but for the fact it was as cold as an ice-box; but at the moment it was like toast.

She sat down on the deep couch against the wall to the side of the fire. It was an old couch but still in good condition. The mistress had been wont to put her feet up on it in the afternoons. Her own feet were the size of two pairs, she could do with getting them up herself. And why not—why not indeed, until himself came back? The other one wouldn't likely be stirring the night if she was so bad she needed a doctor. She went and closed the door. Then returning to the couch, she slowly raised one swollen leg after the other and lay back. Her body felt as heavy as her heart; but aw, this was nice; aw, she hadn't realized how tired she was; she could go to sleep, she could, she could that. An' if she wasn't careful she'd be out for the count.

Twenty minutes later when Paul returned and didn't find Maggie in the kitchen, nor receive an answer to his quiet call from the hall, he clicked his tongue with impatience.

When he entered the drawing-room John Price was standing on the hearth-rug, supporting an elbow in one hand while tapping the index finger of his other against his teeth. It was an agitated gesture. Moving slowly towards the fireplace, Paul kept his eyes on him, and when he reached the couch he stopped and said, 'Well?'

'Paul,' John moved uneasily, 'I'm in a bit of a fix. I've got something to say and I ... I don't know how to say it, or where to begin.'

'In that case, John, you'd better come straight out with it.'

'It isn't as easy as that.' John glanced sideways at him. 'I'm— I'm knocked, I just don't ...'

'Look,' Paul lowered his head and said slowly, 'spit it out. There's something wrong with her, is it cancer?'

'No.' The older man pressed his shoulders back and stretched his chin out of his collar. 'I could say at this minute I wish it was. Paul.' He went closer to him and, his voice rapid and low, he spoke to his averted face. 'I know that things haven't been quite right between you and Bett, not for a long time. Even if I hadn't been your friend and known a little about you, and was just visiting her ... well, I would have sensed things weren't quite normal. Do you follow me?'

'I follow you.'

'Paul, I ... I must ask you something ... pointedly.'

'I'm waiting.'

'Have you been together lately?'

'That's easily answered.' He turned and faced him. 'No. But what do you mean by lately?'

'I mean ... well, within the last few months, the last year.'

'Multiply that by twelve and you'll be nearer the mark.'

'Aw, man.' John Price's hand went to his face and rubbed it in evident agitation, and when Paul said, 'Look, what is this? Spit it out,' he inhaled deeply and his voice now sounding calm, even interested, he said, 'I suspect she has syphilis, secondary stage....'

What happens to a man when he is told that his wife has venereal disease and he knows that he hasn't given it to her? The normal reaction would be hate, disgust, a loathing of the woman and the dirt with which she was impregnated. A feeling of being cheated, of his manhood being indelibly stained. But Paul experienced none of these emotions; what he did experience was a feeling that he had been winded by a kick in the stomach, and that the blow made him want to retch. As if his wits had become dulled with the kick he heard John Price's voice, his words hesitant and limping, coming as if from a distance, saying, 'Of course there's a chance I may be wrong, but I don't think so. Still ... well, you can see for yourself. Her throat's very sore, but a sore throat could be a symptom of anything. It was the papules on her arm that gave me the first indication. It ... it happened when she lifted her hand above her head, and ... and the sleeve of her nightdress fell back. There were two, and one or two brown stains which speaks of recrudescence. I ... I might even have had doubts of my own powers of observation, but when she realized that her arm was bare, and she saw my eyes on it, she covered it immediately and became very agitated, even hysterical.... Paul, it's awful, man, it's awful, but she knows, she knows all about it. She didn't want to see me in the first place. When I went in she called nurse everything for telling me. I thought her attitude was surprise at seeing me so late at night. Then after a while she calmed down; but once she knew that I suspected what was wrong she really did become hysterical.... Well, there it is. I've given her a hefty dose of chloral. She should be well away in a little while, and with your permission I propose to do a Wasserman.... Paul, man, look.'

Paul went to the couch and sat down.

'Will I get you a drink?'

131

After a space of time, during which he sat staring straight before him, he made a small movement with his head.

The glass of whisky in his hand, he looked at it. Syphilis. Bett and syphilis. Of all the people he had to treat it was those with this disease he pitied most. Altogether he hadn't many on his books, not more than three or four. It was a secret disease. People had it, and hid it, and passed it on; and the receivers had it, and hid it, and passed it on. As was sometimes the case, they didn't actually know they had it, they just had spots and were feeling off-colour; and of course they didn't connect the rash with the person with whom they had been cohabiting. As one young fellow had said to him, oh, he couldn't have got it from his girl, she was nice. The boy was seventeen and the girl was his first girl. He'd had to convince them both that they needed treatment. That had been a piteous thing, but it was imperative that they had treatment at once, for this thing, this vile thing, could lie dormant for years then spring on them with frightening consequences, terrible consequences. Very often the only way he could get patients to have treatment was to send them to Newcastle, for they couldn't bear the shame of attending the special clinic, although treatment was carried out everywhere with the greatest privacy.

'Drink it up. Come on, man, drink it up.'

Obediently he put the glass to his lips, but only sipped at it.

John Price sat down on the couch beside him. 'Look, I can arrange for her to go away and have treatment. Not a soul need be any the wiser, so don't worry.'

'Don't worry?' There it was again, that useless, ineffective phrase. He turned his face full towards John and there came the sound of a laugh from his throat while his features remained as stiff as if they had been set in cement. Only his lips seemed to have the power of movement. 'Don't worry, you say. Would it surprise you to know that's all I've done since we married? From the very beginning our nerves have screamed at each other. And just tonight, a few hours ago, I decided that it was the finish, and tomorrow either she or I put in for a divorce. Although I know I stand very little chance of getting it against her, for I won't use the proof I've got, for that concerns Lorna, she has enough on me to knock me flat, finish me.'

'What do you mean? A divorce isn't the end.'

'It will be for me; but at the moment I don't give a damn.' He lay back against the couch and closed his eyes. 'I've had a mistress for the last two years and she's found out about it.'

After concentrating his gaze on Paul's mouth, John Price lowered his lids and said with a laugh, 'Well, it won't be the first time a doctor has done that. She can't hang you for it.'

'She can in this case, she's a patient.'

'Aw, Paul! You above all people.'

'Aye, me above all people.'

'Has she absolute proof?'

'Pretty near. But in any case the mud would stick.'

'And the Board next week, and you on the short list. Aw, Paul.'

'It'll be short all right, if Beresford has anything to do with it.'

'But how? Why him?'

'He knows all there is to know. He received a letter to the effect that I was having an affair with Mrs. Tate, Ivy Tate, who used to work here. Do you remember?'

Paul watched the effect of this last piece of news on his friend. He didn't know why he was telling him all this except that in some way it eased the shock of the disclosure concerning Bett. It was as if in exposing himself he was lessening the disgrace attached to her. Yet he couldn't explain to himself that, feeling as he did towards her, why he should do this.

John Price rose from the couch and walked to the fire, where he stood looking down at it before saying, 'This is awful. You should have told me. Look.' He swung round now. 'We'll have to go into this. You're not going to lose everything because of something that happens every damn day of the week to other men. You know this has always incensed me about our job.... Mustn't have anything to do with a patient. God! You see them stripped, you examine them, and you're supposed to view them as a skeleton in the lecture room. The damned stupid thing about it is, that if the woman concerned is not your patient she's somebody else's. It has always annoyed me that.... Ethics, unprofessional conduct. Taking advantage of someone under your care ... taking advantage. That's funny. Talk about raising a laugh ... when they sit at the other side of the table and rape you with their eyes, and go out disappointed if you don't ask them to strip off for an examination. Look, Paul.' He bent over him. 'Fight this. Anyway, Bett hasn't got a leg to stand on now....'

Paul made no response, he knew why John was letting off

133

steam like this. In the ordinary way Doctor John Price would have supported every maxim in the professional book because he was a good doctor, a good husband, a good father, and a moral man. He was talking as he did to make him feel that what had happened was really of no account; as he had said, this kind of thing happened every day, it was part of the usual routine. But it wasn't true and he knew it. The women who raped you with their eyes were few and far between, and except for the odd one here and there they disliked stripping off. And the odd one would have stripped off for anybody; doctors weren't exceptions in this case.

He said now under his breath. 'How long is it since you gave her the chloral?'

John Price looked at his watch. 'Just over an hour; it should have taken effect by now.'

He pulled himself up from the couch, and slowly they went from the room. He let John precede him up the stairs and along the corridor to the door at the end, and as he entered his wife's room he clenched his jaws and felt the cords of his neck and the muscles of his stomach tighten against the final evidence.

5

It wasn't until Paul saw the side of the Salvation Army Hall with 'The Citadel' painted in large letters upon it, that he realized it was morning and the dawn was coming up. He remained standing at the window until the pale grey light turned to pink and the sun, visible somewhere beyond the roofs, sent its rays like spilt paint into the sky; then he turned and looked about the room. His bed had not been disturbed; his coat lay across the foot of it. On the table to the side of the bed the standard lamp was still alight and looked conspicuously alone in that there was no bottle and glass standing near it. He hadn't touched a drink since John had given him that glass last night. Somehow he hadn't the taste for it; not that he didn't need fortifying, but what he needed more was the power to think clearly, to get this thing sorted out. Except for one instance his feelings had remained at the same shock level of last night. The instance had been when they were standing in the hall after they had come downstairs, and John had said, 'Have you any idea who it is?' and he had answered, 'Yes, I've an idea.' At that moment he'd had the desire to rush out of the house, burst into

Knowles's flat, take him by the throat, and worry him like a bull terrier does another dog.

But later, when he began to think somewhat rationally, he had to admit that Knowles was not all to blame. Knowles could have got nowhere without encouragement, without sanction. Yet this fact did not resurrect his hatred of Bett. It was an odd thing, but not once since he had confirmed without a doubt that Bett had the disease had he felt his rage rise against her. His main reaction still was the feeling of nausea following a shock.

As the night wore on and he had alternately paced the room and sat with his head in his hands, he began to question why there was still no condemnation in him towards Bett. Yesterday, when to him she was, besides being the woman who had tricked him into marrying her, a vicious, unbalanced creature, his hate of her had been something consuming and mighty. Yet now, when he had more reason for hate, it had not increased by one jot. It slowly became apparent that what had happened to Bett was having a cathartic effect.

So, by the first light he faced the unpleasant truth that most of the responsibility was his. He realized that had he tackled her with Lorna's parentage years ago things might have straightened themselves out, her confession might have brought from him forgiveness and pity. The excuse that being the kind of man he was he couldn't bear the slur her deception placed on his manhood seemed thin. The fact that he had withheld himself from her, even while sharing the same room; and when his mother had died he had unhesitantly put the length of the corridor between them, filled him with a deep shame now.

He knew this morning that he had reached the hill of decision; he was on the summit. Whether he was to fall from it in his own estimation depended on what action he was going to take.

Somewhere along the line he knew he had to do something right. He, the supposedly moral man—and he had been a moral man until he took Ivy, for the bottle had been his mistress during the previous years—had to act morally. Bett was frivolous, petty, vain. She had a mania for young fellows, but only, he imagined, to give vent to her skittishness. She would never, he felt sure, have gone with Knowles if it hadn't been for the long corridor. Whatever Bett was fundamentally, she had been, and was still, his wife, and, his conscience continued to tell him loudly, she hadn't deserved the loneliness he had thrust on her.

135

Years ago she had made a mistake, and as a frightened young girl had grabbed at him to hide that mistake. Had he not sympathized with a thousand women in his time because they were frightened of having made that same mistake, of the disgrace it entailed? He had been kind to them, even tender in his commiseration, but when the disgrace touched himself he had seen it as a different kettle of fish.

Anyway, he knew now what he would have to do. Bett was still his concern. She had tried to break him because she thought there was no humanity in him towards herself. Well, he would have to show her she was wrong. He would have to show to her the consideration he gave even to the least worthy of his patients. It wouldn't be easy but he must try. He must think about life with her as something to be lived a day at a time, and no more. Looking at time as the future which meant months and years ahead would get him down. Life as he saw it with Bett could only be taken in small doses.

And there was another thing he must do. As he went to a chest of drawers and took out a clean shirt his stomach muscles knotted on the thought that he must contact Knowles. This in a way would be even harder than facing Bett. But as a doctor he must do this. He stood with the shirt in his hand. Why must he? Could he count on this calmness of mind lasting when confronted by Mr. Knowles? Wouldn't it be better to ask John to deal with it? No. No. This was his concern, and his alone.

After a bath and changing into a different suit, he went quietly downstairs, and there to his surprise he found Maggie with the kettle boiling and the teapot standing ready to hand. She turned at his entry, saying, 'You're early.'

He stood looking at her. 'Why have you come at this hour?'

'Aw, I couldn't rest. I thought I might as well be doing something.'

'You should have waited for me last night.' He peered at her. The permanent bags under her eyes were swollen still further; her old face looked drawn.

She made no mention about having spent the night in the breakfast-room, but said, 'Do you feel like something to eat?'

'Oh, no.' He closed his eyes and shook his head. 'Just make the tea strong.'

'I'll do that.'

Some time later they sat at the table facing each other and drank the hot tea in silence.

'Maggie.' He rubbed his hand across his eyes, then pressed the eyeballs with his first finger and thumb. 'I'll have to have help in the house. Do you know anyone, anyone decent, to be housemaid?'

Maggie looked down into her cup. 'They're like gold dust. If they can get three and nine to four shillings an hour in the factory they're not doing housework for two and six to three shillin's, it stands to reason.'

'But I'll pay anything.'

'Well, that'll be different, for they never got more than half-a-crown.'

'It doesn't matter about the wage, Maggie. Do you know anyone, some woman with a husband out of work? There's a good few of those knocking about now.'

'Yes, yes, I know one or two meself, but as I said, they're all for the factories an' the bigger money. But there's Alice Fenwick. She doesn't like the factory; she'd sooner do housework if it pays. Now I think there might be a chance of gettin' her.'

'Where does she live?'

'In Kibble Street.'

'That's quite near. Do you think you could see her before she goes to work?'

'I'll have a try.'

'Thanks, Maggie.'

As she rose from the table she looked up at him and said, 'Things goin' on as before then?' Her tone was apprehensive.

His head was turned from her when he replied, 'Yes, Maggie, I'm afraid so.' As he walked towards the door he paused and added, quietly, 'Can I ask you to take a tray up later on, Maggie?'

'You can ask.'

'And will you?'

'I will.'

'Thanks.'

He went out into the hall, through the waiting-room, and into his surgery, and sitting at his desk he picked up the telephone directory and found James Knowles's number.

It was just turned eight o'clock when the front-door bell rang and Paul went to open it. On the sight of the pale, smiling, self-assured face all the reasonableness, born of the self-analysis during the night, fled and he had an almost uncontrollable urge

137

to answer Knowles's greeting by bashing his fist between his eyes.

'Hello there.' Knowles had stepped into the hall. 'You want to see me? I didn't know Bett was ill.' His voice had no trace of nervousness, yet there was a wary look in his eyes as if he knew that this visit was not going to be classed under the heading of social.

'Come this way.'

There was a deep indent between Knowles's brows as he followed Paul across the waiting-room and into the surgery, and as he closed the door he said, 'Is it serious? I didn't even know she was bad.' With a slight movement of his hand Paul indicated the patient's chair, then slowly made his way behind the desk to his seat, from which point of vantage he hoped he would be able to deal with the situation in a professional way. But immediately he answered Knowles it was evident that the professional attitude in this case was beyond his power, for he found himself spacing his words in a deadly cold, ominous tone.

'Yes . . . I . . . suppose . . . you could . . . call it serious.'

Knowles was puzzled. He screwed up his eyes as he asked, 'What is it? Why take this attitude with me? What have I done?'

What should be a man's answer to this, a man's, not a doctor's? His whole frame began to shake; it was most noticeable in his hands. There was a pile of bulky correspondence lying on the table, the majority of which, he knew, was from drug firms. He pulled it all towards him as he said, 'I think it's got a lot to do with you.'

'Oh. So there's more in this than meets the eye, is there? Well, come on, come on, spit it out. I don't know what it's all about but I'm willing to listen.' Knowles's voice sounded brittle, cocksure.

The nerve of the bloody swine! But he would have nerve; his type always had; the lady-killers were well equipped. The fury was rising in him. Like a red tide it flooded up to his eyes. With a sweep of his hand the mail went sprawling all over the desk, and bending half-way across it, his anger causing him to splutter, he growled below his breath, 'Would it surprise you to know that she has contracted syphilis?'

Still leaning over the desk, his body rigid, he watched the colour rise into the pale face. He watched the eyes blink, then stretch, as if the man had just woken up. Then what followed took him definitely by surprise, for Knowles, springing up from his chair, thrust his face almost into his own as he barked, 'And you think I gave her that? Me?' He gripped the lapel of his coat. 'By Christ! As big as you are I'll ram that down your throat. Who the hell are you to sit there like some bloated god and say that to me? ... Me give Bett syphilis! Let me tell you, I haven't got syphilis; nor have I ever had it. As for me giving Bett anything——' He drew his head back and screwed up his whole face as if the sight of Paul was distasteful to him, as he went on, in a bitter low tone, 'I suppose it's news to you what I'm going to say, but the fact is I've never been with Bett ever.... Now what do you make of that? Because we've had a laugh together, a bit of a joke, and yes, a bit of slap and tickle, you have to see something else in it. But let me tell you this.' His face was thrust forward again. 'Whatever has happened to Bett there's one person to blame for it, and it's not the one who's passed it on to her, but you.... Oh, she's told me some things about you, big fellow, and nothing that's good. And I'm telling you this: I'm sorry for Bett, always have been, for the simple reason she's had to live with you. She could talk to me and she has, we're pals. Always have been, but nothing else.' He now wagged his fingers about an inch from Paul's face, and Paul, unable to stand any more, took his hand and gave him a push that sent him reeling.

When Knowles regained his balance, he stood glaring across the room as Paul said, 'All right, all right, I've made a mistake, and you've had your say. You don't like me and I don't like you, and I believe you when you say you've never been with Bett, but speaking as a doctor I think that you've found more satisfaction in spewing your filthy stories into her ears than you would have if you had been with her.'

Knowles, his face a dark purple red now, adjusted his perfectly knotted tie and sneeringly he replied slowly, 'Bett always said you were a sanctimonious, big-headed swine, and by God! she was right. But you weren't so sanctimonious that you couldn't do a bit of homework on the side. Your kind make me sick.'

Paul swallowed deeply. 'I think we make each other sick, Mr. Knowles.'

'Ivy Tate! And in this house, under Bett's nose.'

The urge to use his fists was rising again and he had to give himself time before he could say, 'Just to put you right,

Knowles, I will tell you that nothing went on in this house under Bett's nose. Also I would advise you to guard your tongue in case you might have to substantiate what you say, not only to my solicitor but to Farmer Wheatley.'

As Knowles narrowed his eyes Paul went on, 'Mrs. Tate is being married shortly; the wedding has been in the offing some time.... Now I'll let you out.'

When they reached the front door he said, 'I won't expect to see you here again,' and Knowles, turning on the step and looking at him, replied, 'You got me here, sure in your own mind it was me who had passed it on to her, and if you had been right, tell me, what would you have done then?'

'I would have advised you to have treatment.'

'Oh. Oh God! It's as Bett once said, you're as cold as a dead jelly fish. Advise me to have treatment! ... I can't believe it. You know what a man, a real man would have done? He'd have wiped the floor with me, bashed my face in, not just give me a push. No matter what he thought of his wife, he'd have wiped the floor with me. So you would have advised treatment, and now you've got to find out who to advise, haven't you? Well, I can see you'll have to do some detective work ... Doctor; but I'll give you a clue, not in order to help you, but in the hope that it'll worry your guts out. How about starting in the Mayor's Parlour, eh? Good-bye and I wish you luck.'

Paul watched him get into his car before he closed the door, and then he stood supporting himself against it with his outstretched hand. From the moment that Knowles had convinced him that he was speaking the truth he had been shocked into an acute awareness of the magnitude of this thing that had fallen upon him. Behind all the talk with Knowles he had been asking feverishly, Who then? Who? Who? And now the Mayor's Parlour? The Mayor's Parlour? Somebody on the Council? But who? Who? ... The Mayor's Parlour? There wasn't a man younger than himself on the Council. Somebody in the offices? ... The Mayor's Parlour? The Mayor? The Mayor, Arthur Bolton? ARTHUR BOLTON! Don't be ridiculous.... Brian ... Brian Bolton? BRIAN BOLTON, the youngster.... Lorna! He recalled the night he had come in and had heard the rumpus upstairs and Bett clashing about and Jinny sitting on the bed rocking Lorna. What he had made out of this, and only through Bett's tearful yelling, was that Lorna had walked out of a dance because her mother danced with Brian. Then there were the times he had come home and found him in the drawing-room. He had thought he had been waiting for Lorna coming back from school. At these times he said that he had just finished over the road at the Technical School and called in. And then there were the nights Bett was out he had thought she was with Knowles. But Brian ... he was only a boy, nineteen, if that.

No! No!

Now he was really sick.

He was half-way up the stairs on his way to his room when he stopped. On the thought that came crashing into his mind he gripped the banisters. Just suppose! Just suppose.... Lorna had been very distraught of late. She had been sick several times, and she, too, had had a throat. She also had a herpes on her lip. But it could just possibly have been a chancre.

He swung round, dashed down the stairs, grabbed his hat and coat from the hall, went through the waiting-room so as not to give any explanation to Maggie, and out into the garage. Within minutes the car was roaring towards Jenny's.

He rang the bell three times before there was any answer, and when Jenny opened the door, the sleep was still weighting her eyes.

'What is it? Something wrong?'

'No, no, Jinny; I just want to talk to Lorna.'

'She's asleep. She's in the spare room. Will I wake her?'

'No, I'll go in, Jinny.' He went swiftly past her.

'But, Paul, something's wrong....' He had already gone into the room and closed the door before she had finished speaking.

Lorna was lying on her back. Her face, although swollen from her crying, looked beautiful, painfully so. He stood staring down at her for a while before gently touching her shoulder. 'Lorna, Lorna,' he said.

'Yes? Oh! Oh!' She opened her eyes, closed them again, then sat up with a jerk. 'Daddy!' Her tone was high, frightened. 'What is it?'

'Nothing, nothing.' He sat down on the bed and forced himself to calmness. 'I just wanted a little talk.'

'You're not going to stop me going with Aunt Jen ...?'

'... No, no.' He moved his head widely. 'Nothing like that. You're going on a holiday but ... but, there's something I've got to ask you. It's very important and it's very delicate.' He took hold of her hand and smoothed it before saying, 'It's about

Brian.'

Her fingers jerked within his, and she muttered quickly, 'I've finished with Brian, ages ago.'

'I know that, dear, but ... but what I want to say ... what I want to ask you is about the time when you used to go out together.' As he felt her hand stiffen, the sickness deepened in his body, but he went on, 'You know I wouldn't do anything to hurt you, or upset you, not intentionally, and why I'm asking you this is because I love you and wouldn't want the smallest harm to come to you. You understand?'

She was leaning back against the pillows and she stared at him blankly when she said, 'What do you want to ask me?'

This was terrible, terrible. He could ask this of patients, of young girls who denied ever being with a man when he had to tell their mothers they were three months pregnant. He had got used to talking tactfully, easily, soothingly, but none of his past experience helped him now. He looked down at her hand gripped into a fist within his. 'I'm going to ask you a question and you can answer yes or no. . . . Did Brian ever try to do anything to you that wasn't very nice?'

'Yes.' The answer came short, sharp, and coolly, and brought his startled eyes to hers.

'Lorna!' Her name sounded like a pain spilling from his wide-lipped mouth.

'Well, you asked, Daddy.'

'Yes, yes, it's all right, my dear. . . . Can I ask you something else?'

'I can't stop you, can I?' She sounded adult, not at all like a young girl, not at all like his Lorna, and he had to drop his eyes from hers when he put the next question. 'Did you submit to him?'

'No.' The answer came as quickly as the previous one, and the relief caused his body to slump.

'Why did you ask that?'

'Oh, it doesn't matter, it doesn't matter any more.'

'But it does. Why do you want to know that? Why did you ask such a question if it doesn't matter?'

'All I can say is, dear, that Brian isn't a boy you should associate with.'

'Not even to play tennis with? Or go dancing with? Or to the pictures?' The enquiry sounded ordinary.

'No, not even that. I would rather you didn't see him again.'

142

'Oh, you needn't worry about that, Daddy.' Her small nose wrinkled as if with distaste. 'I haven't seen Brian since before Christmas. Didn't you know that?'

'No, I didn't, dear, I knew you weren't seeing much of him, but I didn't know that you had stopped seeing him altogether.'

'Oh, yes. He's got someone else.' Her head was tossing now, and if he needed further confirmation of Bett's association with the boy he had it. My God! And how much did she know? Too much. That was evident, and it might only be a short time before she knew the whole of it. It was imperative that she should be got away.

As he rose from the bed he wouldn't have been surprised if she had said, 'Shall we do a Mrs. McAnulty?' and then gone on, 'I'm bad, Doctor. I've got something with a funny name; it's got three stages and the third stage mightn't happen for years and then it can drive you mad or blind or affect all your bones, and it can be passed on to babies and they can be born blind....'

'Daddy. About Mammy.'

He bit hard on his lip. 'What about her?'

'Well, I don't want to see her before I go. Can Aunt Jenny go and get my things?'

He actually smiled, at least his lips stretched, as he said, 'Yes, dear. Aunt Jinny will come and get your things. And you'd better not go back to sleep; you've got a long journey before you.' He went swiftly back to the bed and, bending over her, took her in his arms and held her tightly for a moment, and when she returned his embrace, he sighed deeply, kissed her, then left her without further words.

In the sitting-room Jenny said, 'I've made a cup of tea.'

'Thanks.' As he watched her pouring the tea out he said, 'Don't let anything stop you getting away as early as possible, Jinny, will you?'

'What's the matter, Paul? What's the matter with Bett?' She kept her attention on what she was doing as she asked him this.

'She's got V.D.' His voice was level and low and he looked straight at her.

'Oh, no. No-o!' She put down the teapot and placed her two hands over her ears as if to shut out the sound. And she rocked her body backwards and forwards in the fashion that Maggie would have done under stress. Then, becoming still, she said,

143

'Who? Knowles?'

'No.' His head was bowed. 'That's who I thought, but I've seen him. No, it isn't him, but it could be...' He found difficulty in speaking the boy's name, for when he linked it with Bett his mind presented him with something indecent. It had nothing to do with sex as such; sex would have covered his wife's association with Knowles, with Brian Bolton it appeared more like incest. 'It could be young Bolton.'

Again Jenny said 'Oh no. No-o!' Then, 'Lorna?'

'That's what I was afraid of, and that's putting it mildly. I nearly went mad when I thought.... Anyway, it's all right, she hasn't been with him, and she doesn't know about Bett.'

'She knows they've been seeing each other, that's what's been upsetting her.'

'Perhaps, but she doesn't know about ... about this other business. I'm sure it would have a dreadful effect on her if she did. In any case her attitude towards men will always be coloured by her mother's attitude, but if she was to know the whole of it ... well! So the sooner you're away the happier I'll be.... You see?'

'But I can't go. I just can't walk out and leave her like this.' Jenny's tone was incredulous.

'You've got to, Jinny.' He came and stood close to her. 'Listen. Listen to me.' He took hold of her arms. 'I'm going to see to Bett, for I realize, now it's too late, that this is mostly my fault. So don't worry. I know where I stand and what I've got to do. I should have done as you said years ago and had the whole business out. But there's no need for you to stay. Maggie's getting me someone for inside the house, and John's going to see about having her sent away for treatment. It will all be done very diplomatically; she'll just be going away on a holiday. And when she comes back ... well then, well, I'll have to try to make amends, won't I?'

'You know I could laugh, I could laugh at you, Paul, I really could. You mean to say you think you can make amends after this? You think you can take up a normal life with Bett or, what's more to the point, she with you? Aw, Paul....' Jenny moved her head in derision.

'Well, I can but try.' His tone was stiff and on the defensive.

'It won't work. I know Bett. It won't work. I've got to say this now, Paul. Bett will never forgive you until the day she dies. You can turn over all the new leaves you like and try to make up to her with everything you think possible, but even before this last, awful, awful business she had worked up a hatred against you that was terrible in its intensity, and now, do you think she'll feel any better towards you knowing what she's got? Why yesterday, when I mentioned your name, she nearly had hysterics; in fact she did; that's why I wanted Doctor Price to see her.'

'You never wanted Bett to leave me, or me her, did you, Jinny? All these years you've tried to keep us together, so what's made you change now?' She could have answered him truthfully and said, 'I worked to keep you together because deep inside I wanted you separated. Work that out, and what's the answer? My conscience was too much for me; it was stronger than my desire for you.' But what she said was, 'I never wanted you to separate before last night, but after that explosion I knew it was too late and that you'll only destroy each other.'

'Well, under the present circumstances what would you have me do, walk out on her?'

'I don't know, I don't know. But what I do know is that, because you've made up your mind to forgive her don't expect her to fall into your arms out of gratitude, because it won't work.'

'Jinny, Jinny, you know me better than to think at this stage of our lives I'd even want that. I just want to do the right thing now because I'm admitting my responsibility for the plight she's in. I expect nothing in the future, Jinny. Nor do I want it ... sufficient unto the day....'

'That's a very reasonable state of mind.'

'Jinny, don't sound like that.' He took hold of her hand and made her face him. 'Don't you turn on me; I couldn't bear it.'

'I'm not not turning on you. I couldn't, even if I wanted to, because, well...' She shrugged her shoulders and her smile held all the bitterness she was capable of. 'You know all there is to know about me, don't you? You know how I feel about you; you always have.'

When she bowed her head, his hands touched her arms, and as he went to draw her gently to him she pulled away, saying sharply, 'Oh, no. That would be the end, wouldn't it? If Lorna saw you holding her Aunt Jenny ... Oh....' She pushed her hand through her thick loose hair. 'I ... I didn't mean it like that. I ... I know it meant nothing. Oh!' She covered her eyes for a moment. 'It's as you say, I think I'd better get away and quick.' She looked at him now standing mutely regarding her. 'Aw, Paul, I'm sorry.' Her manner softened with her voice. 'You're going through the mill with one thing and another, and I'm not being much help. Go on home.' She moved towards the door. 'I'll come as soon as I can and get Lorna's things together, and perhaps you'll run us to the station; then there'll be two less in your hair.'

She was about to open the sitting-room door when he stepped quickly forward, and keeping it closed with one hand he drew her to him with the other. Putting his back against the door he held her pressed fast for a moment; then, lifting her face to his, he kissed her. When next he looked into her eyes they were large and soft and startled.

'Go on liking me, Jinny, please.'

She had difficulty in making out his muttered words. He had not said, 'Go on loving me,' but that's what he meant. She nodded dumbly at him, and he released her and, opening the door, went out.

He was going across the drive to his car when he asked himself why in the name of God had he done that? Why, when his mind was in all this turmoil, when there seemed nothing more that could happen to him had he to go and kiss Jinny like that? He supposed he had done it because she had wanted him to; perhaps because he himself had wanted to. But God hadn't he enough on his plate without getting involved with Jinny in that way? Some part of him must be slightly unbalanced.... It must be. What he should be concerning himself with at this moment was Brian Bolton. Yes, Brian Bolton. He rammed in the gears of the car and drove it full pelt down the drive and into the main road, hardly stopping to check whether the way was clear or not....

There were already a number of people in the waiting-room when he passed through it and into his surgery. Again he consulted the telephone directory, and then he dialled the Mayor's number. It was Mrs. Bolton who answered the phone and replied to his question, 'Oh, Doctor, he's just left the house this minute; this is one of his days for the Technical College. He'll be there in a couple of minutes. Was it anything important?'

It was nothing important, he assured her; he was doing a bit of writing and wanted some technical know-how; he thought that Brian might be able to help him.

146

Mrs. Bolton assured him, too; Brian would be delighted. She asked after Bett, and Lorna, and remarked on it being a lovely morning.

He replied that indeed it was and then rang off.

Passing through the waiting-room again, he went down the courtyard and stood at the outer door. The Square was busy. Three lorries were being loaded up with carcasses outside the Pearson's factory. Across the road opposite the Technical College the cars were parked tightly against the kerb. A number of motor-cycles came whizzing into the square and went round the side of the college where there was parking space. Young men, in twos and threes, came hurrying up the street and went up the steps into the building. And then he saw Brian in company with another young man. He was wearing a leather jacket, drainpipe trousers, and painted black shoes. His apparel seemed to emphasize his youth and stamp him as of another world.

Stepping quickly into the roadway, Paul called, 'Brian! Hi, there!' And he had to call again before he brought the boy's attention to him.

Brian had been laughing and demonstrating something with wide gestures of his hands, and when he heard his name called and saw the doctor his hands became stationary in mid-air for a second, and the smile slid from his face. As Paul beckoned he left his companion and came across the square. But not until he was close to Paul did he speak, and then he asked, 'You want me?' not 'Good morning, Doctor,' or 'Hello, Doctor,' but, 'You want me?'

'Yes, I want you. I would like you to come to the surgery for a moment.' As he spoke Paul was forced to turn away, but after taking a few steps he stopped and looked over his shoulder to where Brian was standing, straight, stiff, and unsmiling.

'I can't come now, classes are about to start.'

'You can make your excuses about that later; I will leave that to you; but at the moment I would like to speak to you.'

Paul had turned fully round again and they were staring at each other. If there had been any doubt in his mind as to whether he was on the right track in following Knowles's lead of the Mayor's Parlour it was gone. In the face of the young man before him was a mixture of defiance, fear, and guilt.

'We get into trouble if we're late.' Brian's voice was surly.

'You'll find yourself in greater trouble if you don't come with me, and at once.' He was growling at him now, his words mut-

147

tered and thick. 'I haven't much time to waste on you. I phoned your home. Your mother asked me what I wanted. I said I was doing a paper and wanted some technical advice. It's up to you. If you come into the surgery now we can leave it like that, if not, then I must advise your parents of my real reason for wanting to see you.'

He saw the boy's face turn grey. He heard him utter something that sounded very much like, 'To hell with you!' He remained still while Brian passed him, his step slow, and defiance emanating from him. Then he followed him to the house, through the courtyard and into the waiting-room.

The sight of the number of people waiting seemed to take Brian aback slightly, for after glancing behind him he allowed Paul to pass him, then followed him into the surgery. And when he had closed the door he stood just within the room.

Going to his desk, Paul said, 'You'd better sit down.'

'I don't want to sit down.'

'I think you'd better; I may have to shout if you stand at that distance, and perhaps you wouldn't want the patients out there to hear what I have to say.'

Slowly Brian moved towards the desk. His body still looked stiff with defiance, but there was open fear on his face now, and as Paul looked at him he found that he couldn't sustain the fierceness of his own anger. He almost saw the boy as a patient. Perhaps it was the chair, and the desk between them, and the atmosphere, but he wasn't seeing him as his wife's lover; at least not until Brian, poking his head out and speaking below his breath, hissed rapidly, 'It's about her, isn't it? Well, it wasn't my fault, she kept chasing me. I tried to push her off but it was no use, she kept on.'

'Be quiet!'

'I won't. That's what you got me here for, isn't it? Well, this is my side of it. She was determined from the word go. She broke Lorna and me up. . . .'

'That's about the only thing I'm thankful for; I'm grateful to my wife that she accomplished that.'

'What d'you mean?'

'Have I got to put it into words for you, or are you going to do the talking?'

'I don't know what you're getting at. I did nothing to Lorna.'

'That wasn't your fault, was it?'

'Now look here. . . .'

148

'No, my boy ... you look here. If it had to be either my wife or my daughter I would prefer it as it's happened, and that it was my wife who contracted your disease and not my daughter.'

As Paul took out his handkerchief and wiped the sweat from his face he watched the boy's jaw sag, and his eyes widen. His expression was very much like that of James Knowles, and for a moment it brought a feeling of horror to Paul with the thought that he might be making a mistake for the second time.... But no, as he watched Brian's hands go up to his face he recognized the confirmation of the boy's fear.

'I ... I've got nothing wrong with me. I couldn't have given her ...' The finger that came out and pointed towards Paul was trembling. 'You can get into trouble for saying a thing like that; it's taking a fellow's character away. Look. Look, I admit to being with her, and I've told you how it was, but there's nothing wrong ... I tell you there's nothing wrong with ...'

'You have syphilis, Brian.'

The quiet tone in which this statement was made and the look on the doctor's face, which at this moment was not that of an enraged husband, deflated the boy. His body sagged like a punctured tyre and he pressed his hand over the lower part of his face and bent his head over the desk.

'How long have you had this?'

It was a full minute before Brian spoke. 'I ... I thought it was gone. Honest, honest, Doctor.' He raised his eyes to Paul's. He was seeing him no longer as Bett's husband, or Lorna's father, but just as the doctor, his doctor, for he was on his panel, and he began to gabble: 'I was a bit off colour about a year ago, spots and things, and then ... then they got better. I didn't know it was anything, and then a few weeks later they came back. I had a sort of cold. I was going to come to you, but I happened to tell a fellow about it and he said ... well, he said I'd caught it. I felt bad, awful, then it passed away and ... and this fellow said if it cleared up like that I was all right, I wouldn't have it again.'

The face before him was dead white, the eyes were full of a mixture of fear and shame, and when the boy's voice, almost a whimper now, said, 'I'm clear again, no scabs or anything,' Paul replied softly, 'You have syphilis, Brian; it's in your blood. But we'll have your blood tested and that'll make sure.'

'Can I ... can I be cured?'

'Yes. Yes, you can be cured.'

149

'But ... but my father; he'll go mad, he couldn't stand it. He couldn't live in the town, the Mayor and all that, you see....'

Yes, Paul saw; he saw what effect news such as this would have on Arthur Bolton. It would break him, and his wife.... Oh yes, it would surely break her up. Their respectable lives would be shattered. Bolton himself was an honest, conscientious, good man, but he was an ordinary man, and as such this would hit him as a terrible, shameful catastrophe, magnified a thousandfold because of the position of honour he held. It would still matter if no one else in the town knew a thing about it; once he possessed the knowledge of his son's condition that would be enough. He said slowly and emphatically, 'Your father needn't know, he need never know. I—I couldn't inform him, anyway, without your consent.'

'But he'll—he'll get to know somehow if I have treatment in this town.'

This was indeed true, although there was a social service making contacts with V.D. patients and this was done with the utmost tact and secrecy, so much so that contacts didn't often realize at all that they were being investigated for V.D. Yet in the case of this boy, whose father was the Mayor and whose family life was open to the public, greater caution than ever would be needed. He said, 'I'll make arrangements for you to go to Newcastle, after I've taken a blood test. You needn't worry; everything is strictly confidential. I will be kept in touch with your progress, and when you come to visit me here you can be coming to give me information for my paper.'

He watched the boy's chest expand and his head droop as he muttered, 'I'm sorry, I'm sorry about...'

There was a short silence before Paul said, 'Well, you can prove that.'

'How?' His head came up a little.

'You can tell me how many girls ... or women, you have been with since you first knew you had contracted this, and ... and, by the way, do you know from whom you got it?'

He watched the boy straighten his shoulders and swallow a number of times, then smooth his hair back.

'I was with a woman in Newcastle.'

'Do you know her name?'

'No.... No. Well, she was just one of those....'

Paul wetted his lips. 'You're sure it was from her you got it?'

'Yes.'

'Before you noticed anything wrong with you were you with anyone else?'

Brian's head drooped again. 'Yes.'

'Can you give me her name?'

'I ... I couldn't do that.' Brian wagged his head from side to side. 'She lives in the town; she would get ... Well, her people would go mad.'

'We can approach contacts in a very diplomatic way. She may be on my books or a patient of one of my colleagues.... Don't worry, don't worry.' He put his hand up as he saw the boy's agitation. 'No one will know from where I got this information, I promise you that. But in the course of taking an ordinary blood test, or an examination, we could perhaps accidentally discover if this girl has been infected. You see what I mean? Now give me her name.'

'Fay Baldock.'

'Fay Baldock!' Paul repeated the name in a whisper. 'But she's going to have a baby.'

'Yes, yes, but that wasn't me, she's been around with a number.'

Paul leaned back in his chair. A girl still at school was going to have a baby and perhaps already she had given it an inheritance that might cause it to be blind and a thousand and one other things.

'Are there any others?'

Brian shook his head wildly. 'Aw, I can't remember.... Yes, yes, one. Susan Crabb. She lives in Bogs End, although she's all right.' He jerked his head upwards. 'Quite decent.'

Quite decent! 'Was there anyone else?'

'No, no, I don't think so.'

'Think hard. It's very important that the girls you've been with should be traced, because it's more than likely they don't know they have anything the matter with them, anything serious that is.'

'There's nobody else.' Brian's head was lowered again, and as Paul looked at him he knew that he was not telling the truth, but he supposed that this was enough for the time being.

He said now, 'I'll take a blood test, then I'll want you to come back tomorrow morning. By then I'll have made arrangements for you to begin treatment....'

'Where are you going to take it from?'

'Your arm; just a little prick.'

Brian sidled up from the chair, his head still hanging. 'You'll promise you won't tell my father?'

'Your father won't know, or anyone else who matters, if you follow my instructions.'

It was strange but he felt no reluctance when he touched the boy. 'There, that's done.' He dabbed at the small puncture; then went towards the door, and as he put his hand on the knob Brian looked at him and said again, 'I'm sorry. Believe me, I'm sorry for—for everything.'

'I believe you.' He opened the door and the boy went into the waiting-room, pushing his shoulders back as he did so, erecting the façade once again.

After closing the door Paul stood looking around the room. He felt like a man who had been in an earthquake, dazed, slightly stupid, knowing that it was impossible to attach the blame for the eruption to anyone, yet knowing that if Lorna had been concerned, vitally concerned, his reactions would have been totally different. Yet that boy had cohabited with his wife. He had, in doing so, infected her with a filthy disease. Shouldn't he, as Knowles had said, have wanted to bash his face in, wipe the floor with him? Did being a doctor make you less of a man? The truth was, doctor or no, if he had loved Bett in the slightest he would likely have done all that Knowles required as proof of a man. Yet had he loved her he couldn't have borne to live with her after this. It was because his feelings were mainly compassionate now that he could tolerate the thought of staying with her. And there was something more. He had never been able to satisfy Bett. Even at the very beginning, when he had thought he loved her, he had still been incapable of satisfying her; he was, as she had so often said and in so many ways, ineffectual. . . . But look at Ivy. What had been the cause of the physical barrier that he couldn't surmount with Bett? Was it the deep rooted illogical feeling against small women? Big men were supposed to be attracted by small women, yet since he was very young he had always felt an antipathy towards them. Had he allowed himself to be married to Bett to prove something? He didn't know.

He went out now and across the waiting-room again, and noticed with a feeling of irritation, even aversion, that it was almost full.

In the kitchen Maggie said, 'Sit down and have a bite.'

'Nothing to eat, Maggie.' He shook his head at her. 'A strong coffee, that's all.'

'You won't last long at that rate, you've got to eat. Look, it's ready for you an' they can wait.' She nodded towards the surgery. 'I do believe it's a form of entertainment with some of 'em, especially the afternoon lot, the ones that have nothing to do. It's a meeting place for 'em to exchange their symptoms with their pals.'

She went on talking as she busied herself about the kitchen, until he broke in on her, saying, 'Did you take a tray up, Maggie?'

There was a pause before she answered, 'Aye. Didn't I say I would? She was asleep. I spoke three times, but she didn't let on, so I left it there. I didn't know whether she was awake or not. An' about Alice Fenwick. I caught her, an' she'll be round to see you in the dinner time.'

'Thanks, Maggie.'

He finished his coffee, pulled down his waistcoat, and went out to begin the business of the day.

6

Jenny arrived at the house about half-past nine. She could see that Paul was still in surgery so she entered by the kitchen. When she saw Maggie wasn't about she went through the hall to the playroom, and there, collecting two cases, she took them upstairs to Lorna's room. It didn't take her more than ten minutes to fill the cases; and this done, she placed them outside the door, and as she did so Maggie's voice came from the bottom of the stairs, saying, 'Who's that up there? Is it you, Miss Jenny?'

'Yes, Maggie.' She leaned over the banister. 'I'll be down in a minute.'

'All right, all right. It's just that I heard sombody above me head in the child's room.'

Jenny now turned and looked towards the far end of the corridor. What was she going to say to Bett? Well, whatever she said she couldn't appear other than callous in leaving her. And what was to be her attitude? Was she to let her know that she was aware of her condition? Or pretend that she was just leaving her with a cold?

It was Bett herself who decided this. When Jenny knocked at

153

her door and pushed it open she saw her sitting propped up in the bed. Her face was white and pinched, yet on it there was a look of determination that hadn't been there last night. It was as if she had made up her mind that nothing was going to floor her, not even this detestable state.

'How are you?' said Jenny softly.

'Well, how do you think I'd be, eh?' Bett raised her eyebrows with the question. 'And you needn't look so shocked; you know all about it, don't you?'

Jenny turned her head towards the window. She couldn't find anything to say, but Bett didn't leave space for an embarrassing silnce. 'I'm not the first one it's happened to; half of them in this town are rotten with it. All very quiet and hushed up, special clinics, but I know. I could burst a few balloons if I liked, and in some very respectable residences at that.... All right, I was unlucky and I'll have to put up with it, I suppose. And nobody's going to say, you're too small, and too nice, and too respectable for this to happen to you. Besides, you're a doctor's wife and it couldn't happen to a doctor's wife.... Look at me, Jenny. Jenny!' She was leaning over the side of the bed now, her tone demanding, and when Jenny turned her head towards her she said, 'When you're busy blaming me, ask yourself, would this have happened if I'd been treated right? If I hadn't been kicked to one side? ... Now if in the beginning he'd ignored me because I'd got this then it would have been understandable, but he kicked me to the end of the corridor because I had committed the great sin of having a baby....'

'... No, no, be fair,' put in Jenny quickly. 'What you did was to hoodwink him into marrying you. You know you did. But if you had told him the circumstances, even after you were married, he would have got over it. But no, you kept it up. And from the beginning you pretended you wanted him because you were in love with him, mad about him, couldn't live without him, when the only thing you were mad about, Bett, was to get a wedding ring on your finger.... I'm not defending him from any blame but ...'

'...Huh! That's news. You're not defending him you say; why, you've done it with every breath and every look for years. You've always been daft about him. I knew that the day you introduced us.'

Jenny, staring down at this cousin of hers, experienced a feeling akin to that which Bett's tongue had engendered in Paul

154

over the years, a feeling that urged the hand to come out and strike.

'Not that I mind a damn. And when the divorce is through the way will be open for you. And why shouldn't you try your hand now that you've been remodelled? And he'll likely fall into your arms by then; anyway, he'll need a nurse to help tend his wounds and somebody to keep him, so your money'll come——'

'Stop it! Bett ... Stop your bitchiness. Oh, if you weren't ill I would tell you some home truths. I've been tempted to many a time in the past but——'

'Well, why didn't you, eh? You know why you didn't? You didn't because you couldn't risk having any rows with me. You wouldn't do anything that would stop you visiting the house, would you?'

Jenny's eyes were as hard as Bett's now, and her tone more deeply bitter as she said, 'The only thing you know at the present moment is that you're hurt and that you're determined to hurt in return. When I came in I was sorry I was going away; I had the idea that you might need me; but I see now that you don't and it'll make things easier.'

'You know, Jenny, you're so naïve. You always have been. But now for you to be surprised that I'm kicking out, that I want to hit back, well!'

'I'm surprised at nothing you do, Bett. You've always done what you wanted to irrespective of what anyone felt. And you've used me for years, you've always used me, and I was willing to let you go on using me....'

'Oh, come off it. You're like him, holier than thou, and, like him, you're a damned hypocrite, for you've had your fun on the side. You can't tell me a man's going to leave someone like you—like you were—forty-seven thousand for giving him blanket baths. He might have been paralysed and incapacitated....'

Jenny did not listen to the rest; she had never banged a door so hard in her life before. She was shaking so much that she had to put her hand out against the corridor wall to steady herself. Her whole body was sweating as if from a high temperature; it was in her eyes blurring her vision. When she saw the bulky outline of Maggie before her she blinked rapidly and wiped her eyes; then she allowed Maggie to take her arm and lead her to the landing. Neither of them spoke, not even when at the top of the stairs she looked towards the cases and, Maggie leaving go of

155

her arm, she went to them and picked them up, and slowly followed the old woman down the stairs. But when she put them down on the kitchen floor, she bowed her head and, her long body shaking again, she began to cry.

'Aw, lass, lass, don't. Don't give way. She's not worth it, she's not worth your little finger. She's an ungrateful sod, and I'm not asking God to forgive me for saying it, for that's what she is. Sit you down an' I'll make you a good cup of tea.'

'No, Maggie, no thanks. The—the taxi will be back at any minute; I said in half-an-hour.'

'Well, sit down till he comes; you look like a piece of lint.'

As Jenny went to sit down, the taxi came into the yard, and she said, 'Here it is, Maggie.' She wiped her face quickly and, picking up the cases, went to the door which Maggie opened for her.

'Good-bye, Maggie.'

'Good-bye, Miss Jenny. And don't you fret. Don't fret, I tell you. Try to enjoy yourself.'

For answer Jenny said, 'Tell the doctor I've been, will you, Maggie? He's coming to pick us up later.'

'I'll do that, I'll do that.' Maggie remained standing at the door until the taxi left the yard. Then going slowly through the kitchen and the hall, she stood at the foot of the stairs and, looking up them, said to herself, 'The Devil found habitation the day you were born, and he won't be without a house until the day you die, for you're neither good for man nor beast.'

It was twelve o'clock when Paul saw Jenny and Lorna off from Newcastle. He did not indulge in the usual platitudes, exhorting them to have a nice time and to enjoy themselves, but when he had found them seats he took Lorna in his arms and kissed her, and was again grateful for her response. Then taking Jenny's hand he held it for a moment as he looked at her, and there came a softening to his face when he said simply, 'Thanks, Jinny.'

She let him go along the corridor without a word, but when she saw him alight on to the platform she called, 'Paul! Paul!' and hurried after him. Looking down on him she said what was usually said at partings: 'Take care of yourself'; but her tone wasn't light and her words were heavy with meaning.

'I'll do that.' He smiled again.

'Let me know what happens, won't you?'

'I'll write. But don't worry; I don't think anything more can happen. Good-bye, Jinny.'

It was as if the incident in her sitting-room had never taken place.

As he passed down the platform he saw Lorna standing at the corridor window and he paused and looked up at her, then moved on.

When he got outside the station he knew a sense of relief—relief that Lorna was going away—yet the relief was coupled with a sense of loss. But the loss wasn't attached to Lorna, it was attached to Jenny. Sometimes he never saw Jenny for months on end, as during the period of this last post of hers; yet he knew now that it had been a comfort to him that she was always within reach, within a car ride or a phone call. Well, he could still phone her; distance was no object to phoning. Yet now it was different. This morning had made it different. He would never phone Jenny or contact her in any way.

When he returned to the house at lunchtime he was struck immediately by the silence. There was no banging of doors and running feet and swirling into rooms. . . . That was Lorna. Yet she hadn't swirled, or dashed about the house so much of late, which he had put down to her growing. How blind you could be to those nearest to you. He even missed Bett's high voice reprimanding or criticizing someone or other.

As he took his hat and coat off in the hall his eyes were drawn to the stairs. He had to face her some time.

He walked slowly into the kitchen, and Maggie, turning from the stove, said, 'They got off then?'

'Yes, they got off.'

'Doctor Price has been. He said to tell you he'd be back later.'

'Oh!' He paused, then asked, 'Has she had anything?'

'She had a drink around eleven.'

He was about to walk out of the kitchen when she said, 'I'll serve you now.'

'Hold it a minute, Maggie. I'm going upstairs.'

'Take my advice and have somethin' to eat first.'

'I won't be a minute.'

Outside Bett's door he braced himself before knocking. When there was no answer he knocked again; and when there was still no answer he slowly opened the door and went into the room. She was lying well down in the bed. Her face looked swollen, hot, and sweaty. What could he say? How could he begin?

How could he convey to her that he wasn't repulsed by her, that he understood, that he had to share the blame for what had happened to her? He forced himself to look at her kindly as he would at a patient who was frightened and ill, and he said, as if to that patient, 'How are you feeling?'

'Huh!' She stared up at him over the rim of the bedclothes. Then again she said, 'Huh!' And the sound was rough and rusty and told him of the soreness of her throat. 'How do you expect me to feel? But then you wouldn't know how I feel, would you?' Her voice was uneven, the words cracked.

'You ... you can soon get well.'

'You think so? You think I can ever be the same again? Go on, tell me, tell me how I'm to go about it?'

'We'll talk later, when you are feeling better.'

'Oh, for God's sake come off your pedestal.' For the first time her body moved, and bringing up her hands she covered her eyes as she went on speaking, 'I could bear you shouting, storming, better than this sanctimonious front. And it doesn't cover up anything, I can see through it. Oh, I know you ... I know you would like to kill me.'

'Strangely enough, Bett, I don't. I've been wrong and you've been wrong. I mean it when I say we've both got to bear the consequences.'

'Oh, for God's sake go away. Go away! I tell you I can't bear you like this. It's worse than when you are your natural big-headed self.' She took her hands from her eyes and glared at him. 'Look, we don't change, we're still the same under the skin.'

Striving to keep the seemingly calm demeanour, he picked his words. 'We can try. At least in our attitude.'

Her body became quite still again, and looking down the length of the bed, she said, 'I don't want you to forgive me, not about anything, you understand? I couldn't change towards you, not in a hundred years, ever. It's over, finished. As soon as I'm able I'm going away. As I said yesterday, when everything's settled I'll have enough money to live on. Even if you bring this out in the divorce you'll still have to stump up, because what's happened to me now is through your neglect, and judges are sympathetic to women, especially wives who have been neglected.' She raised her bright, hard eyes to him. 'You see, I couldn't change. I'll feel this way about you till the day I die.'

Gazing down at this fragile-looking woman, he again thought of the compressed fierce driving power of small women. Their frames never seemed big enough for their emotions, and when the emotion was hate ... She was right, she could never change.

He turned from the bed and walked towards the door, and as he opened it she said to him, 'Where's Lorna? I haven't heard her.'

'She's gone away for a holiday.'

'What!'

He turned and looked at her again. She had raised herself up on her elbow. 'She's gone with Jenny to Switzerland. They left on the twelve o'clock from Newcastle.'

'Damn her!'

He watched her drop back on the pillow; then he went out, closing the door softly. It wasn't Lorna she was damning, he knew, but Jinny, who she had used all her life, Jinny who had always taken her side. And now Jinny had left her when she most needed her. Not only that, she had taken Lorna with her. He pondered at this moment that Jinny, who must have always loved him, had for the first time in their long acquaintance tipped the scales in his favour.

As he went down the stairs he heard the bedroom door being pulled open and the next moment Bett's voice came croaking loudly at him. 'You and her won't get away with this. She's mine. You have no claim on her and she's coming back here. She'll take a holiday when I say so. D'you hear?'

He heard.

7

Paul awoke to Maggie's voice saying, 'Come on now, sit up and have this cup of tea. Come on now.'

With an effort he pulled himself up through the thick layers of sleep; then turning on to his side he forced his eyes open and grunted, 'What's the time?'

'It's turned eight.'

'Turned eight!' The sleep slid from him and he sat up and pressed his two hands over the top of his head.

'How far turned eight? You shouldn't have let me lie so long.'

'Aw, just about ten past. I'll run you a bath. Get yourself into it an' you'll be as right as rain. Drink that tea first.'

His hand shook as he lifted the cup from the side-table, just

159

as if he'd had a skinful, yet he had got to sleep last night through sleeping tablets, not the bottle. He had needed that sleep. He rested his head against the bed panel, and as Maggie went towards the door he said to her. 'Did you have a good night?'

'Aye, I didn't raise me head until after seven, that old couch is better than a bed.'

'Were you warm enough? That morning room's like death.'

'Aw, warm as toast. I left one bar of the fire on.'

'Maggie . . . have you taken a tray along?'

'Not yet.' She had her back to him as she spoke. 'I'm just after setting it. I'll get your breakfast first, then see to it.'

'Take it up now, Maggie, will you? See to it now.'

She made a movement with her shoulders which said she would do as he wished, then went out.

Slowly he got out of bed; he still felt a bit dopey. After his bath he had a cold shower and a brisk rub down, and he was naked when he went back into the bedroom, there to come to a dead stop when he saw Maggie standing with her back to the door. She looked as if she was leaning against it. As he grabbed at his pants and pulled them on he asked quickly, 'What is it? Are you feeling bad?'

He went to her and took hold of her arms and watched her trying to speak. 'Maggie! Maggie! What is it?'

'Put . . . put something on,' she said. She pointed to his trousers. 'You'd . . . you'd better come.'

He glanced to the side of her, towards the wall, in the direction of Bett's room; then pulling on his things he went hastily along the corridor, Maggie following slowly.

Bett's door was open. Bett herself was lying sprawled across the floor. The bedside table was overturned and on the floor was a travelling clock, a glass, and a bottle. He knelt down and turned her over and felt her heart; then reaching out he picked up the bottle. It was the one from which he had taken his two sleeping tablets last night. The same bottle that he had locked up in the medicine cupboard in his surgery. That was after he had handed John two tablets to bring upstairs to her.

He looked down at his wife. Her features were contorted as if she had died in an agony or struggle. Oh, the pity of it. Oh, the waste, the waste of energy and temper, of bitterness and resentment. He wanted to lay his head down on her small breast and cry. He knew all about the remorse that comes with death.

Remorse for not having done enough for the one who has gone. This happened to people who had no need to feel such remorse. But now he himself was filled with it, justifiably filled with it. Oh! Bett, Bett. This was what was meant by the irrevocability of the last chance. He knew, as he knelt there looking at this girl who had been his wife—and she looked a girl, for the years had not turned her into a woman—he knew that until the day he died he would carry with him fragments of the feeling that was in him now.

He lifted her on to the bed; then turned about to see Maggie standing, not in the room, but out in the corridor. He went towards her and they stood looking at each other in guilty silence. He had no doubt that she, too, was experiencing some of his own feeling, for she had been against Bett from the beginning. He saw that her old body was shaking, and so, taking her arm, he led her down the stairs to the hall, and after sitting her in a chair, he went to the phone and got through to John Price.

It was forty-eight hours later when John Price, standing in the drawing-room and facing Paul squarely, said, 'I know you'll think it a callous thing to say, Paul, but, between you and me, it's the best thing that could have happened to her ... and you.'

'Perhaps.' Paul held his hands out to the fire as if he were cold, and it was some seconds before he added, 'But I can't get rid of the feeling that she must have been in a dreadful state of mind to do it; it wasn't like her. You know yourself self-preservation was her slogan, and although she was ill she was full of life, aggressive life, when I last spoke to her. She was still determined to go through with everything she had set her mind to.'

'That was likely just a front she was putting on. A thing like that happening to her was bound to affect her. The very fact that it might become known must have worried her.'

'Will ... will it have to come out at the inquest?' He slanted his glance towards John.

'No, of course not, you know that. Not publicly anyway, but ... well,' John Price bit on his lip, 'I think there's one man in particular who should be told of it.'

'One man? Who?'

'Beresford.'

'Beresford! Good God, no. No! Anyway, why him, him of

all people?'

'You mentioned self-preservation a minute ago. Well now, this, to my mind, is a vital matter of self-preservation. You see, Paul, I was talking to Beresford yesterday, and if I hadn't known already about that letter, the letter Bett sent him—oh yes, she told me it was she who did that—I would still have thought his manner slightly odd when speaking of you. But as it was I could see him putting two and two together. He's got a good idea now who sent that letter ... if he hadn't before, and he's just got to say a word in the right quarter and what will happen at the inquest? There'll be an investigation. Wait a minute, wait a minute, Paul.' He held up his hand. 'You were, let's face it, having an affair with another woman; your wife found out about it, and she wrote to your colleague; the colleague in turn spoke to you about the matter and you were furious.... Moreover, and what is much more important, you were the only one in the house with her who had access to the medicine cupboard; in fact there was no one else in the house that night except Maggie, and I think we can rule her out.... Now you see what I mean? You see how one thing can lead to another? Now what I propose to do is to go and have a talk with Beresford. As Bett's doctor I can do this. And once he has the facts he'll see things in their right perspective. He'll have the reason why she took her life.... You know the first thing he asked me was had I informed the police, and I told him of course I had. And what you must realize too, man, is, that if such a rumour started it would put paid to your chances of getting that appointment.'

'That's been put paid to already, for the simple reason that I'm not going before the Board,' Paul put in quickly.

'Don't be a damn fool, Paul. This time next week when the inquest's over you'll feel differently. You've got on the short list and you're going before that Board, if I've got to drag you there.'

'It's no use, John.' Paul began to pace the floor between the window and the couch. 'Beresford's had it in for me for a long time. I would rather lose my practice than you go to him, I'm telling you.'

'Paul, look, you don't seem to have understood me. It'll be more than the practice at stake if I don't go. Now you leave this to me. But with regard to the appointment you lay too much stock on Beresford; he's really very small fry in that quarter.

You talk as if he were actually on the Board.'

'He might as well be, he's a pal of Bowles, and his son trained under Bowles too. Oh, don't underestimate Beresford's connections. Do you think his locum would have got on the short list without Bowles's aid? ... But look, John, don't think I'm ungrateful. I'm grateful in all ways, for I don't know where I'd have been these past few days without you, but I'm just not bothered any more about the appointment. A few days ago it was important, I meant to fight to get it, but now I don't feel that way, it just doesn't matter, so I'm going to withdraw my application.'

'You're a damned fool, Paul.'

'Maybe, but there'll be other posts, if not here, in some other place.'

'You know what Beresford will think? He'll think he's frightened you off.'

'Well, let him have that satisfaction and then he can go to church and give thanks to God for his benefits to a just and moral man.'

'Well, I suppose you'll have it your own way. Look, let me take surgery for you tonight. Crawford will do mine.'

'No, no thanks, John; you've done more than enough this week. No, I've got to start some time, the sooner the better.'

'By the way, when are you expecting Jenny and Lorna back?'

'I'm not.'

'You're not? What do you mean?'

'I haven't told them and I'm not going to.'

'But, man!'

'Look, John, I think it's too soon for Lorna to come back. She's got to do a bit of thinking on her own, to adjust herself to the new relationship with me, and Jinny is the right person to help her. They were to be away for a month, so I'll leave it like that. I'll tell them just before they return, that's if they don't see anything in the papers. But I doubt it, out there.'

'There's always the possibility of someone talking, someone from these parts on holiday.'

'Well, I'll have to take that chance, but that's the way I want it, John.'

'It isn't right you being left here on your own; it isn't good for you.'

'I'm not quite on my own, there's Maggie. She's a rock is Maggie.'

'Well, just as you say. But I don't agree with you; I think you should let them know. Now I must be off. I'll look in tomorrow.... You wouldn't like to come round for a drink after you're finished?'

'Not tonight, John, thanks.'

'All right. I'll be seeing you.'

'Thanks for everything, John.'

'Oh, be quiet.... Until tomorrow then.'

After John Price had gone Paul stood in the drawing-room staring before him. His mind was taken up at this moment with a question which centred around Beresford and the selection committee. What, he was asking himself, was the real reason he wasn't going before the Board? Was he really afraid of Beresford and what he might say about the circumstances of Bett's sudden death? To this he gave an emphatic no. Then what was the reason, if not fear? He could find no answer to this except to say he was tired, tired of it all.

He looked around the room. The cushions in the two big armchairs were rumpled; they would never have been like that if she had been here. Nor would the evening paper be lying on the table; it would have been in its correct place in the paper rack. Her finickiness in this way had always annoyed him, yet at this moment he had a longing for her to walk in, and in her maddenning way put the room to rights. His world was suddenly empty; everyone that mattered in one way or another, for good or bad, had gone from him. Ivy, Lorna, Jinny, Bett. He had a sudden longing for company, not company outside his house as he would have had if he had gone to John's, but company inside, family company. As the loneliness weighed on him he began to think of Ivy. Had she heard about Bett, and what did she think? Did she wonder if he would have married her? Would he? He didn't know. But she'd be committed now. Ivy was as dead for him as Bett was. He had a sudden impulse to go and phone Jinny. He had only to phone her and she would be home like a shot. But as he had said earlier to John, he had Lorna to consider. This news coming so soon on top of the revelation of her birth might affect her adversely; she wasn't ready to receive another shock so soon, because she, too, would suffer in the same way as himself. She, too, would be filled with remorse, for she hadn't loved her mother, she hadn't even liked her. He had been long aware of that. In a way he had taken Lorna from Bett. It had been a form of retaliation for Bett's deception, subconscious perhaps but nevertheless real.

The clock in the hall struck the quarter hour. It would soon be time to start surgery, but he would go in the kitchen and have a cup of tea with Maggie first.

In the kitchen, Maggie said to him, 'I would like to slip into Newcastle; it's me niece, she's bad. There was a letter waitin' for me at the house when I slipped along a while ago. I could be back by nine or so.'

'You go on, Maggie, and do what you want to. And look, I'm all right here, get yourself home to bed tonight.'

'I'll do no such thing. I'll stay here until Miss Jenny and the child comes back. And if you want my opinion I think you're mad not to let them know.'

'Perhaps I am, Maggie, but I've worked it out it's better that way.'

'Have your own way then, but don't tell me to go until they're in the house.'

He put his cup down, patted her shoulder as he passed her, and went to his surgery.

Elsie as usual had placed the patients' cards on his desk, and he began to look through them. Annie Mullen was the first. He hadn't seen Annie for months. It came back to his mind the very night she had paid her last visit; it was the same night as Jinny had come back and said she was married. It was also the same night that Bett had told him that one day she would get him where she wanted him. He shied away from the thoughts that might lead to renewed recrimination of his wife. She was gone; let her rest. He felt nothing but pity for her now. . . . Was that all he felt? Wasn't his big body really light with the feeling of release? He quickly passed on to the next card. This read: Harold Gray. Well, Gray was due for another visit. He looked back at Annie Mullen's card and saw that he had signed them both off the same evening. Funny how things link up. He pressed the bell on his desk, which would show a light outside his door. The next minute there was a tap on it and Annie Mullen entered.

'Hello, Annie. Sit down. How are you?'

'Middling, Doctor, just middling.' She sighed. 'But before I start yapping on about meself I would like to offer you me condolences. 'Twas sorry I was to hear of your dear wife's passing. It was tragic, tragic.'

'Thanks, Annie.'

165

'The mind can only stand so much, that's what I say. You know I often think, Doctor, that the body is stronger than the mind. At least, I can stand pain in me body but I can't put up with the naggings at me mind.'

'Has she been on again, Annie?'

'She's never stopped, Doctor. Anyway I'm after thinkin' I won't have to put up with her much longer.'

He looked at her grey, drawn face and said, 'Now, now, Annie, you mustn't get despondent. Come along, tell me what the trouble is.'

'It's me stomach.'

'You've had pain?'

'I could say so.'

'A great deal?'

'I'd be tellin' a lie if I said no.'

'Go and take your things off'—he nodded towards the screen in the corner of the room—'and get on the couch.'

She nodded back at him and went behind the screen, and as he listened to the rustlings of her undressing he looked back over her case history, to which he added hard work, worry, and sorrow, which had brought her to where she was now, and at sixty-nine she was about to die. He knew it, and she knew it.

A few minutes later, when he came from behind the screen and returned to his desk, he talked to her as she dressed again. 'I'm going to get you a bed in hospital, Annie. Now you mustn't worry; you'll be under Doctor Fenner, he's a grand man. I know him well and I'll have a word with him about you. You might be in for a week or two and when you come out I'll make arrangements for you to go to a convalescent home.'

To all his talking she made no answer until she was seated opposite to him again, and then, looking him in the eye, she said, 'Do you believe I'll ever come out, Doctor?'

'Mm! It's an even chance, Annie,' he said. He should have put the percentage at ninety-five but truth was cruel and age had to suffer enough cruelty. 'It all depends if you put up a fight.' He put his hand out and patted her broken-nailed, blue-hued fingers, where they lay on the edge of the desk.

'Well, we'll see, Doctor, eh? We'll see about the fight. . . . But about what you promised me.' She brought her face nearer to his. 'You won't be able to do anything for me if I'm in the hospital.'

'Don't you worry.' He picked up her hand and pressed it.

166

'They'll see to it. You'll be in much less pain than you are in now. You know, Annie, you should have spoken about this years ago when you first felt the pain.'

'Aw, Doctor, if I kept runnin' to you with every pain and ache I would have been camped on your doorstep for years.'

He came round the desk and put his hand on her shoulder and led her to the door, and looking down at her he said, 'They don't come like you today, Annie; they're made in a different mould.'

'Will I be seein' you again, Doctor?'

'Good gracious, Annie, of course you will. Now goodnight, and don't worry; you'll be hearing from me very shortly.'

'Goodnight, Doctor, and God bless you. And thanks for all the kindness you've shown me all these years.'

When he was seated behind the desk he did not immediately press the button. Poor Annie. Poor Annie. And when she was in hospital he wouldn't be able to visit her, at least not professionally. It wouldn't be in his province; that kind of thing was the privilege of the consultant, or assistant physician.

He pressed the button and there was no tap on the door before Harold Gray entered. He didn't look at the man but went on writing as he said, 'Good evening, Mr. Gray. What's your trouble now?'

'It's me back again, Doctor. I'd be all right if it wasn't for this back.'

'Oh, yes, yes. Well, I've been thinking about your back, Mr. Gray.' He raised his eyes. 'It came to my mind when I was down in the physiotherapy department. Now I think I'll send you for some massage. Since the X-rays have failed to find anything we'll try some massage. How about that?'

'It's up to you, Doctor, it's up to you.'

Yes, it was up to him ... and old Peter Willings. Old Peter could spot a phoney a mile off. He wondered why he hadn't thought of him before in connection with Mr. Gray. He said now, 'I'll give you a note making an appointment. Mr. Willings will give you a good do over.' ... 'And how!' he added to himself. He'd like to gamble that Mr. Gray's back would be better in a fortnight. He wrote rapidly on a sheet of paper, put it into an envelope and sealed it. If Mr. Gray decided, as he very likely would, to steam the envelope open, he would find only some medical terms which he wouldn't be able to translate.

'There you are.' He handed the letter and certificate across

167

the desk to Mr. Gray. 'You take that letter to the hospital, to the physiotherapy department, and ask to see Mr. Willings. Ask to see him personally.'

'I will, Doctor.' Mr. Gray stood beaming down on Paul. His smile said there was one born every minute, the secret was to know how to handle them. 'Goodnight, Doctor, and thank you.'

'Goodnight, Mr. Gray.'

He sat looking at the closed door. It took all kinds. The world was filled with the Annie Mullens and the Mr. Grays, but how he loathed the Mr. Grays....

It was five past seven when the last patient left the surgery and, gathering up the cards, he went across the waiting-room and into Elsie's office.

'Anything in, Elsie?'

'Yes, two calls, but I put them through to Doctor Price.'

'Now why did you do that?'

'Because he told me I had to.'

'Yes, for the last two nights....'

'... And for tonight. He got through to me just after he left here and he gave me my orders.' She bounced her head at him. 'And now you go indoors and get yourself something to eat and sit down and have a rest.'

There was a faint smile on his face as he answered her, and in the same vein as she had spoken to him, 'And you get yourself away home and leave that lot until the morning. I'm always telling you. Goodnight.'

'Yes, you are. Goodnight, Doctor.'

Elsie's tone was crisp and normal sounding. Everything had returned to normal; at least it would appear so. He crossed the empty waiting-room and stood on the step above the courtyard looking up into the sky. The long northern dusk was creeping over the Salvation Army building. The figures he could see crossing the Square through the open gate were dim, mist-shrouded.

He shivered and turned indoors, and going to the door marked 'Private' he entered the hall. Once inside, the silence and emptiness of the house hit him. He was instantly conscious that Maggie wasn't in the kitchen. He walked slowly across the hall and down the length of the passage that led to the play-room. He switched on the light and looked inside. It had been his nursery, and Lorna's nursery, but now it was full of discarded pieces of furniture and old books. Why had he come

168

here? He closed the door, walked back down the passage and into the morning room. It had always struck cold, this room; it was too big for a morning room. Bett had been right there, but he had opposed her, even to the extent of not letting her take the old couch away. The couch now was made up as a bed for Maggie. She had refused to sleep upstairs, either in one of the spare rooms or in Lorna's. He bent and switched on the electric fire; it would be warm for her coming back. Next he went into the dining-room. He had always liked the dining-room, always liked to eat here, but of late years it had been used less and less. It was a good-shaped room with good furniture, the oval dining-room table surrounded by Hepplewhite chairs. The glass-topped sideboard with the wine cabinet built in. The china cabinet ornate but beautiful, which Bett had considered a monstrosity. He would like to use the dining-room more. He closed the door after him and went into the drawing-room. Here the emptiness of the house was more telling. The easy chairs, the couch, and no one sitting in them. The baby grand in the corner with the top closed, the music stacked neatly in the cabinet. But then the piano wasn't often used; he hadn't played it for a long time. He had the urge to go to it now and open it up, but the thought seemed indecent. He put some coal on the fire and stood with his back to it; then slowly he began to inhale, deep, deep breaths that expanded his chest and pressed out the muscles of his stomach. And do what he might, he could not check the feeling of release and relief from rising in him. All day he had been pressing it down, pushing it away, ignoring it, telling himself it was too soon for that, she was hardly cold yet; it wasn't decent. Wasn't he full of genuine remorse for the part he had played in her life and the awful end it had brought her to? Yes, yes, he was. And there was part of him just as vitally aware now, as it had been when he saw her lying on the floor, that always he would carry the deep secret feeling of guilt within him. But it was a guilt bred mostly from things undone, and not the big things, such as lack of understanding and not being able to forgive her for using him, but the small things, small unkindnesses like preventing her from moving the couch out of the breakfast room, although he himself had always considered it an eyesore. . . . Yet all this apart, he had to face the fact that the feeling of remorse was being overwhelmed at the moment by that of release. He began to pace the floor. Be as conventional as he liked, wear a face of mourning, yet to himself he knew he must own to the truth. This feeling was telling him he was free; after sixteen years he was free. It went further: it told him he was just turned forty, that he could start another life, that he was still young enough to achieve something.... Here he stopped in his pacing as the words of Annie Mullen came back to his mind. 'But you won't be able to come and see me in hospital, Doctor.' He began to walk again, but more slowly now. There'd be more Annie Mullens and more times when he'd know the frustration of not being allowed to follow a case to the end. Once patients went into hospital they were on an island and he couldn't make contact with them until they returned to the mainland and came under his jurisdiction again.... Did he want to be able to follow them to the island? Again he stopped, and the answer was almost verbal. Yes, he did. It wasn't true what he had said to John, he still wanted that appointment, but he knew he didn't stand a chance in hell of getting it if Beresford told Bowles about the letter. Even if they didn't connect it in any way with Bett's death he wouldn't have a chance, for Bowles too had his cronies. Sir David Cooper, for instance, who was also on the Board. And you only need two such men to give their heads an almost imperceivable shake and it would be over. There was the reason for his fear; being ignored or overlooked, being considered unfit to fill a post of responsibility. The humiliation would be too much.

There came a pause in his thinking, and he turned his steps towards the hearth again and stood looking down into the fire, and as he stared into the flames there was borne right home to him, and it came in the form of a shock, the fact that unless John made Bett's death clear to Beresford there would, as he had said, be more than the post of Assistant Physician at stake, more than even his practice; there could be his liberty. There was only Maggie's word to prove that she'd heard someone moving about around twelve o'clock, and thinking that it was himself she had got up from the couch in the morning room and gone to the door, and when she saw her mistress going up the stairs she went back to bed.

Of a sudden he began to sweat. They could question whether Bett would have been able to come downstairs if she had taken the two sleeping tablets prescribed for her. John had said he had left them on the side-table, together with a glass of water. But if she had intended to acquire more of the tablets she wouldn't have taken them, would she? He recalled the moment when

John had told him that he had left the tablets on the table. He'd had his back towards him and his voice had sounded odd. He could recall it now, muffled, muddled.... Was all this imagination? Had John really given her the sleeping tablets? If so, it would have taken a mighty effort of will for her to keep awake until twelve o'clock. But then Bett had had a mighty will.... And what was John thinking?

He began to breathe deeply again, but it brought no feeling of relaxation now. He was imagining all kinds of things, but what he mustn't imagine was that John suspected him of doing Bett in.

This is what came of being alone in the house. He wished Maggie were back or that someone would call. He went and poured himself out a large whisky, and after drinking it at a gulp he again made an inspection of the house, upstairs too now, all except Bett's room. For although her body was no longer there her presence would be heavy in it.

He stood on the landing looking about him, seeing things that he had forgotten were there. The black Chinese dragon-carved chair, which, taking into account its sloping back, had never been made to sit in. The set of Chinese prints along the landing wall. His father's tastes had run to the Chinese, and he had done quite a bit of collecting in his later years. He stood on, pondering, as if undecided what to do with himself; then releasing his lip, which had been held tightly between his teeth, he ran down the stairs and went straight to the phone and rang John Price.

'Hello there,' he said. Then, 'Oh, hello. Is that you, Muriel?'

'Yes, Paul. How are you?'

'Oh, not too bad. I just wanted a word with John.'

'Oh, he's out, Paul, he's gone along to Doctor Beresford's. Some consultation about a patient, I think.... Why don't you come over? Now, why don't you?'

'Aw, I'm not fit company for a dog, Muriel, not tonight at any rate, but I'd be glad to keep you to your invitation tomorrow, say.'

'Any time, Paul. Just suit yourself.'

'Will you ask John to phone me when he gets in, Muriel?'

'Yes, yes, of course.'

'Goodnight, Muriel.'

'Goodnight, Paul.... Take care of yourself.'

'I'll do that. Goodnight.'

When he replaced the phone he kept his hand on it, and as he stood thus he became conscious of the tick of the hall clock. He had never heard it so loud before. It seemed to boom through the empty house. Many a time over the years he had longed for a period of peace and quietness. Well, now he had the quiet, utter quiet, and it was terrible.

When the door bell rang his hand jerked on the phone, almost lifting it from its rest, and before going to the door he wetted his lips and pulled his collar straight. And when he opened it and saw the white face of Brian Bolton looking at him, he again wetted his lips and after a moment said, 'Yes?'

When the boy did not speak but moved his head from side to side, Paul said briefly, 'Come in.'

In the hall, his head hanging, Brian still made no effort to speak.

Paul, his tone even, asked, 'You want to see me?'

'Yes ... but ... but not about that.' His head was slightly raised now but his eyes were still downcast. 'I haven't been able to sleep since I heard. I ... I can't get it out of my head that she did it because.... Oh God!' He turned sideways and leant against the wall and buried his face in his hands.

Paul remained apart, standing looking at him. It was strange, but he had hardly given this boy a thought since Bett had died. It hadn't really entered his mind that if this boy hadn't infected her she'd be alive today. Why hadn't he thought like that? Because, he supposed, there were more factors than her contagion that had led her to take her life. The disease had merely been the last straw. Not having blamed the boy in his own mind for Bett's death he was finding it somewhat of a surprise that Brian himself should have taken on the responsibility. He hadn't given him credit for a conscience.

He found it easy to put his hand on his shoulder and bring him from the wall. 'Come along,' he said. 'Let's talk this out.'

He did not lead him into the drawing-room, for he did not know what memories that room might evoke for the boy, but went through the waiting-room and into the surgery.

After Brian was seated in the patient's chair Paul rested against the edge of the desk within arm's length of him and said, 'Well now, tell me about it.'

Brian wiped his face with his handkerchief, then blew his nose before saying, 'I've ... I've got the feeling that I've killed her. I ... I can't get rid of it. If she hadn't got this ... con-

172

tracted this ...' He closed his eyes and shook his head frantically. 'Well, if she hadn't got it she would never have taken her own life, would she?' He looked up at Paul and went on under his breath, but rapidly, 'She was so full of life, so jolly. I know she was older, a lot older, but she wasn't like other women. She was like a girl; she sort of ... well'—his head was shaking again—'loved living, and I ... I can see her face all the time, laughing as she twisted. She always used to laugh as ... she ... twisted.' As his voice trailed away his body slumped until his head was in line with his knees.

As he looked down at him, Paul realized, with a sense of pity, that youth had fled from this boy. He also remembered that it was he himself who had first brought him into the house, and, what was more, that he had thought at the time that this was the kind of boy he would like for Lorna: open-faced, clean-looking, manly. How wrong could you be? He prided himself on being a judge of character—he'd had enough practice in that line—yet when he had first seen this boy and passed his opinion on him, Brian Bolton had already been with a number of women, and infected them. How, just how could you tell what was below the skin? And could you blame yourself for not being able to tell? As he stared at the dejected figure he knew he had the power to mar this boy's future. He had only to let him assume all the blame for Bett's suicide and it would remain with him, and with what dire reactions, for the rest of his life.

As he made a swift decision, he knew, as he had done two days ago that his magnanimity was possible only because Lorna was not involved. Had she been, he had not the slightest doubt but that his attitude would have been ruthless. He said now, 'You mustn't blame yourself. She didn't take her life because of that, not entirely.'

'How do you know? Did ... did she leave a letter or anything?' There was fear in Brian's upturned face.

He shook his head. 'No, nothing.'

'Then how do you know?' His tone was despairing, insistent.

Paul looked down, and gripping the edge of the table with his hands, did a sort of swaying motion with his body before saying, 'It's a long story. There were many things that led up to her taking her life. All her laughter and high spirits were a form of cover up. She ... she was really very unhappy.'

'Bett unhappy?' Brian's face screwed up in disbelief.

'Yes, she was unhappy. She was unhappy because ...' How

was he going to put this? How was he going to give this boy something to hang on to, something feasible that would bring him back on balance? He had no intention of telling him about the impending divorce, yet to be convincing he must give him part of the truth. He blinked his eyes rapidly and rubbed his hand over his face. 'Well, she was unhappy because she liked youth. You see, my wife was thirty-six years of age, but she was still a young girl in her mind, and I was perhaps'—he jerked his head—'too old for her.'

This latter statement had no truth in it, yet he could see that the boy had grasped it and was holding it fast. His expression said that he could comprehend this, and this was made evident as he said, 'Well, you're not all that old.'

'I'm turned forty.'

'Aw yes.' It was a telling sound, and the single upward movement he made with his head gave it emphasis. And this was followed by a deep intake of breath.

'I am past being frivolous. My wife liked the company of young men, so our life wasn't entirely compatible, you understand?'

'Yes, yes.'

He saw that the boy's breathing was easier.

'She was very dissatisfied with life. Although her death came as a shock, it . . . it wasn't entirely a surprise.'

'No? Then you don't . . . you don't think it was because of the other?'

'As I've been trying to tell you, not entirely.' The eagerness in the boy's attitude here warned him that it might be wrong to take all responsibility from him. It might be better to let him carry some of it, if only as a deterrent against passing on his crippling gift. 'We all do things we're sorry for,' he went on, 'but very often if we face up to ourselves these very mistakes help us to be more sensible.' The triteness of the remark, the smugness that it conveyed, checked him from following this line.

As he brought himself sharply up from the support of the table Brian, his head low again, muttered, 'I'm going to get away. I've got a cousin in the South. He's . . . he's got a good car business; he's offered me a job.'

'What about your career? Couldn't you carry that on from some place else?'

'I don't want to; I want to make a complete change.'

174

'What has your father to say about this?'

'We—we've had words, a row yesterday.'

'And your mother?'

'She's terribly upset. She—she senses something's wrong and if I don't get away I'm afraid I'll blurt it all out.'

'You mustn't do that. That would upset them both much more than your going away. They'll get over you going away but I doubt whether they'll get over the real reason for your going.'

'I know, I know.'

'And what about the treatment?'

Brian rose to his feet and buttoned his coat, and he kept his eyes on his hands as he replied, 'I mean to see about that, I do.' Now he was looking at Paul and after a short silence he repeated. 'I do. I'll see to it.'

'It'll be wise, if only for your own sake, for, remember, this thing can rear its head twenty years from now. Well now,' he moved towards the door, 'you go home and try not to worry.'

He led the way out of the surgery, across the waiting-room and unlocked the door leading into the courtyard, and when he stood aside with the door in his hand, Brian paused, and, looking up at him from under his lids, said in a shamefaced way, 'Thanks. You've been kind when you needn't have been. All along you've been kind. I feel a bit better than when I first came, yet—yet I know now that I'll always feel that somehow I'm to blame for what she did.'

'That feeling will wear off with time. If it's any comfort to you, I feel the same way.'

Brian remained a moment longer looking at him; then briefly he said, 'Goodnight, sir.'

'Goodnight.'

Paul closed the door. The boy hadn't said 'Goodnight, Doctor' but 'Sir'. It put him into focus somehow. It was like a pointer to the boy's future life. It seemed to foretell that he would make an all-out effort to regain his self-respect, yet at the same time Paul knew that Brian might never succeed, for, as the boy had said, he would always feel responsible for her death. If he was inclined to be pi he could say that it was only justice that he should carry the weight with him for life, but who wanted justice? Justice was an over-estimated quality. It was odd that this last thought should bring James Knowles to his mind. He'd had no word from him, and he'd been expecting some word either through a letter or a phone call, and either form to convey abuse. It was very unlikely that he hadn't heard, the whole town knew. He had no fear of him mentioning Bett's contagion, for Knowles was sensible enough to know that other people would link it with him. One thing Paul knew was that Knowles would place the full responsibility for Bett's death on him. Well, whatever move he made he felt capable of meeting it. He wasn't afraid of anything Knowles could do; at least he was sure of this.

As he went through the door marked 'Private' the phone rang again and when he lifted it he heard John's voice, saying, 'Hello there! That you, Paul?'

'Yes; yes, it's me, John.'

'I've just got back from Beresford's.'

There followed a pause. 'You shouldn't have done it, John, but how did it go?'

'Very well, very well indeed. I think putting him in the picture will have made all the difference.'

'You do?'

'Yes, indeed.'

'But ... but what do you mean, John, by putting him in the picture? You didn't tell him everything?'

'As much as was necessary.'

'You didn't mention about Bri— about the boy?'

'No. Well, not exactly. What I mean is, no names were mentioned.'

Paul ground his teeth lightly, then said, 'What if he talks?'

'He won't. I can answer for his discretion. And after all, Paul, no matter what you think about him he's a doctor, and in his old-fashioned way he's good one; and you know this won't be the first secret he's kept.'

'I'll take your word for it, John, but I'm not easy in my mind. But ... please don't misunderstand me, I'm most grateful for what you've done, but well, knowing old Beresford, I suppose I'm prejudiced.'

'Well, you're not the only one who is prejudiced against him. I'll give you that—he's got more enemies than friends in the town—but I've always seen his good side, and he has one, By the way, I tapped him about the post.'

'You did?' Paul waited.

'Yes, we had quite a natter about it. Naturally, he's backing Rankin, but by what he said he still expects you to stand. And there's another bit of news I've got for you. Sir David Cooper is off the Board, resigned, ill-health so I understand, and Baxby's in his place.'

'Baxby? You mean from the Royal?'

'The same.'

'Oh, I know Baxby very well.'

'Good. Well, what do you say now? You're going to take a chance?'

There followed a lengthy pause before Paul said, 'Yes, John, I'll take my chance. I've done a good deal of thinking since you left and I know I must do something besides the ordinary grind.'

'Fine, fine. Oh, I'm glad.... Now you're sure you won't come over and have a drink?'

'No thanks, John, not tonight. I told Muriel, Maggie's gone out for a while and I'll have to stand on call. And by the way, I'm on full duty from now on. It'll do me good to keep going; it'll keep my mind off things. But thanks again, John. I can't put into words what I feel. I'll look in tomorrow.'

'Good. And I'm delighted you've altered your mind about the other business. Goodnight, Paul.'

'Goodnight, John.'

He walked slowly from the phone towards the drawing-room, but before he reached it he turned about and went into the kitchen. Of a sudden he felt hungry. He hadn't had a proper meal for days. There was a tray all nicely set on the table, and he knew there would be something tasty in the oven. Going to the Aga he opened the bottom door and lifted out the covered dish and set it on the tray, and when he raised the lid his mouth watered: curried chicken. Maggie was a dab hand with curried chicken. There should be a bowl of rice in the oven too. Bending down he pulled a dish from the back of the oven and placing this too on the tray, he carried it into the drawing-room.

When some twenty minutes later he brought the tray back into the kitchen as from habit he put the dishes into the sink and ran the hot water on them, and as he stood with his back to the sink drying his hands his eyes roamed round the familiar room. The plastic-topped stools under the table offended his eyes. He looked to the corner where Maggie's armchair used to stand but which space was now taken up by the washing machine. Then his eyes settled on the corner near the stove where stood a small chair which would not have held one of

Maggie's buttocks. Slowly he went out of the kitchen and down the passage to the playroom, and there he selected from the discarded furniture the larger of two armchairs. This he carried to the kitchen and placed it to the side of the stove. Then sitting down in it he tested it for comfort. It felt good, easy; it was a chair made to take a lot of weight. Maggie would be pleased about this. He stretched out his feet until they came opposite the lower door of the oven. Yes, Maggie would appreciate this. He must see that she got off her legs more from now on; he must get extra help in the house. She'd had it pretty tough of late years. It was a wonder she had put up with it, even taking into account her loyalty to him. Bett had been a swine to work under. It was no use trying to varnish that truth. She hadn't had the remotest idea of how to control a staff. Of course, it must have been irritating to her when Maggie loaded her blouse each night. But then, as he had said time and again, who was paying for the stuff Maggie took? In his mother's day she hadn't needed to help herself, her basket had been packed for her. During the hard times she had brought up her family on what his mother had given her. Looking quietly back now, he was amazed at the patience Maggie had shown since Bett had taken over, for she had a tongue of her own and would use it at times; but what Bett had never seemed to understand, what he couldn't get her to understand, was that underneath Maggie's rough exterior lay a thoughtful, kind creature who wouldn't hurt a fly.

It was at this point of his thinking that the door bell rang once more.

He did not wonder who the caller might be as he approached the door, there was just someone at the door, so when on opening he found himself enfolded in Lorna's thin arms he stood helplessly, his own arms hanging slack, looking over her head to where Jenny, carrying only a small case and her handbag, went past him into the hall.

'Oh, Daddy! Daddy!'

He put his hand on Lorna's head, while he looked at Jenny, and he said weakly, 'Why didn't you tell me?'

Jenny's back was towards him and she turned her head over her shoulder but did not look directly at him when she answered, 'Tell you? Why didn't you tell us?'

He put out his hand and closed the door. Then leading Lorna, who was now crying unrestrainedly, past Jenny towards the drawing-room, he muttered below his breath, 'I had my reasons.'

In the drawing-room, his arm still about Lorna, he pressed her to him, saying, 'There now, don't cry.'

'Aw, but, Daddy, Daddy, it's awful.' She raised her tear-stained face to his and, shaking her head slowly, she repeated, 'Awful, awful.'

'We all feel that way. Come along, take your coat off.'

He now took her hand and led her towards the fire, and, pulling a chair forward, said, 'Sit down; you're frozen. When did you leave?'

'First thing this morning, around ten.' She sniffed and her head bobbed each time.

'How . . . how did you find out?'

Lorna did not answer but turned her drenched face to where Jenny was entering the room, and she left the answer to her. But Jenny did not speak until she had seated herself stiffly in a chair to the side of the couch, away from the fire and Paul, and then looking at him she said flatly, 'We were going into breakfast when we met the Turnbull family, the accountant. They had just arrived last night. They seemed surprised to find Lorna there and they sympathized with her about her mother's death.'

Paul lowered his gaze and bowed his head. 'I'm sorry. I did it for the best.'

Jenny gave a little sigh which took some of the tenseness from her body and her voice sounded less stiff as she said, 'I suppose you did. But it would have been better, I think, if you had let us know.' Again she sighed. Then turning to Lorna she said, 'Do you think you could make us a cup of coffee, Lorna?'

It seemed a surprising request to make of the girl, the state she was in, and Paul said immediately, 'No, no, sit where you are, I'll see to it.' As he made to move from the hearth Jenny said quickly, 'Let Lorna do it, please.'

Lorna looked from one to the other, and when her eyes were held by Jenny's she rose and went past her father, and as she rounded the couch Jenny touched her gently on the hand, saying, 'Just make it in the cups, as long as it's hot it'll do. All right?'

'Yes, Aunt Jenny.' Lorna's voice was submissive. She was aware that her Aunt Jenny wanted her out of the room, and she knew why.

The door had hardly closed behind her before Jenny, leaving

her chair, went to the fire and resting her forearm on the mantelpiece stared at the frame of the picture as she said, 'Now tell me what happened.'

Paul stood looking rather helplessly at her back. He didn't know where to start. Jenny seemed alien. Whatever her attitude when they were to meet he hadn't expected it to be like this. 'Well,' he began, 'I don't know whether they told you or not, but she took her own life.'

'They told us all right. Mrs. Turnbull has a flair for shock tactics. I couldn't believe it at first, I couldn't take it in. But that wasn't Lorna's reaction; she took it in immediately and has hardly stopped crying since. You know something.' She swung round and faced him. 'She blames herself for Bett's death.'

'Nonsense.'

'No it isn't not with her way of looking at it. Not when she remembers what she's been wishing on her mother for a long time now. Do you know she'd been wishing that Bett would die, that she would drop down dead, or be knocked down—anything as long as she was out of the way?'

'She told you this?'

'Yes. She's talked of nothing else the whole journey.'

'Well,' he hunched his big shoulders, 'it's not unusual for children to wish death on their parents, not unusual at all.'

'But she's not a child, Paul. Don't you realize that? she's a child no longer. And what's more she's older than her years.... Oh,' she put her hand up to her head, 'why didn't you get in touch with us and bring us back?'

'It wouldn't have made any difference, would it, if she thinks like that? I can't see that it would have helped in the least.'

'Of course it would. It would have been different coming from you. But having it shot at her in that strange hotel miles away, and then to face that awful journey feeling like that.'

'I'm sorry, I'm sorry.' He sat down on the couch and leant his elbows on his knees and supported his forehead with his hands. 'It wasn't that I didn't want you back. I—I thought, coming so close on everything else it might affect her.'

'You would really have let us stay there a full month and not told me? I cannot understand it.'

'No, perhaps not.' He shook his head wearily.

She stood looking down intently at him for a moment. Then slowly she lowered herself into a chair to the side of the hearth and asked, 'Who found her?'

'Maggie.'

'That Mrs. Turnbull said she had taken a full bottle of sleeping tablets. Is that right?'

'Yes. She came downstairs around twelve and went to the surgery cupboard. It was the easiest thing in the world; she knew where the keys were.'

'And it wouldn't have happened if I'd been here.'

He brought his head up quickly. 'What! Now don't you be silly, Jinny.'

'I'm not being silly. I know for a certainty in my own mind that if I hadn't gone away she would never have done it. I knew I shouldn't have left her. She was ill, almost demented—yes, almost demented, and I left her with you and Maggie, and neither of you had a grain of sympathy for her.'

He looked at her steadily before saying, 'But there you are wrong. I felt more kindly towards her that last day than for many a year, and I told her so as best I could. But it didn't make the smallest difference to her; she was determined to break me.'

'If that's the case, what made her take the tablets?' Her mouth now fell slightly agape and she eased herself up from the chair by gripping the back rail. 'Paul, you . . . you . . . ?'

'. . . No, no, I didn't, Jinny.'

'I'm sorry.'

'You needn't be, for I won't say there weren't times I didn't think about it. But my opinion is she took her life because she couldn't bear the thought that she had contracted the disease.'

'Yes, that's what I think too, and that's why I'll never be able to forgive myself for leaving her.'

'Now, now don't be silly.'

As he made a move to go to her, Lorna came into the room carrying a tray, and after placing it on the table she silently handed Jenny a cup and then one to her father, and taking the other cup she sat down on the edge of the couch and slowly and methodically she began to stir her coffee.

They were sitting now like three strangers in a waiting-room, quietly ill at ease, waiting as it were for a signal to move. When the silence of the room became unbearable, Paul, leaning towards Lorna, said, 'Are you very tired, dear?'

'Yes.' She nodded, still looking down into her cup.

'Have an early night, eh? You'll feel better in the morning.'

Again she nodded.

'We'll all have an early night. I'll go and switch the blankets on.' He was in the act of putting his half-empty cup on the table preparatory to leaving the room when Jenny said, 'I'll be going home, Paul.'

Before he could protest, Lorna exclaimed loudly, 'Oh no, Aunt Jenny!'

'Yes, Lorna, I think it's better this way, but I'll be back in the morning.'

As Paul stood looking helplessly at Jenny's profile he sensed in her face the beginning of a battle that would be harder for him to fight and win than the straightening out of the relationship and re-establishing the love between himself and Lorna. Just a short while ago he had pictured what it would be like to have them both in this room. Now the picture had come alive and the reality held no promise of happiness, not even contentment, it simply posed another problem. How had he expected Jinny to react? He had known that she would be upset, but not that she would take the blame for Bett's death on her own shoulders.... Brian, Lorna, Jinny, and himself, all feeling responsible for Bett's death.... And she wasn't worth it. The thought appeared blasphemous, but he held on to it and attacked it by repeating, no, she wasn't worth it. In life she hadn't done one good thing that he was aware of, and in death she had the power to rob four people of their peace of mind. Well, he wouldn't let her. He had already done what he could for the boy. He was positive he could explain Lorna's guilt feelings away. For himself he was damned if he was going to let her get the better of him after all; he would deal with his own conscience.... But could he deal with Jinny's? He would have to talk to her. It suddenly became the most important thing in life that he should get things straight with her. But he must go careful.

When he heard Lorna say, 'I think I'll go up, Daddy,' he asnwered quickly, 'Yes, yes, dear, I think that's the best thing you can do. I'll come in and see you in a little while. Go on now.' He went to her and kissed her gently and said softly, 'It'll be all right, it'll be all right.' Then he watched her go to Jenny and cling to her for a moment before turning swiftly away and running from the room, not like an adult as Jinny had suggested, but, to him, like a very young girl. And he saw this as a hopeful sign.

When the door had closed he did not turn immediately to

Jenny and say, 'Why do you want to go home?' It was some seconds before he spoke, and then he forgot all about going careful for he said outright, 'You're going to hold the whole thing against me, aren't you? I can see by your face you are.'

It was a full minute before she said, 'No, not against you, against myself.'

'Oh, that's nonsense. You did everything possible you could for her for years. You did more for her than anyone else.'

'Except when she needed me most.' She turned and faced him fully now. 'Paul, I knew that morning I shouldn't go. I almost didn't take the plane; I had a dreadful feeling on me. I might as well tell you now that we quarrelled bitterly before I left the house, but when I'd time to think I realized it was because she was ill and lonely and frightened. I phoned twice and couldn't get through; I wanted to say to you I was coming back. I tell you I had a premonition that something was going to happen. And now,' she spread out her hands, 'it's with me for life.'

He moved slowly towards her and when he was within touching distance of her he stopped. 'Jinny.' His voice was soft and had a note of pleading in it. 'I know how you feel, believe me, for there's part of me eaten up with remorse, but we're human beings and time will bury these feelings. Later on we'll be able to look to the future . . . we will, Jinny.'

'You think so?' She was staring into his face. 'You really think so? I wish I could feel the same.'

'You will.'

'I doubt it.' Her lips were trembling and she began to pluck at the front of her suit with her fingers, and when his hand came over hers she screwed her eyes tight and the tears pressed from beneath her lids and rolled down her cheeks.

'Jinny. Jinny, don't. Please.'

'You . . . you know how I feel.' She was sobbing and gasping now. 'There's no need to go into all that, but as impossible as the situation was for me when she was alive I felt nearer to you. . . . But . . . but now, well now, her going has made a gulf so wide that I can never see myself crossing it.'

He brought her hands to his breast and held them tightly and he looked at her long, still ordinary-looking face, drenched with her tears, and he knew that in her and her alone lay his future peace and what happiness there still remained for him. He knew now that he had always needed her, but he needed her most at this moment. Yet he also knew that if he were to press

183

that need he would lose her, perhaps for good.

'When is ... when is she to be buried?'

'Monday.'

She withdrew her hands from his, and turning slowly from him she walked towards the door, saying, 'I'm going back to work as soon as I can.'

Again he took the opposite course from that which his mind and caution prompted. He knew this was neither the time nor the place, but he had to say it. 'Jinny. There's a job waiting here for you if you want it.'

She stopped but she didn't turn round. 'Thanks, Paul.'

He stood still as he said, 'You don't consider taking it? I mean, just to look after the house ... and us?'

'I couldn't. But thanks all the same.'

He warned himself again, but it was no use, he had to ask her. 'Do you think you would later on?'

'I don't think so, Paul. I don't know. Don't ask me now ... the way I'm feeling....'

When he moved to her side and took her arm she looked at him and all the hidden sadness of her life was in her face. For years and years she had dreamed of what it would be like to be loved by this man. She'd had to fight her jealousy and envy of Bett. She had thought that if he would only love her, take her once, just once, she'd live on it for the rest of her life. And here he was, offering her everything and she couldn't take it. She doubted whether she'd ever be able to take it, for what he didn't know, and what he wouldn't lay much stock on, if she were to tell him, was that she, like Lorna, had wished Bett out of the way. That it had been a deep hidden wish, and that she hadn't really acknowledged it until Lorna had blurted out her feeling for her mother, she didn't alleviate her guilt. She felt almost buried under it. She doubted if Paul would ever understand how deep her feeling of responsibility for Bett's death went.

'No one knows the weight of a conscience except the owner.' She'd heard that somewhere and now she knew just how true it was.

'What did you say?'

'Nothing. I—I was just thinking.'

'Try not to think too much, and don't judge anything on the way you're feeling now. I won't press you, I'll leave it to you. But the job will always be there, Jinny. I just want you to know that.'

She bowed her head deeply; then turning from him, she went into the hall. And as he watched her there came to his nostrils a scent, a scent that he had always associated with Bett, a particular perfume she used; it was as if Bett herself were crossing the hall, passing between them. And now the scent was a smell and he actually felt Bett's presence. For a moment he imagined he heard her laughing as she turned his own phrase, indicating her victory: 'She's tipping the scales towards me again.'

Dead or alive, it seemed that Bett would win. The hell she would! At this instant there came the sound of movement from the kitchen. Maggie was back.

As if attacking the still warm bitter spirit that stood in the space between him and Jinny he gripped the door and flung it wide, bouncing it back against the wall.

When Jenny turned her startled face towards him, he advanced to her, smiled, and, taking her arm firmly in his hand, led her towards the kitchen saying, 'Maggie's just come in. Let's go and have a natter with her, eh? Her home-spun wisdom has a habit of clarifying things. Oh, to be as uncomplicated as Maggie! What do you say, Jinny? Wouldn't life be simple if we could accept things like Maggie does?'

Jenny, seeing him through her blurred vision, thought that at the moment he looked boyish, and that there was even something child-like about his way of thinking, as child-like as his Maggie's.

FIVE

MAGGIE

It was many years since Maggie had been in Newcastle and she felt slightly lost when she walked out of the Central Station, but, she reasoned, Northumberland Street would still be in the same place, and St. Clement's Church wasn't likely to have moved itself. Nevertheless, she noticed, as the bus took her towards St. Clement's, that there had been some changes over the last few years, and also that some were desperately needed still. She alighted from the bus and went along a street that she remembered well, and when she saw the old iron and taggerine heaped up in the little railed gardens in front of the houses she thought to herself, 'It's a bulldozer they want along here; you would have thought that they'd have pulled such streets down years ago.' But still, she had to concede when she came to a square that held towering blocks of new flats that they were getting on with it.

St. Clement's, as she surmised, was still in the same place. It had always served the poorer quarters and would likely go on doing so, new blocks of flats or no. They had always held confession here on a Thursday night and she hoped to God they still continued to do so, or her journey would have been in vain.

When she entered the dim church and saw half-a-dozen people scattered in the pews before the confessional to the right of the door she thanked God; then taking a seat she slowly lowered herself on to the wooden kneeler and prepared herself for confession.

By the time her turn came there were at least another eight people waiting to go in after her, and for this she also thanked God.

When she entered the confessional box she had to grope for the arm rest and the kneeler, and when she was settled she raised her eyes and saw the outline of the priest's hand that was

186

cupping his face. His nose protruded beyond the stub of his little finger; it was a fleshy nose as far as she could make out, with wide nostrils. The rest of him was all in shadow, beyond the light of the solitary candle.

'Father, I want to make a confession.' It wasn't the set type of approach to the making of a confession, which usually began along such lines as, 'Pray, Father, give me your blessing for I have sinned.'

'Make your confession, my child.'

Child is it, she thought. It was nice to hear that again. It was many, many years since she had heard that phrase.

'Make your confession, my child.' Aw yes, it was nice, sort of comforting. So she began: 'I haven't been inside a church for years, Father.'

'When did you last make your Easter duties?'

'Oh——' She stopped herself from saying begod! 'Oh, many a long year since, Father; I've lost count.'

'Ten? Twenty years?'

'Oh, I've been about twice in that time I should say, but I've done no harm to anybody in my life up to recently. I've got a sharp tongue, I'll admit, but I'm loyal, aye, I'm loyal in me way.'

Maggie stopped here and the priest waited. This certainly wasn't the usual line he had to listen to. When the penitent didn't go on he proffered in a whisper, 'And now you've done some wrong to someone?'

'Aye, in a way, Father. Aye, yes, that's it. To tell you the truth I've poisoned a woman.'

The priest's middle finger knocked sharply against the end of his nose, and then, his voice lower still, yet the words piercing, he said, 'You mean you've committed a murder?'

'You could say that, Father, but I don't look upon it like that. It was somethin' I had to do.'

'Nobody has to commit murder; it—it's the greatest of sins to take a life.'

'There are different ways of killin', Father. You can watch someone being killed slowly each day. An' you can see them bein' driven to the limits of their endurance until you expect them in their turn to kill. . . .'

'Was she old?'

'No. No, she was youngish, but she was bad. And she'd got a disease.'

187

'And you killed her because of that?' There was the sound of horror in the young priest's voice.

'No, not because of that, but because her husband had been goin' to divorce her because he couldn't stand any more. And then she goes and gets this thing from goin' with other men. And I could see him sacrificing the rest of his life to her because he blamed himself for what had happened afore, or what hadn't happened for years atween them. It's all the way you look at it. You see, they hadn't been like man and wife from shortly after they were married, and I could see him goin' on until he was an old man tryin' to make amends an' being broken on the wheel of her. I just couldn't let it happen.'

There was a long pause before the priest asked, 'How did you do this?'

'I got some sleeping tablets and I mixed them up in a glass, and I woke her out of her sleep—she'd already had a few of them—and I made her drink it.'

'This is terrible, terrible.'

'Perhaps you bein' a priest of God may think like that. It's understandable.'

'Don't you? Aren't you laden with remorse?'

'Truthfully speaking, no, Father.'

'Then why have you come to confession?'

'Well, I thought I'd make me peace with God, because this is atween Him and me entirely. He knows the rights and wrongs of the case, He knows me motives. He knows that there was no personal feeling in it at all, for although I didn't like her, I wouldn't have got rid of her on me own account. He knows the real reason why I did it, that's why I've come.'

The priest was stunned by this logic. He knew that the person on the other side of the grid was no longer young, over middle-age, perhaps old, yet the voice gave no indication of age, for it was strong and vibrant. He had a duty here that was clear; he must make her see that this crime, for crime it was, was not only between her and God, but between her and man, her and justice. He said to her, 'I must talk to you further about this. Would you be willing to see me after confession?'

She paused for a moment before saying, 'Yes, Father, as you will.'

'Then go out into the church, go to Our Lady's altar and begin on the sorrowful mysteries. I'll be with you shortly. Now make a firm, firm act of contrition.'

She hadn't said an act of contrition for years, but the words came back to her mind as if she had only used them yesterday: 'Oh, my God, I am very sorry that I have sinned against thee because thou art so good and by the help of thy Holy Grace I will not sin again. Amen.

'Thank you, Father.'

She went out of the box and made straight for the church door, and from there she hurried up the dark street. She was no fool, she told herself; that was why she was glad there had been people going in after her, it would keep him occupied for a time. She had done what she had felt compelled to do, and her conscience was at rest, and that was all there was to it. He might look in the paper to find the suicides. Well, there was never a week went by but there was a number of them.... Death from Misadventure. Death while the balance of the mind was disturbed. He had served his purpose. She wasn't goin' to have him haunt her for the rest of her life, however long or short that was. What she had done was, as she had told him, atween her and God, and she would do it the morrow again if called upon. And now she must get back to himself for he'd be feeling lost in the house on his own. It wasn't good for a man to be on his own.... Yet better that than have his brain turned and have him do something he'd suffer for.

As she got out of the bus and went towards the station the thought came to her that if by accident she should happen on Miss Jenny's address there'd be no harm in droppin' her a line to ask if she was enjoyin' her holiday, and to say what a great pity it was about the missus. She had always known that the poor plain body was a bit taken with himself, and she'd had proof of it when she'd gone and got her nose done, but she hadn't imagined for one minute that that little snipe had been aware of it. And then for to throw it in the poor soul's face as she had done the morning she left.... Well, she was where the good God pleased at this minute and she'd try to think no more ill of her. Her concern now was with the living, with one human being, to see him settled and happy afore her time came. She had always seen to his needs as far as it lay in her power. Hadn't she manoeuvred Ivy into his bed? She had made the excuse that he couldn't do the stairs, knowing that a full-blooded young widow like Ivy couldn't wash a man down and remain cool; an' hadn't she been right? She only wished to God Ivy had come to the house years ago. But now from what she could gather

189

Ivy was no longer in the picture, and all things considered it was just as well, for he could never have married her. No, that would never have done. An' she herself wouldn't have stood for it ... Ivy as mistress of the house! That would have been more intolerable than seeing him sacrifice himself to a dirty disease-ridden woman. But with Miss Jinny ... well, she was a different kettle of fish. She would know her place and realize that the kitchen, particularly the larder, was a very minor part of it.

As she gave the porter her ticket she said it was a nice evening and it was good to see the days drawing out, and he said in reply, it was indeed. And he told her to be careful how she went for she seemed a little unsteady on her feet. It was thoughtful of him to tell her to be careful; people were kind. Oh, aye, people were kind.

As she sat in the train she wished she was home; she didn't think she'd ever visit Newcastle again, and she told herself she wouldn't miss much.

At Fellburn station she hailed a taxi to take her to the house. And why not, why not indeed! The circumstances, she felt, warranted such a luxury; it wasn't every day in her life that she went to confession.

When she entered the house by the kitchen door she sensed immediately that there was company in; the kettle wasn't in the place where she had left it, and there was the coffee tin on the table and three cups missing from the rack.

She had just taken off her hat and coat, put on her apron and made her way to the stove when the door opened, and as she turned and looked at Jenny and himself standing side by side, there entered into her a beautiful feeling. It was as if her body was filled with light; it was a good feeling and she took it for a sign of God's utter forgiveness; that Miss Jenny was back in the house at this time showed that the Almighty, like herself, was working towards one end. And she thanked Him as she went forward, her hands outstretched towards Jenny, for she said. 'Thanks be to God.'

THE END

Further examples of Catherine Cookson's renowned ability to capture the flavour of the Northern scene and its people, past and present:

THE DWELLING PLACE

When Cissie Brodie's parents were taken by the fever in 1832, Cissie suddenly found herself the head of a family of nine brothers and sisters. She was just fifteen and the youngest was but a babe in arms, yet she decided that rather than have the family split up in the workhouse, she would try to find work to keep them all, for they would be happier together. But how? And where would they live?

In *The Dwelling Place*, Catherine Cookson tells with compassion and warmth of Cissie Brodie's heroic fight to rear the family under appalling conditions of cold, near starvation and persecution in the class-conscious society of nineteenth-century England.

0 552 09217 7—65p

FEATHERS IN THE FIRE

Every once in a while circumstance traps a group of people in a pattern of tragedy and violence from which they struggle vainly to fight free. Thus it was with the Master of Cock Shield Farm, Angus McBain, who was too easily tempted to sin, too sinful to escape a hideous retribution . . . and Jane his gentle daughter who devoted her life to caring for her deformed young brother . . . Amos, the legless child whose tortured spirit transformed him into a demon capable of every cruelty—even murder . . . and Molly Geary, the 'fallen' servant girl, whose love for the child she had borne in shame gave her strength to become a truly courageous woman . . .

552 09318 1—65p

A SELECTED LIST OF FINE NOVELS THAT APPEAR IN CORGI

☐ 09475 7	A RAGING CALM	Stan Barstow	60p
☐ 09274 6	A KIND OF LOVING	Stan Barstow	40p
☐ 09277 0	THE DESPERADOES	Stan Barstow	30p
☐ 09278 9	JOBY	Stan Barstow	30p
☐ 08419 0	THE FIFTEEN STREETS	Catherine Cookson	50p
☐ 08444 1	MAGGIE ROWAN	Catherine Cookson	65p
☐ 09305 2	THE INVITATION	Catherine Cookson	50p
☐ 08821 8	A GRAND MAN	Catherine Cookson	30p
☐ 08822 6	THE LORD AND MARY ANN	Catherine Cookson	35p
☐ 08823 4	THE DEVIL AND MARY ANN	Catherine Cookson	35p
☐ 09076 X	MARRIAGE AND MARY ANN	Catherine Cookson	30p
☐ 08538 3	KATIE MULHOLLAND	Catherine Cookson	85p
☐ 08849 8	THE GLASS VIRGIN	Catherine Cookson	75p
☐ 09217 7	THE DWELLING PLACE	Catherine Cookson	65p
☐ 09318 1	FEATHERS IN THE FIRE	Catherine Cookson	65p
☐ 09373 4	OUR KATE	Catherine Cookson	35p
☐ 09617 2	THE CONSERVATORY	Phyllis Hastings	40p
☐ 09904 X	A VIEW OF THE SEA	Margaret Maddocks	40p
☐ 09256 4	THE LOTUS AND THE WIND	John Masters	40p
☐ 09230 4	BUGLES AND A TIGER	John Masters	40p
☐ 09796 9	HOUSE OF MEN	Catherine Marchant	50p
☐ 08507 3	THE HERITAGE	Francis Parkinson Keyes	35p
☐ 08525 1	THE MARIGOLD FIELD	Diane Pearson	35p
☐ 09140 5	SARAH WHITMAN	Diane Pearson	50p
☐ 08946 X	THE RUNNING FOXES	Joyce Stranger	30p
☐ 09462 5	LAKELAND VET	Joyce Stranger	35p
☐ 09399 8	A DOG CALLED GELERT	Joyce Stranger	35p
☐ 09891 8	CHIA THE WILD CAT	Joyce Stranger	40p
☐ 09892 2	ZARA	Joyce Stranger	40p
☐ 09893 0	BREED OF GIANTS	Joyce Stranger	40p

All these books are available at your bookshop or newsagent: or can be ordered direct from the publisher. Just tick the titles you want and fill in the form below.

CORGI BOOKS, Cash Sales Department, P.O. Box 11, Falmouth, Cornwall.

Please send cheque or postal order, no currency, and allow 10p per book to cover the cost of postage and packing (plus 5p each for additional copies).

NAME ....

ADDRESS ....

(JAN. 76)...

While every effort is made to keep prices low, it is sometimes necessary to increase prices at short notice. Corgi Books reserve the right to show new retail prices on covers which may differ from those previously advertised in the text or elsewhere.